NIGHT

OF

MANY

DREAMS

ALSO BY GAIL TSUKIYAMA

Women of the Silk
The Samurai's Garden

GAIL TSUKIYAMA

NIGHT
OF
MANY
DREAMS

St. Martin's Press

New York

NIGHT OF MANY DREAMS. Copyright © 1998 by Gail Tsukiyama.
All rights reserved. Printed in the United States of America. No
part of this book may be used or reproduced in any manner
whatsoever without written permission except in the case of brief
quotations embodied in critical articles or reviews. For
information, address St. Martin's Press, 175 Fifth Avenue, New
York, N.Y. 10010.

Design by Songhee Kim

Library of Congress Cataloging-in-Publication Data
Tsukiyama, Gail.
Night of many dreams / Gail Tsukiyama. — 1st American ed.
p. cm.
ISBN 0-312-17194-3
I. Title.
PS3570.S84N54 1998
813'.54—dc21   97-40807
CIP

First Edition: January 1998
10 9 8 7 6 5 4 3 2 1

FOR MY FAMILY,

NEAR AND FAR

Acknowledgments

I wish to thank my mother and brother for their constant faith and support. And Dorothy Buckley for all her wisdom. Many thanks also to my agent, Linda Allen, and to my editor at St. Martin's Press, Sandra McCormack, for their care and guidance.

I am deeply grateful to Catherine de Cuir, Cynthia Dorfman, Blair Moser, and Abby Pollak for their ongoing generosity of spirit. And to Norma Peterson, whose life and words will always remain in my heart.

Home would be *here*. I'd made it, unconscious, and the

roots were deep.

—Reynolds Price, "Kate Vaiden"

The Floating Family — 1940

EMMA

All the other women in the Lew family were beautiful. Emma saw it time and time again, in the striking faces of her mother and sister, in the old yellow-edged photos of her ancestors. The difference that set her apart from Mah-mee and her older sister, Joan, haunted Emma. It wasn't that she was ugly, but in photos of herself, even as a baby, she saw a too-large nose, a too-round face, that made her feel awkward and conspicuous. She sometimes wondered what kind of fate had caused generations of Lew beauty to be withheld from her.

Emma sat at her father's desk in her parents' bedroom watching her sister get dressed to go out to collect money. Ever since she was a little girl, Joan had tried to appear older by borrowing her mother's clothes and cosmetics, disrupting the neat row of jars and bottles that lined the dresser, upsetting Mah-mee when she was home. Now fourteen, Joan worked as carefully as an artist, darkening the mole on the left side of her upper lip, then applying makeup and dressing so perfectly, Emma thought Joan must be the most beautiful young woman in Hong Kong.

Emma glanced at the silver-framed photo sitting on one side of the desk. She leaned forward and pressed her fingertips against the two girls in the black-and-white snapshot taken almost two years ago in front of their house. In it, Joan was twelve, five years older and at least a foot taller. Emma looked hard at herself. Her flat features stared back. She stood skinny and pale, dressed in a Western-style cotton dress with puffed sleeves and a Peter Pan collar, while Joan looked beautiful in a sleeveless silk cheungsam that Emma remembered had been the color of jade. Emma recalled posing for the camera, standing on her toes so she would appear taller, leaning lightly against Joan so she wouldn't fall. Still, they looked more like acquaintances than sisters. Ever since the picture was taken, Emma had tried to catch up, as if the years that divided her from Joan were simply a space she could cross over.

Ba ba had snapped the photo during the summer of 1938, a few months before the Japanese invaded Canton. Not long after the invasion, Joan had started collecting receipts from the shops and department stores that owed money to their father. Emma could tell by the relaxed smile on Joan's face then, that the photo had been taken before these monthly money-collecting days began. Even the mole on Joan's upper lip appeared faded, less serious now.

Until 1939, their father's trading company, Ten Thousand Profits, had done very well. From his main office in Japan, he exported everything—bolts of silk, lacquerware, antiques—to Hong Kong and throughout China. While their father and mother traveled to

Japan and China on business, sometimes for six months at a time, Emma and Joan stayed in Hong Kong with their gold-toothed servant, Foon. They were also looked after by their mother's first cousin Auntie Go, who lived two houses away.

Not until her father's business began to falter did Emma really understand that a war had begun. Salvaging his company meant staying longer in Japan, so Ba ba had decided to send out fourteen-year-old Joan to collect his outstanding debts. Ten Thousand Profits had always been a family-run business. In the absence of sons, Joan was his only choice. Besides, she already knew some of the shop owners through longtime family dealings. Any money Joan collected was used for household expenses in Hong Kong. More often than not, they barely scraped by from month to month.

Emma wondered how Joan could be so brave. For almost a year, on every last Thursday of the month, Emma had sat outside their house and waited nervously for her return. Emma worried incessantly about money. In the beginning, if Joan returned empty-handed, Emma actually felt physically ill, a dizziness filling her head that made her pause. But nowadays, when Joan finally came into view, walking slowly up the slant of the hill, Emma looked hard for the slightest sign of how her day had been. She relaxed when she saw Joan's familiar smile, the darkened mole, knowing that however anxious she was about the money, at least her sister was safely back home.

Emma glanced up from the photo as her sister unscrewed the lid from a jar. Joan sat in front of the mirror gently patting makeup onto her cheeks and forehead. Emma couldn't remember how many Thursdays she had sat watching the ritual of Joan's preparations for collecting debts. Most of the time, Emma loved to sit on the red and green silk-embroidered bedspread, which was forbidden to her when her mother was home. And she loved smelling the sweet scents that reminded her of department stores. While Emma would never waste so much time in front of a mirror, she watched mesmerized as her sister sat gazing at her own reflection, outlining the red lipstick, darkening her eyebrows into pencil-thin half-moons, dabbing on Mah-mee's Shalimar perfume. The final touch in Joan's attempt to appear older was to put on their mother's black cashmere coat with the beaver collar, matching black gloves, and a hat. When Joan was finally satisfied with her creation, she sighed softly, then turned around like an actress prepared to go onstage and said in a deep, throaty voice, *"I'm ready to go."*

"Garbo?" Emma guessed, continuing a game they'd been playing for years.

Joan laughed. "Right. You're getting good, or else I'm getting better." She rolled her eyes and tilted her head back, imitating a scene from the movie *Camille*, which they'd seen together.

Ordinarily, Emma would watch and remain quiet. But on this particular clear and cool February morning, before Joan had a chance to turn away from the mirror, Emma caught her eye and asked, "Can I go with you?"

Emma swallowed and waited for an answer. She had been wanting to ask Joan for months, hoping she could be of some help.

Joan glanced back at her, then adjusted her hat in the mirror once more. "You're too young."

"I'm almost ten," Emma argued. "Besides, don't you want the company?"

Joan was silent a moment, staring at her little sister's reflection in the mirror. "I guess, just this once," she finally answered. "But keep quiet. Let me do the talking."

Emma held lightly on to the back of Mah-mee's black coat as Joan walked confidently through the crowd and down Queen's Road. Emma felt dizzy with the blur of passing faces, and proud that most of them were watching Joan. Years from now, she knew she'd remember the soft feel of the cashmere, and the sweet, thick scent of Joan's perfume, which drifted through the cool air, protecting them.

They turned onto a small street and entered a crowded shop filled with ornately decorated vases, mother-of-pearl-inlaid jewelry boxes, woven rugs from India. Emma loved all the muted colors of saffron, orange, and brown, which reminded her of desert tombs, the intricate black and gold designs that carried hidden meanings. The shop smelled of sweet incense and faraway places. She moved closer to Joan and took hold of her hand as the spell was quickly broken by the high, excited voice of the shop owner, who lashed out at them. He thrust the bill back in Joan's face.

"I have no money!" he cried. "Look around you, my stock hasn't moved from the store! Those Japanese devils have scared everyone away from buying! You be good girls now. Go home to tell your ba ba I will pay him as soon as I can."

Emma watched the man closely. He was thin, with a high forehead and a full head of very black hair. He smiled insincerely as he inched them across the crowded room toward the door.

Joan stopped, refusing to be moved farther. She turned around and said in a strong, self-assured voice, "If you can't give Mr. Lew money now, he will take something as collateral until you can pay him."

Emma let out a gasp and froze behind Joan. How did she find the courage to say such things? Emma had always been quiet, unlike Joan, preferring to study, read, and draw. Forever with a book in her hand, Emma would have been heartbroken not to be among the top three in her class.

The shopkeeper remained silent for a moment. His eyes narrowed as he looked at them. Then, in a lower, more controlled voice, he asked, "What do you want?"

Emma stepped back, but Joan slowly took off her gloves and moved around the store like a cat. Emma held her breath and watched her sister, who had always loved shopping. When Joan spied what she wanted, she stopped and smiled, then turned back to face the shop owner. "That," she said, pointing to a vase sitting under a glass case on a polished table.

"Are you crazy? That's worth twice as much as I owe your father!"

"Then I'm sure you'll want it back as soon as possible." Joan's calm, sultry voice never flinched. "We'll send someone to pick it up this afternoon."

When they finally left the shop, Emma was floating on air. She'd never been prouder of Joan. She thought of the Chinese movie *Maiden in Armour*, which was one of Joan's current favorites. It told the story of Hua Mulan, the lady general who had disguised herself as a man and led a frontier Chinese army to defeat the Mongols. Joan had done no less, Emma was certain. She let her body relax against her sister's and they walked triumphantly down the street in the direction of the Wing On department store.

By the end of the afternoon, Emma was tired. And she could tell Joan had lost much of her fortitude. Her shoulders slumped forward, and Mah-mee's black cashmere suddenly looked too large on her. If she failed to collect enough money to carry them through the month, she would have to wire their father in Japan, mumbling to herself that she had let down the family.

At other stores they visited, Emma had remained in cramped waiting rooms stacked high with boxes and papers, while Joan cleared her throat, straightened her stance, and entered one office after another. Through the flimsy walls, Emma could hear Joan's strong, determined Joan Crawford voice, followed by a man's laughter, then words that fell hard and flat when the door opened again.

"What are you doing collecting money?" the men would spit

out. "You're much too beautiful. You should be in the movies!" In the doorway, they handed Joan their cards, with promises of money as soon as possible.

As Joan and Emma walked home, crowds pushed against them. In the past few months, Emma had seen so many refugees from China pouring into Hong Kong that she could barely walk down the street without coming upon entire families living out of cardboard boxes, begging with empty wooden bowls. She was glad for the cooler winter months that allowed the crowds of refugees to breathe. Now, she kept her head bowed low and tried to avoid bumping into people who appeared to be deliberately blocking her way. The high, crying voices of the vendors rang out unrelentingly. She could feel Joan's exhaustion. Even her Shalimar seemed stale.

"Can we stop here a minute?" Joan asked, her voice sounding young and familiar again.

She pulled lightly on Emma's sleeve, then pointed to a small, crowded shop. Emma waited just inside the doorway, pressed up against a wall to avoid getting in the way. She never took her eyes off Joan, who, she knew, waited anxiously every month to buy the latest Chinese and Hollywood movie magazines with lucky money she'd saved from the Chinese New Year. Now, Joan's face finally relaxed as she leaned forward to pick up each precious copy. On their slick covers, Emma could see the handsome, smiling faces of Gary Cooper and Ronald Colman. She watched her slim, elegant sister pay for the magazines, then felt Joan grab her hand and happily pull her through the noisy crowds until they reached home.

As they made their way back up the hill, Emma saw a small, thin figure pacing to and fro outside the front door of their gray-stone, two-story building on Conduit Road. From the distance, in a black tunic and pants, she resembled any other servant, but as they approached, Emma recognized Foon's high forehead and dark, intelligent eyes.

"Is anything wrong?" Emma asked. It was unusual to find Foon waiting for them.

"Your mah-mee has returned a week early," Foon warned.

Emma turned toward Joan, who stood stone still, clutching the movie magazines to her chest. Emma felt Joan's eyes rest heavily upon her. Both knew that their days would change now, again filling with the sharp, efficient click of the mah-jongg tiles as their mother socialized and planned Joan's future. Emma was still young enough to escape Mah-mee's ambitions, so all the attention was focused solely on Joan. Over and over again, Emma heard how Joan's good looks and family connections could easily reward her with the kind of husband and life she deserved, and Mah-mee had taken it upon herself to see to this. The only one who dared to speak up to Mah-mee was Auntie Go, but she was often busy with her struggling knitting business.

Joan turned to Emma and tried to smile. "We better go in, Mah-mee's waiting for us."

Emma nodded, her throat dry. She knew that Joan was thinking that with Mah-mee back home, everything was different. Now, their lives would be arranged and calculated. It always felt as if they were trading one life for another. Emma reached over and grabbed on to Joan's sleeve as they climbed the stone steps to their second-floor flat.

Emma glanced into their large, antique-filled living room, then beyond, to the opened double doors that led out to the terrace. Mah-mee wasn't there. She peeked into the dining room, dominated by a large round table and chairs. Then she and Joan hurried down the hall, past both of their rooms, following the thick trail of Mah-mee's perfume.

They rushed to greet her when they found their mother unpacking in her room. Mah-mee looked up quickly from her suitcase when she saw them coming. She was wearing a maroon silk cheungsam that Emma thought made her look particularly beautiful.

"Mah-mee!" she and Joan said, almost in unison.

While Emma ran to hug her mother, Joan remained behind her, simply kissing Mah-mee lightly on the cheek when Emma moved out of the way.

"I thought I would come home earlier since I'm not sure when Ba ba will be finished with his business. He'll be home when he's through, and I was tired of waiting around. It's good to be home. How are you, moi-moi?" she said to Emma.

"I went to collect money with Joan today," she answered, smiling. In spite of all the changes, she was always happy to see her mother again.

"How did it go?" Mah-mee looked over Emma's head toward Joan.

"They say business is slow," Joan quickly answered.

"The devils! They take your father's merchandise and then tell us they have no money. They just don't want to pay their debts. It would be different if you were a son. They see a pretty young girl and they think they can take advantage. I told your ba ba it's not right to send you. A young girl like you shouldn't be worrying about anything except finding a good husband."

"She was able to get a nice vase," Emma volunteered.

"A vase doesn't put food on the table," Mah-mee snapped, throwing her silk stockings on the bed. "When your ba ba gets back, I'm going to put an end to this money collecting. How does it look for the Lew girls to be out begging for money, even if it is money owed to us. Your ba ba can go out and collect his own money!" Then Mah-mee calmed down and said, "Anyway, the Japanese are just about to put a stop to everything."

Emma swallowed hard, knowing that despite her mother's protests, nothing would really change. Whenever her father and mother were back in Hong Kong, Joan would return to what she loved most—the movies. Her dark eyes would gleam for hours every week as she watched Nancy Chan and Li Qinian, or Greta Garbo and Robert Taylor. Foon often waited for Joan after school in front of the King or Queen's Theatre to collect her books before the movies began. Emma tagged along whenever she could. During those two hours of movie magic, she saw Joan enraptured as she sucked on the small, salty-sweet dried plums or the hard strips of Chinese beef jerky she savored. Joan never tired of watching the same film over and over again, though Emma saw each only once, preferring to return to a good book.

For the next few months Joan would be freed from having to collect, but Emma knew that once her parents left Hong Kong, Joan would have to become her father's bill collector again.

Emma turned around and watched Joan, suddenly paralyzed with the fear that she might say something disrespectful back to their mother. Emma hated it when they argued. It usually began with simple words as short and sharp as quick slaps: *I won't . . . You must . . . I can't.* But this time Joan remained quiet, her smooth face absolutely calm. Emma knew Mah-mee could be right. Joan's money-collecting days might nearly be over. China was being devastated. As each day passed, rumors moved through school of how the Japanese devils were moving closer and closer to Hong Kong.

Watching her mother unpack, Emma breathed in the flowery air and leaned back just enough to feel the warmth of her sister behind her.

* * *

By June of 1940, Emma began to see serious signs that life in Hong Kong was changing. Westerners began to leave, taking their families with them. One morning two weeks before the term was over, many of Emma's European classmates were suddenly evacuated from Hong Kong to Australia. The sky rumbled, then rained, leaving a damp smell of concrete behind.

"Will your father leave with you?" Emma asked her friend Mary Clarke.

Mary slowly cleaned out the last of the colored pencils from her desk before she answered. "No, he can't. He must stay to fight, in case the Japs dare to invade Hong Kong." She looked down, avoiding Emma's eyes.

"Do you think you'll come back after all this is over?"

"I suppose so." Then Mary glanced up toward Emma. "I was born here, you know."

"So was I."

"Well, then, we're sure to see each other again. Here, you can keep these for me until I come back." Mary handed Emma the colored pencils like a bouquet of flowers.

Throughout the summer, other signs of war began to appear in careful, measured ways. Sandbags were piled against the Government House and important banking buildings in case of bomb blasts. There were periodic practice blackouts and halfhearted drives to sell war bonds. Emma watched the people in Hong Kong move through each exercise as if it were some kind of game. No one, herself included, believed the Japanese would ever really come this far. Otherwise, life in Hong Kong remained the same. The Pan Am flying boats arrived on schedule, while mah-jongg games and afternoon teas were a daily ritual. Joan talked excitedly about the all-China premiere of *The Philadelphia Story*, starring Katharine Hepburn and Cary Grant. All around her, Emma heard reassurances: "The Japanese will never attack us. We're part of the British Crown."

By the fall of 1941, Ba ba had returned to Hong Kong from Japan. He looked tired and thin after months of trying to save his business. Emma was just happy he was safe and back home having dinner with them.

"There's nothing more I could do," he said, shaking his head. "The Americans and British have imposed embargoes on all exports of steel and oil to Japan. It has increased tension throughout the Pacific. The Japanese have confiscated much of my merchandise, but I've hidden some pieces away in warehouses and cargo containers until this is all over."

"What if they find out?" Joan asked.

"I have many friends there who will cover for me."

"What does it matter anyway," Mah-mee said, waving to Foon to begin serving. "As long as you're not caught in the middle of it all."

Emma knew her father had been fortunate that the Japanese hadn't found all of his goods. So many others had lost everything.

Foon emerged from the kitchen carrying a large covered soup tureen. When she raised the lid, a strong, pungent smell of seaweed filled the room. Emma wrinkled her nose, but kept silent as she watched Foon generously fill a bowl and present it to Ba ba.

By early December, the war turned their lives into a nightmare none of them had ever really believed possible. Auntie Go shut down her knitting factory, just before the Japanese crossed the Chinese border into Hong Kong, bombing Kai Tak Airport and crippling the Royal Air Force. Within four days, the radio announced that Japanese troops had swept through the northern New Territories, reaching the Shing-mun redoubt.

Mah-mee tried to keep some semblance of calm and routine. She even made Emma practice piano one hour every afternoon.

"What's that?" Emma asked, abruptly stopping her Chopin polonaise. She cocked her head sideways listening, then stood up and went to open the terrace doors.

"What are you doing?" Joan asked, throwing her movie magazine down on the sofa and following Emma.

"Don't you hear it?"

Mah-mee stepped out and joined them. "Hear what?"

"That!"

From the distance faint strains of music drifted toward them. They could just make out the static, crackling notes of "Home Sweet Home," coming from the direction of the harbor, followed by the words, "We have come to liberate you from British imperialism," repeated in English and Chinese.

"Will those devils stop at nothing!" Mah-mee snapped, turning back into the flat. "Come, moi-moi. You have to practice."

A thin bead of sweat glistening on her forehead, Emma looked at Joan and said, "Come on, we better go in."

"I'll be right there," Joan said, her thin body leaning back against the stone wall.

Emma went inside, sat down at the piano, and began to play loud and furious.

For days the air was filled with the high shrill of air-raid sirens. Positioned on the Kowloon peninsula, the Japanese began shelling Hong Kong Island. Again and again, Emma retraced her anxious footsteps over the cracked pavement as they made their way to one of the designated bomb shelters. Usually, these were nothing more than crowded, rat-infested basements. Emma sat on the cold floor, crushed between Ba ba, Mah-mee, and Auntie Go. Joan's eyes were squeezed shut, most likely dreaming of the last movie she'd seen. A child cried as her mother whispered, "Be quiet, be quiet, be quiet," in a frantic chant. Emma tried to imagine that the explosions were firecrackers filling the air and prayed that the long, sad wail of the all-clear signal would sound before they all suffocated in the hot, musty air.

Most of the time, Emma and her family stayed inside as much as possible. The heavy woolen blankets draping the windows for the blackout left them cocooned in their flat. One morning, after days inside, Emma and Joan begged to go to the market with Foon. Mah-mee hesitated, while Ba ba watched his daughters, then said, "I'll go along with them." They willed themselves invisible. Ba ba and Foon moved through the devastated streets like ghosts, while Emma and Joan sidestepped large craters, like deep, jagged wounds in the streets. The corpses of those killed by the bombings often lay in the streets for days, as the nauseating stench of death and dying enveloped Hong Kong.

"They're coming! They're coming!" Emma would wake up sweating from bad dreams. Often, she tiptoed across the hall to Joan's room to sleep. Each day she became more terrified. Just the thought of the approaching Japanese made her sick to her stomach.

From their rooftop, Emma and Joan watched stunned and helpless as the Wanchai district went up in flames, and Statue Square drowned in a thick, suffocating smoke. "It's all 'Gone with the Wind,'" Emma heard Joan whisper. Emma wanted to guess Vivien Leigh as Scarlett O'Hara, but when she opened her mouth, no words emerged. Finally, on Christmas Day, 1941, the British surrendered Hong Kong to the Japanese.

*   *   *

The Japanese occupation brought life in Hong Kong to a near standstill. An eerie silence descended upon the city as Emma and her family held their breath and waited. All the while Mah-mee insisted Auntie Go move in with them.

"Aii-ya, a woman alone, at a time like this! Go, quit your foolishness and move in with us. Those Japanese devils will stop at nothing!"

Emma watched Auntie Go weigh Mah-mee's words, which lingered heavily in the air. Emma knew independence was something her aunt guarded as closely as treasure. What Mah-mee considered foolishness was something Auntie Go cherished. Unlike other Hong Kong Chinese women her age, Auntie Go had never married and often wore Western clothing, sometimes even slacks like Katharine Hepburn. She had made a life of her own running a small knitting business. Now in her midthirties, Auntie Go did as she pleased and was in some ways closer to Emma and Joan than their mother was.

"I'm only two houses away," Go finally said, sighing.

"For the girls," Mah-mee continued, knowing Emma and Joan were Go's weak spot. "They'll worry if you are alone."

"I have Ming and Chen."

Mah-mee waved her hand through the air, as if slapping Auntie Go's words away. "They're servants. What do they care if the Japanese soldiers take everything? They will be gone out the back door before those devils reach your front door! Please, Go. Come and stay with us."

Auntie Go remained silent. She looked over at Emma and smiled and then relented. "All right, Kum Ling. But Ming and Chen come with me."

Emma was delighted Auntie Go was moving in with them. Whenever possible, Emma went over to Auntie Go's house to hear the stories of her business travels. Emma sat and listened engrossed, sucked into the exotic tales of different people and places.

She'd been with her aunt just the afternoon before. "And what about New York?" Emma had asked.

"Big and noisy," Auntie Go had answered, "but also very exciting. The first time I saw the Statue of Liberty, I understood why immigrants felt America was such a great country."

"Why?"

"Because of her size and strength," Auntie Go had answered, then sipped her tea.

Emma had smiled, reminding herself to move New York up on her list of places to visit when the occupation was over. It would be second to Paris, just before Egypt.

Every day, Emma watched the Japanese impose their own image upon her once vibrant city. All the streets, hotels, and even restaurants were given Japanese names. She could never get used to shopping at Matsuzakaya's, instead of Lane Crawford's, or having tea at the Toa, which had been the Peninsula Hotel. Royal statues made of iron were removed and sent back to Japan to be melted down. The rising sun fluttered from flags on buildings and automobiles. Foon flatly refused to walk down Nakameiji-dori, which just the previous week had been Queen's Road.

Emma and Joan spent the first few weeks of the occupation trading one set of rules for another. They kept their eyes fixed on the ground in front of them and learned to bow low to any Japanese soldiers they weren't able to avoid. One afternoon, they watched terrified as a young Chinese man was repeatedly slapped for not bowing low enough to satisfy a Japanese sentry. Emma still saw the thread of blood that had run from the man's lip as they dragged him away. In her mind she wanted to scream, *"Stop them! Stop them!"* to all the Chinese men and women who simply stood passively by, watching. Surely they outnumbered these Japanese devils! But in her heart, Emma knew they were as frozen as she was, shocked into disbelief at what was happening right in front of them. Even Joan averted her gaze and stared blindly toward the ground.

And the horror stories multiplied. Emma heard that most of the remaining British officials and their dependents were being herded into Stanley Camp, beside the seaside village less than an hour away. Emma was glad her friend Mary Clarke had left the year before. She missed the cheerful, colorless faces of her other English classmates and wished she could make all the Japanese soldiers disappear.

But day after day, low whispers moved through the heavy air telling of the torture of Catholic Maryknoll fathers and civilian doctors, who were bound hand and foot and suspended from the ground with a rope tied around their neck. They were then made to stand for days, without food and water, on a narrow piece of bamboo for support. Emma even heard Mah-mee and Ba ba whispering of the countless English and Chinese nurses and servants who were beaten and raped in broad daylight.

"What does *rape* mean?" Emma had asked.

Mah-mee's eyes darted over to Ba ba, then back again. She cleared her throat. "It's when someone forces himself on you without your consent. Do you understand what I mean, moi-moi?" she said in a dark, serious voice.

Emma trembled, felt the hairs rise on the back of her neck. "Yes," she whispered back, not daring to look at Ba ba.

Emma saw little of Mah-mee during the first weeks of the occupation. Her mother spoke perfect Tokyo-dialect Japanese, having spent a great deal of time there with Ba ba's business, and was often called away by frantic friends who begged her to negotiate with the Japanese commanding officers. All Chinese and British possessions were being systematically confiscated—money and jewelry, furniture and automobiles—much of which was then sent on ships back to Japan. Her mother worked day and night saving small, priceless family heirlooms: a brush and comb set, family photos, a porcelain vase handed down through generations. Foon shook her head and would no longer smile for fear of losing her gold tooth.

And while Mah-mee saved whatever she could for family and friends, Emma and the rest of the family struggled like everyone else to obtain food, waiting in long lines for nothing more than a handful of rice and a few stringy pieces of bok choy.

Foon became an expert, bargaining and bartering through the black market for a chicken or two. Once she had even brought back several cans of goose-liver pâté. Emma could still taste its salty smoothness against her tongue as she licked the pâté off a hard, dry biscuit.

Occasionally, Emma would wake up before sunrise and accompany Auntie Go to wait in the Central Market rice line. When they arrived, Emma stood in line and watched the hordes of men, women, and children push and shove their way forward. Voices rose and fell. The persistent smell of salted fish, sweat, and urine filled the air.

"Why are they pushing?" Emma asked. "There's no one selling rice yet."

Auntie Go looked around and quickly inched forward in line. "Everyone's trying to get up front. There's never enough rice for everyone. Those in the back will most likely go home empty-handed."

Emma felt someone push her from behind. She stood her ground, pushed back using elbows and hips. When she turned around, Auntie Go was gone. Emma felt another push from behind and squeezed onward and glimpsed her tall aunt ahead. Emma pushed forward again, felt someone scratch her arm, but didn't look back when she finally caught up.

Auntie Go leaned over and whispered, "When I get our rice, we must leave immediately. Sometimes there's trouble from those who don't get their share."

Emma nodded. She'd heard of riots and fights over a few grains of rice, which ended in cracked skulls when the Japanese intervened.

When Auntie Go finally maneuvered her way to the front, the Japanese soldier's glare sent shivers through Emma. His small eyes narrowed at the sight of them, as if he were intoxicated by the power of holding their fates in his hands. He mumbled something in Japanese that sounded rude and coarse, then laughed out loud. Auntie Go didn't flinch, her face smooth and calm as she held out her burlap bag for a few scoopfuls of the precious grains.

Emma was hot and exhausted by the time they had their small bag of rice and headed home. She felt the lightness of the rough burlap bag held tightly in her hand, calculated it would last them two, maybe three days, and shivered at the thought of Auntie Go having to wait in line again.

Schools were also closed after the invasion, much to the delight of Joan, who never liked studying. During the first month, Emma sat home and reread translations of *Little Women* and *The Scarlet Letter*. At last, her mother arranged for them to study Chinese classics with Professor Ying, a well-known scholar of poetry and classical essays. "It is a great honor," Mah-mee repeated to them. "Do you think he will take just anyone? His time is like gold."

Professor Ying lived in an old apartment, just off a narrow alley that smelled sour with urine and garbage. Inside, his rooms were dark and damp. Emma knew at once that Ying, who appeared to be in his eighties, was too old to be a teacher. Mah-mee couldn't have known that his reputation had long outlived his teaching skills. He had neither the energy nor the patience to deal with young students and gave each of them the same assignments, though Joan was so much older.

In the end, it didn't matter. Only Emma did any of the written work, while Joan sat and daydreamed or stared into a locked glass cabinet in the small dining room where the professor stored his food. Professor Ying, only too happy to be paid for his services, never said anything to their mother about Joan's lack of participation. He simply turned all his attention to Emma, who recited poems every week as he sat listening with his eyes closed and his head tilted down as if he had fallen asleep. The memorized lines seemed to float from her lips.

> *Her black hair must be wet with the dew*
> *Of this autumn night, and her white*
> *Jade arms, chilly with the cold; when,*
> *Oh when, shall we be together again*
> *Standing side by side at the window,*
> *Looking at the moonlight with dried eyes.*

Emma also kept quiet about Joan's indifference. Emma was sometimes irritated by her sister's brazen lack of respect, but she couldn't bring herself to tell their mother, who only wanted to better her daughters' futures, and whose anger was sometimes provoked by much less. Only after they'd left Professor Ying's dark, sour apartment and begun the walk home with Foon did Joan come alive again in the fresh air.

"Why does he keep all his food locked up with that huge padlock?" Joan asked, laughing, after one of their lessons. "He lives by himself, and anyone who wants to can just reach in and take his dry crackers and powdered milk through the missing glass panes in his cabinet."

Foon made a snickering sound.

"Maybe it makes him feel better!" Emma snapped back, defending the professor, though she often wondered the same thing.

Emma had heard stories from her mother and Auntie Go of how the war brought out hidden peculiarities in people. There was the woman who would no longer bathe or change her clothes because she had taped all her jewelry to her body, or the young boy who had suddenly become stone blind, though there was no medical reason. She knew that everyone had to find his own way to survive. Most of the time she tried to lose herself in a book, while Joan went to the movies as often as she could.

"I think it's absolutely crazy." Joan laughed out loud. "I think Professor Ying's crazy too!"

Emma tried to keep a straight face until she felt Joan's elbow nudge her lightly in the side. Then she elbowed her sister back, bursting out in laughter.

chapter 2

Maiden

in

Armour —

1942

JOAN

All day long Joan pored over old Chinese and Hollywood movie magazines trying to catch something she might have missed the hundreds of times she'd studied them before. When she'd memorized the way Hedy Lamarr wore her hat tilted slightly to the left, or how Nancy Chan lifted her hand just so, Joan smiled to herself, then slapped the magazines shut and threw them onto the stack already on the floor. Restlessly, she got up from her bed and moved from one room to another, feeling caged. Most days she and Emma stayed close to home, but on this particularly humid April afternoon, after months of confinement, Joan needed to breathe again.

Her parents were out helping friends deal with Japanese officials who were inspecting their homes, and Emma had gone with Auntie Go to wait in yet another line for a meager cup of rice or a box of powdered milk. Joan could hear Foon moving around in the kitchen, but knew better than to disturb her when she was trying to prepare dinner with what little she had.

In the living room, Joan picked up a copy of the *Hong Kong News*, an English-language newspaper printed by the Japanese. It was still lying on the sofa, where earlier she'd heard Emma reading the Japanese propaganda and small advertisements out loud to Auntie Go. "Look!" Emma had said. "It says the Hong Kong Hotel's snack bar has been turned into a tempura grill, and there's a Japanese lesson here, '*do-mo ar-ri-ga-to,* thank you,' " she'd repeated several times.

"Thank you for what?" Joan mumbled to herself. She turned the page and glanced down at a column called "About Town," which read, *Now with local hostilities laid to rest, Hong Kong movie theatres will begin operating again on a limited basis.* Joan breathed in the stale air. It had been months since she'd last seen a movie, *In Name Only,* with Carole Lombard. Just the thought of going again lifted her spirits.

Since the start of the occupation nearly five months ago, Joan and Emma had been forbidden by their parents to be out after dark, or to walk alone, without Foon. Still, at checkpoints along Robinson or Bonham Roads, Japanese soldiers whose rifles hung ominously from their shoulders often stopped and harassed Joan whenever she dared to venture out. "Shall I walk you home, sweet thing?" a snake-eyed soldier asked. "Wouldn't you like to keep me warm tonight?" another whispered. When Joan came home anxious, Mah-mee shook her head and said, "No matter how you try to camouflage yourself under big coats and hats, those guards are like animals! You can't hide yourself from them. Do as Ba ba says. Just stay indoors where you'll be safe."

Joan sighed. In spite of Mah-mee's warning, she wanted to go out more than ever. She put down the *Hong Kong News,* then moved gingerly toward the kitchen. It was a small, square, gray room toward the back of the flat, with stone-slab counters lining two walls, an enamel washbasin, and charcoal fires enough for two woks.

There was also a small space in back where Foon slept. Ever since they were little, Joan and Emma were forbidden to disturb Foon's sleeping space. Originally a pantry, the narrow closet had been Foon's room for as long as Joan could remember. Once, when Foon was at the market, Joan and Emma had stolen into the kitchen to peek behind the faded red curtain that draped the opening. It was like a game to them. Emma was only six or seven and had a hard time stifling her giggles. Joan turned and covered Emma's mouth with the palm of her hand until she stopped laughing. The kitchen was cold and sterile, dark in the winter light. Joan grabbed the coarse cloth and pulled it slowly aside as Emma hovered behind her. A strong, musty smell hit them first, which Joan later discovered came from the dry mushrooms sitting on the shelf. There was no window, and the space was too dark for them to really see anything clearly.

Joan turned and whispered to Emma, "Go watch out for Foon."

Then Joan sneaked forward, raising her hand in search of the string that turned on the light. With a quick click, Joan surveyed the cramped space, just enough room for a makeshift bunk bed on one side and shelves on the other. There was so little there, mostly dry foods Foon used for cooking. Only the bottom bunk had a sheet and blanket on it, the top holding Foon's few possessions—two small piles of clothing, a padded jacket, a worn straw hat she wore to the market during the hot summer months. It was the first time Joan realized Foon existed on so little. It seemed barely enough to represent a life.

"What's in there?" Emma giggled. She didn't dare to leave her place at the door.

"Just a bed and some clothes." Joan swallowed. She quickly turned off the light, but the memory of Foon's spare life had always stayed with her.

Joan pushed open the kitchen door slowly, and right away the rich, pungent smells of Foon's herbs filled her with longing. Every night Foon would surprise them with culinary delights, despite the meager food rationing. Strange soups and vegetables appeared on the table, made from dry herbs and plants Joan could only guess at. It was as if Foon were a magician, creating something out of nothing. And if she was lucky enough to bargain through the black market for a chicken, or a piece of meat, they ate well and never questioned her sources.

The windows facing the courtyard were open, but the kitchen still felt sweltering. Joan cleared her throat to let Foon know she was there.

"What do you need?" Foon asked as she continued to mince garlic without looking up.

Joan shifted from one foot to the other. At sixteen, she still felt like a little girl around her old servant. "When will dinner be?" she finally asked, thinking it better to ease into a conversation with Foon.

"Same as always." Foon raised her head and eyed Joan closely. "Why?"

"I was wondering if I could go out for a little while. I'll be home before it gets dark. I promise I'll be very careful."

Foon looked back down and continued to mince. "Your mah-mee wants you to stay home."

"She won't know. I'll be back before she comes home."

"Too dangerous," Foon said, never looking up.

Joan lingered, watching the quick movements of Foon's hands as she scooped the minced garlic into a bowl.

"Can I just go to the end of Robinson Road to meet Auntie Go and Emma?" Joan asked. At least she would be outside.

"No farther?"

"No."

Foon picked up a wilted bunch of green onions. "Go then," she said, holding up her cleaver and bringing it down with a swift chop.

Joan skipped down the stone steps to the dark, cool entryway of their building, which always smelled of mildew and incense. She walked quickly down Conduit Road, wrapped in one of Mah-mee's cashmere sweaters over her cotton cheungsam. She wished she could disguise herself as well as Hua Mulan, the maiden warrior. At the end of the block, Joan paused and looked around. The streets were empty of Japanese soldiers. Only a few women and servants hurried home with their precious rations. Joan hesitated a moment, deciding whether to continue down to Central. Her mind raced with an urgency to know if the theatres were operating, hoping that the one thing she loved most might be returned to normal. The same road she had walked down thousands of times lay before her, quiet and inviting. She felt certain Kate Hepburn would keep walking, knew Hua Mulan would.

Halfway down to Central, Joan was perspiring from the late-afternoon warmth, and the guilt of having lied to Foon. She wanted to take off her sweater, but decided against it. So far, she'd found it easy to avoid all the Japanese checkpoints, but there was something unsettling in the sticky air that made her keep Mah-mee's sweater wrapped around her. When she walked past St. Paul's Middle School, Joan thought she heard someone call out her name and stopped long enough to realize it must have been her imagination. The closer she came to Central, the more sounds and activity besieged her. High-crying voices pierced the air, while the squeaking wheels of hand-pulled carts moved all around her.

She looked down and walked carefully around the concrete rubble still littering the streets from the countless bombings. Storefronts she had walked past since childhood stood ransacked, their broken windows boarded up against the light. Bone-thin vendors sat slumped against walls selling their meager, unwanted wares of pencils and combs. When she came to the end of Flower Street, Joan saw a group of Japanese soldiers loitering a half block away. They appeared no older than she was, dressed in uniforms that didn't seem to fit, that sagged or pulled at places they shouldn't. She quickly looked away and crossed the street toward the Queen's Theatre. For a moment, Joan wondered if she'd made a mistake going out alone, but her heart raced when she looked up and saw the marquee still advertising *His Girl Friday*, starring Cary Grant and Rosalind Russell. As she entered the cool shade of the theatre, Joan glanced around, hoping the soldiers hadn't spotted her. Satisfied that she was alone, Joan walked up to a piece of paper posted on the theatre door. Written in both Chinese characters and English, it read, *Queen's Theatre will reopen by the end of the week. Now under Japanese management, a series of Japanese films will be shown first, as a way to acquaint those in Hong Kong with the Japanese ways.* Joan stepped back, disappointed that it wouldn't be a Hollywood film, angry that the Japanese devils had taken even the movies away from her. She was about to turn around when someone grabbed her arm from behind. Impulsively, she pulled away, but the grip only closed tighter, twisting painfully. She jerked around to face a young Japanese soldier, and the thought flashed through her mind that he looked like a boy who might be in her class.

"Come with me," he snapped in Japanese.

Joan's stomach began to turn. The heat felt oppressive as she tried once more to pull away from the soldier's grip. She couldn't help but think how angry Mah-mee would be that she'd gone off alone.

"What do you want?" she whispered hoarsely.

Grasping the back of her sweater, the soldier swung her around and half-dragged her back into the doorway of the theatre. When she tried to scream, he covered her mouth and yanked her hair back with such force, she thought he would break her neck. For a moment, Joan's mind went blank. She smelled the oily scent of metal and faintly heard the soldier hiss something in Japanese. When he slammed her against the wall and pressed himself against her, Joan thought, *It can't be like this; it's never like this in the movies!* He clawed at her clothes, trying to pull up her cheungsam. Then, as if suddenly awakening, Joan struggled against him, pushing and scratching at his face. He swore at her, but when Joan knocked off his glasses, he fell back enough for her to jerk up her knee hard into his groin. Her heart jumped at the sound of his low grunt and the sharp intake of air that might have been her own as he stumbled back just enough for her to push him hard and run.

Joan ran blindly until her lungs felt as if they would burst. Faces blurred as she passed them. She looked back once or twice, but there was no sign the Japanese soldier was following her. Still, she couldn't take any chances. She dodged in and out of buildings and down narrow alleys. Hiding in a bathroom stall at the Hong Kong Hotel, she couldn't stop shaking for almost an hour. At last, in a hot rush, she jumped into a taxi and returned home, sick to her stomach.

By the time Joan arrived home, the sky had turned a dusty gray. A dull ache was in her muscles and her legs felt as heavy as lead. She straightened her hair. Her clothes felt disgustingly dirty. Joan didn't think she would ever forget the soldier's oily-metal smell. Slowly she pushed open the front door and stepped inside. From the hall she saw Foon in the living room pacing back and forth, muttering to Emma, "Good thing your mah-mee's not back yet." Joan had never seen Foon so worried, and it sent a terrifying numbness through her to think about what could have happened in that watery light of night if she hadn't escaped.

"I'm so sorry." Joan stepped into the living room. "I didn't mean to go so far."

Foon looked up, her gold tooth fully exposed. Emma ran to Joan, but stopped when she held out her arm as if to keep Emma at a safe distance.

"Auntie Go's out looking for you," Emma said, her voice high and excited.

Whatever Foon was thinking, she remained silent. Joan saw the glaze of fear in her eyes and the thin film of sweat on her forehead as she continued to pace back and forth across the room. Her eyes narrowed as she looked Joan up and down for what seemed like a long time, then she stopped and said, "Hurry! Go change before your mah-mee returns."

Emma followed Joan into her room and quickly closed the door behind them. "What happened? Where were you?" Emma asked in one breath.

Joan began unbuttoning her cheungsam, her fingers numb and clumsy. Her tongue felt thick. "I was followed by a soldier," she whispered.

Emma moved closer. "Are you all right?"

Joan nodded her head and tried to remain calm. "Yes. Of course. I lost him. I hid in the ladies' room at the Hong Kong Hotel. I caught a taxi from there."

The smell of the humid streets still lingered on her sweater and cheungsam. Joan took them off and wrapped herself in an old robe. Her hair hung heavy down her back. She lifted it off her neck, then let it drop again at the thought of the soldier's oily fingers tangled in its length. She steadied herself as a wave of nausea passed over her. Faintly she heard Emma asking again if she was all right. But when Joan saw how scared her sister looked, she avoided Emma's large, questioning eyes, pressed her lips together, and kept quiet. Then, instead of placing her clothes neatly on the bed as she usually did, Joan flung them in a pile on the floor next to the black lacquer chest.

Joan took a deep breath to calm herself. She opened the door and, with Emma following closely behind, stumbled out of her room into the bathroom. From the teak cabinet, she took Mah-mee's steel shears, then turned to face the mirror. Slowly and deliberately, she cut her hair as short as a boy's. Watching her hair fall away, Joan was surprised at how easy it was to become someone else. The face that stared back at her in the mirror already appeared younger, lighter. With each quick, sharp snip of the scissors, more and more silky black hair lay coiled and limp on the floor, like a dead animal.

That evening at dinner Joan ate little. It was hard to follow the conversation. Auntie Go's and Emma's words seemed to float all around her. When Mah-mee saw Joan's short hair, she simply said, "Short hair is much easier to take care of. Besides, it will grow out again when the time is right."

Joan breathed a sigh of relief when she closed the door to her room. She somehow felt safer in the small, familiar space. She prayed that the soldier would soon fade from her mind like a bad nightmare. A sourness rose up into her throat and she swallowed it back down. She touched her naked neck, then the close-cropped head of hair that felt as if it belonged to someone else. Not until hours later, when the milky, gray light of morning filled the room, did Joan dare to reach over and turn off the light.

* * *

On a hot, airless afternoon toward the end of July, Mah-mee called Joan and Emma into the living room. Joan glanced at the piano, the pearl-inlaid lacquered boxes sitting on the table, and the vase she had collected a few years ago from a store that owed her father money. They remained untouched. Joan held her breath for the day when their house would be inspected by the Japanese. In one quick sweep, they would take everything they wanted, until all that was left were empty walls. She had heard rumors that even bathroom fixtures were being removed and sent back to Japan.

Mah-mee had just arrived home and was still clutching her handbag as she waited by the tall terrace windows. In the slant of sunlight that fell around her, Joan thought how Mah-mee, who had just turned thirty-eight, looked not much older than herself.

"I've applied to the Japanese government for permission to move to Macao," she said as soon as they sat down. "Ba ba and I think it would be much better for the two of you."

"When?" Emma asked.

"As soon as possible," Mah-mee said.

Joan glanced over at Emma, who was smiling and clapping her hands in excitement. Joan swallowed hard. Trying to remember what it was like to feel that happy took all her strength. It had been weeks since the Japanese soldier had left her feeling anesthetized. Joan watched as Emma ran to hug Mah-mee, whose handbag dropped heavily to the floor.

While they talked, Joan gradually let the idea sink in. She and Emma had gone to Macao several times as young girls to visit friends and relatives. The sweet taste of fresh mango pudding and coconut candy came to mind. Her mouth almost watered. The Portuguese colony had long been neutral territory, as well as a gamblers' haven for the Chinese. According to the papers, the Japanese had more than welcomed their exodus, hoping to reduce the Chinese population and replace it with their own. Macao had a

romantic feel that reminded Joan of the movie *Algiers*, with Charles
Boyer. For the first time in weeks, something inside her stirred.

Less than two months later, their emigration papers to Macao
were approved. Mah-mee called them into her room, handed Joan
and Emma each a suitcase.

"Take only what you can carry," Mah-mee told them. "The
steam ferry will be crowded enough."

"Is Ba ba going?" Emma asked.

Mah-mee shook her head, straightened the collar of her cheungsam, then answered, "Auntie Go and Foon will be going with
us. Ba ba has to stay here and watch the flat. Apparently, his only
compensation for having done business in Japan for twenty years is
an untouched flat! When things settle down, he'll come to visit."
Mah-mee waved her hand at them. "Hurry now, go pack."

Joan closed the door to her room. She hated the thought of leaving Ba ba, wanted to say something as she touched her cropped
hair. She couldn't wait to leave the strict confines of Japanese-
occupied Hong Kong. Maybe in Macao her nightmares would go
away. Sometimes, she tried to keep herself awake all night to escape
the dark shadows that visited her sleep. The next morning, Joan was
always so tired she could barely get through the day. Only then, if
she was lucky enough, could she sleep through the night.

Orphan
Island
Paradise —
1942—45

EMMA

The instant Emma stepped off the Macao ferry that afternoon in
October of 1942, she felt protected, safe at last from all the Japanese devils. She turned to Joan, who appeared serene in a half-trance,
her short black hair fluttering in the warm, salty wind. More than
anything, Emma wanted her sister to regain her spirit, to laugh and
act out movie scenes again. Ever since the night Joan was followed
by the Japanese soldier, Emma had worried. Most of the time Joan
seemed guarded, her words measured and brief, and when she did
talk, Emma felt something cold and distant in her sister's voice,

some dark shadow in her mind that Emma prayed their time in Macao would help to erase.

Emma could feel their move already working. Back on the enclosed deck of the ferry, Mah-mee and Auntie Go had stood up and squeezed through the crowds to get tea. All around them high, whining voices reverberated in the crowded, airless space. Knowing Joan couldn't resist Garbo, Emma hoped for some reaction when she called after them, "Give me a whiskey . . . and don't be stingy, baby," a terrible version of Garbo in *Anna Christie*.

Joan had sat motionless on the wooden bench, staring blankly out at the water. Emma waited for her to give any sign that she'd heard. The slightest smile would do. But Joan remained silent. Emma had shrugged and returned to reading her battered copy of *Wuthering Heights* when Joan's hoarse whisper suddenly grazed her ear. "Gif me a viskey . . . and dawn't be stingy, baby."

Many of her family's friends and relatives had already settled in Macao, and Emma was glad to join them in the safety of the tree-lined streets and Mediterranean architecture. Even as a little girl, she had dreamed of going to the faraway lands she'd read about, the wide open spaces of America, or the broad boulevards of Paris or Berlin. Hong Kong sometimes felt like a crowded room, the walls closed in all around her.

On the wharf, women sat behind crates selling fruits and flowers. Emma turned around to make sure Auntie Go and Foon were following. She wanted to laugh at the sight of her aunt almost a head taller than Foon as they walked side by side. She held on tight to her mother's and Joan's hands as they hurried away from the dock and through a lingering crowd. Along the main Avenida Amizade stood a line of tricycle-drawn, two-seater pedicabs, the drivers scrambling and hustling for customers. Foon hissed at them, "Get away, get away." As they walked on, Emma felt both delighted and appalled that life in Macao had continued without pause, while less than three hours away, the war continued to turn lives around. The fresh air tasted faintly of exotic fruits. She breathed in great mouthfuls, unable to get enough.

With the help and connections of relatives, Mah-mee sold some of her jewelry to rent a small, comfortable house with a veranda that wrapped around it like a ribbon. Emma and Joan shared one bedroom, while Mah-mee and Auntie Go had the other. Foon occupied a small space off the kitchen.

Emma liked the house immediately. It was barely half the size of their Hong Kong flat, but there was something romantic about its simple, white stucco walls and red-tiled roof. She could already feel Joan more at ease, the small house somehow embracing them, keeping them safe from the Japanese.

The room she shared with Joan looked out on a quiet street lined with umbrella-shaped palm trees. One morning not long after they unpacked and settled in, Emma heard some sweet, melodious voices coming from outside. She ran to her bedroom window and peered out at a group of Macanese children skipping rope and dancing to tunes they sang aloud. Auntie Go had told her the children were a wonderful mixture of Portuguese, Chinese, Brazilian, and African. Emma envied their smooth, dark skin and quick steps. At twelve, she still felt as clumsy as a small child. When one of the Macanese girls looked up and caught her eye, Emma felt a warmth touch her cheeks before she shyly turned away.

The tiny Portuguese colony also gave Emma a taste of another world. Faint threads of Portuguese echoed through the cobblestone streets, sounding an exotic music that she loved. Macao never slept, but moved in a rhythm all its own. You could buy or sell anything for exorbitant prices. Enterprising men who had tapped into the black market became rich. No one knew when the war would end, and many were willing to pay dearly for luxuries such as cigarettes and silk stockings. Every day on their way to school, Emma and Joan tried to ignore the singsong call of "Missee, lookee, missee," from merchants trying to sell them their wares. The girls walked freely down the wide, shaded boulevard of Avenida Almeida Ribeiro with many of their old Hong Kong friends. Sometimes they laughed and talked with the sweet, fragrant air of forgetting. But other times, they spoke wistfully of friends who had remained behind.

In some ways, Emma found each day in Macao similar to life in pre-occupation Hong Kong. Mah-mee resumed her social activities of leisurely lunches and mah-jongg games. Auntie Go worked in the garden and revived plans for her knitting business once the war was over. Foon spent more and more time in the kitchen. But it was Joan whom Emma watched most closely, quietly waiting for her to resemble again the sister Emma had always known.

Every morning when Joan picked up her hairbrush, Emma wondered what she was thinking as the bristles sailed through her short hair.

"Do you miss it?" Emma asked one morning, poised against the doorframe.

"What? Hong Kong?" Joan looked up as if noticing Emma for the first time.

"No. Do you miss your long hair?" Emma watched Joan stare back into the mirror, her hand sliding down the back of her head to the nape of her neck.

"Sometimes."

Emma touched her own shoulder-length hair, her fingers loosening mild knots. "Me too."

From the time they were babies, she and Joan had balanced on each side of their family seesaw, tilting more to one parent than the other in looks or temperament. Though they appeared so different and were almost opposite in personality, Emma sometimes saw the slightest similarities in their gestures, and in the way they laughed. But it was by their lustrous dark hair that they most resembled each another.

Emma loved going to the casinos and nightclubs that enlivened evenings in Macao and added to the prosperity of the colony. The loud hum of urgent voices in the casino below their favorite Chinese restaurant intrigued her. To reach the restaurant, she had to walk through the large, smoky casino filled with determined people betting on everything from *pai gow* to craps, oblivious to whether it was day or night. To Emma the gamblers seemed to be under some sort of spell, yelling wildly at dice and cards to do as they commanded.

"Seven! Seven!" one man sang to a pair of dice resting in the palm of his hand. The dice tumbled onto the worn green table and turned up a three and a one. "Death to you!" he yelled at them, his face becoming an angry mask.

Emma stopped and watched for as long as she could, until her mother or Auntie Go pushed her along.

While waiting for their food, Emma begged to play *dai-sui,* a numbers game in which she selected either a small number between one and nine or a larger number between nine and eighteen. If she chose with luck, she doubled her money. To humor Emma, Mahmee and Auntie Go usually let her play a round. Then Emma would stop eating and anxiously wait. When the dice were rolled, and the bulbs began lighting up, Emma's eyes flashed to the board, her eager stare darting up and down between the number on the wall and the one on the piece of paper she held tightly in her hand. Even Joan, who often appeared bored by all the activity around her, stopped and watched as the bulbs came alive.

In the sultry winter nights of Macao, Emma delighted in watching Joan slowly unwind and become herself again. Within two months of their arrival, Joan's hair grew into a short pageboy that for a while made her resemble Joan of Arc. On Saturday mornings, Emma and Joan often accompanied Foon to the market to help shop for their evening meals. After months of so little to eat in Hong Kong, they found rice, meat, and vegetables abundant, although expensive. Emma loved the musical cries of the vendors and the wooden crates stacked high, filled with everything from chickens to snakes. They stood by, entertained by Foon, who picked and haggled over everything, from oranges to bok choy.

"Too much! Too much!" Foon argued.

"You pay for what you get!" an old, toothless man returned. He dropped the dark green leaves into a bag, held it out to Foon. "You want it or not?"

Foon wavered. She picked up a bunch of green onions, wilted slightly at the tips, and held up the long, flowerless stems. "Include this, then I want it."

The old man grinned, then nodded. "Okay, okay." He leaned forward and opened the bag, mumbling something to himself as Foon dropped the green onions in.

At the same time, Joan began to show a real interest in cooking. The theatrics of the marketplace were far more entertaining than the same old Portuguese melodramas that played in the local theatre for months. Emma and Joan had seen them so often, they began to memorize the dialogue by heart, though they could never fully understand all of it. Lying in their beds at night, Joan mimicked the fluid Portuguese lines. *"Eu te amo com todo cor a ção,"* I love you darling with all my heart, Joan spouted without a mistake.

"I do too," Emma answered in English.

"Fique comigo para sempre," come be with me for the rest of our lives, Joan said, and both of them burst out in laughter.

Still, Emma was amazed at how convincing Joan was, even in a foreign language.

Emma often found her sister in the small, hot kitchen, where Foon sliced slivers of beef and peeled lotus roots or turnips. Joan watched, absorbed, while softly reciting to herself the five great grains of Chinese cooking—wheat, sesame, barley, beans, and rice. Soon, she was slicing and frying alongside Foon, learning the small secrets of how to keep crispy chicken moist, or just how long to fry glass shrimp with ginger and garlic. "As soon as they turn milky white," Foon directed, "don't hesitate, don't wait!" It wasn't long before Joan could prepare a meal almost as well as Foon.

Emma remembered one time Mah-mee caught Joan in the kitchen cooking. Mah-mee stood on the threshold of the door, her flowery perfume mixing with the aroma of frying food. "Are you finished with your studies?" she asked Joan, her voice flat and stern.

Joan looked up, surprised. She had just begun tossing Chinese green beans and thin slices of pork in a large wok. "Yes," she quickly answered, looking back down at the spitting oil.

As Foon ladled soup into four bowls, Mah-mee remained perfectly still, eyeing Joan. The kitchen felt hot and crowded. Emma stood quietly as she watched Mah-mee's lips part then close again as if tasting the thick air. "Be careful," Mah-mee finally said, turning around to leave. But even after the door closed behind her, her perfume lingered.

One afternoon in late February when Mah-mee and Auntie Go were out, Foon refused to let Emma into the kitchen. "No, no, not yet," Foon said, pushing her back outside. Curious, Emma strained to look beyond her into the cluttered kitchen where Joan had been cooking. Soon, exotic aromas drifted through the closed door. Emma detected the sweet scent of coconut and curry, an aroma unlike that of any dish Foon had cooked in Hong Kong. Emma pressed her ear to the kitchen door thinking of any excuse to get in. Not that she had any real interest in recipes, but she wanted to know what the big secret was. The low, intimate whispering between Foon and Joan gave nothing away. Emma pushed hard against the locked door once more and gave up. She'd have to find something else to do.

Emma stepped out the front door and closed it softly behind her. It was the first time she had ventured out alone in Macao. The rains of the past few days had left a moist, pungent smell of earth. Cool and refreshed, the air enveloped her instantly and made her feel better. She was glad to be wearing a long-sleeved shirt and overalls. Emma skipped down the stone steps and stood under the cover of a large palm tree, not knowing which direction to go. At the sound of a sharp whistle, she turned to see the Macanese girl who lived next door standing a few feet from her. Since she'd first seen the girl singing and jumping rope outside her bedroom window, Emma had felt curious about her, often standing by her window watching the large, boisterous family at play, too shy to approach them.

"You going out?" the girl asked in heavily accented English. She held on to both ends of a jump rope, which she swung back and forth, wrapping and unwrapping it around her sturdy legs above open-toed sandals.

"Yes," Emma shyly answered. The girl, no older than Emma, was slightly taller. Her curly hair was wild and she wore a light cotton jumper.

"You maybe want company?"

Emma heard the Portuguese lilt that laced each phrase. "If you'd like. I'm only going for a short walk."

Without another word, the Macanese girl dropped the jump rope on the wet grass and Emma fell in step beside her. As they walked in silence, Emma glanced at the girl's arm, where a long, faded white scar rose from her elbow to her broad shoulder. Her skin was the color of pale tea, and Emma thought she smelled faintly of cinnamon.

"You from Hong Kong like all the others?" the girl asked.

"Yes, I'm here with my family. All except for my father. He's still back in Hong Kong."

"My *papai*'s dead. He died in a fishing accident just after my youngest brother, José, was born."

"I'm sorry."

The girl kicked a rock out of their way, and Emma wondered how she didn't hurt her toe. She turned to Emma and smiled.

"My name is Maria Theresa Felicite Barbosa, but most call me Lia."

"I'm Emma Lew." It was too humid to go through the slew of Chinese names given to her at birth.

"Hong Kong is *grandioso* I have heard."

Emma nodded. "Hong Kong's also noisy and crowded, not like here."

"All kinds come to Macao," Lia said, nudging a small lizard across the road. "Most now because of the Japanese. Others for the gambling, though I don't know what they see in it."

"I think it has to do with the excitement," Emma blurted out. "Like chasing some kind of dream." She couldn't help remembering her own experiences playing *dai-sui*.

"Why chase something you can't catch?"

Emma didn't have a ready answer. She wanted to say because it was fun, but decided to keep quiet.

"I've never been farther than the islands," Lia continued.

"Which islands?"

"Taipa and Colôane." Lia swept her dark, curly hair out of her face. "They're not far. Trees and hills mainly. My uncle Arturo takes all of us over in his boat."

"How many brothers and sisters do you have?"

"Four brothers and one sister. All younger," Lia said in one easy breath.

Emma smiled. "I have an older sister."

"The short-haired one? Very *bonita*."

"Yes, we're very different."

Emma felt Lia's gaze fall heavy upon her, making her uncomfortable. She shoved her hands into her pockets.

"But isn't that good?" Lia finally said. "What good is it if we all look and act the same?"

Emma shrugged and stopped. She felt herself blush, and she quickly changed the subject. "We better turn back now," she said, thinking she ought to return home before Foon noticed her missing.

As they turned around, Lia began to hum a tune softly. Emma listened as the notes rose and filled the misty air. She was reminded once again of how she liked Macao, and of how she already liked this tea-colored girl with the wild, dark hair.

Just two days earlier, Joan had anxiously been waiting for Emma to come home. Joan took her by the arm the moment she stepped through the door. Joan's face was dark and serious, her lips pressed tightly together.

"What's wrong?" Emma asked when she saw her sister looking so despondent.

"Mah-mee doesn't want me to spend so much time with Foon in the kitchen. She thinks it takes away from my studies and social life. I don't know what I'll do if I can't cook." Joan's voice sounded tense and urgent.

"What can I do about it?" Emma asked, already knowing the answer.

"Talk to her, tell her how important it is to me," Joan pleaded.

She doesn't want you to cook, Emma thought to herself. *You're her only hope. She knows how beautiful you are and wants you to marry into a good family and have many children,* Emma almost blurted out. Instead, she said, "I'll try, if you think I can help."

Joan smiled, coughing up a laugh. "Of course you can, Mah-mee loves you best."

Emma often wondered how much her mother really loved her. She remembered waiting for all the approving smiles, the quick brush of Mah-mee's cheek against her lips, the uncertainty of whether Mah-mee's potent smell of Shalimar perfume meant she had just arrived or left the flat. Her mother's affection had always felt like playing hide-and-seek to Emma—a game she always disliked.

That night at dinner, Foon and Joan sat Mah-mee, Auntie Go, and Emma down at the table, then disappeared back into the kitchen.

"Foon, what are you two up to?" Mah-mee called out, tapping impatiently on the arm of her chair.

"Be patient, they have a surprise for us," Auntie Go said.

"What kind of surprise takes so long?" Mah-mee paused for a moment, then rose from her chair just as the kitchen door swung open.

"Coming, coming," Foon said, holding open the door.

Joan emerged carefully carrying a large, covered bowl. Heat and steam had pressed her short hair close to her head. She placed the bowl on the table, stepped back, and said, "Portuguese chicken, made from the freshest Macao ingredients!"

Auntie Go clapped first, followed by Emma, then, at last, by Mah-mee. Joan smiled at her applause, bowed, and sat down next to Emma.

Foon carried in a plate of Chinese mustard greens and a large container of rice. "Eat, eat," she commanded.

"What's in it?" Emma asked.

Joan smiled and rattled off a list of ingredients in her calm, steady voice. "Chicken, potatoes, coconut, tomato, olive oil, curry, olives, and saffron."

Foon hovered over them as they ate. Even Mah-mee seemed to loosen up and enjoy herself once she had tasted Joan's Portuguese chicken. "Very good," she muttered under her breath.

"Excellent!" Auntie Go said. She dished more sauce over her rice.

Emma turned to Joan and nodded her head in approval, careful not to talk with her mouth full. Joan smiled back. In the short silence between them, Emma once again caught a glimpse of the confident, bill-collecting actress who was her sister.

They had almost finished eating when they heard the first scream, high and harsh, so unexpected, so out of place, that no one moved at first. When the second scream pierced the air, Auntie Go leapt from her chair and ran to the window.

"Something's happening next door," she said, hurrying toward the front door.

Emma and Joan dropped their napkins and followed without a word. The air was still thick and wet as they rushed toward Lia's house. Emma felt the earth soft beneath her shoes. Seeing the big, rambling house, she felt odd intruding on her new friend's family, but a third scream that raised the hairs on the back of her neck convinced her something was terribly wrong.

The door to the house was standing wide open as they approached the front steps, but the loud screams had become a muted, almost rhythmic crying. Auntie Go turned around and told them to wait for her outside, just as Lia came shuffling out of the house, pulling and pushing three boys and a girl with her.

"Are you all right?" Auntie Go asked, her voice calm yet urgent.

Lia looked up, and when she saw them, Emma thought her friend was going to burst into tears. Instead, Lia swallowed and said in a soft, distant voice, "My brother José."

Auntie Go ran up the steps and into the house. Emma and Joan didn't move, though Emma felt Joan take hold of her arm. Lia, her sister, and the three boys stayed huddled on the porch, as if they'd forgotten that Emma and Joan were there. Emma tried to say something, but her mouth felt dry and useless. She stood there staring at Lia, watching as she calmed the four children, wiping their noses and pressing down stray hairs. In that moment, she seemed much older to Emma than the girl she had watched singing and jumping rope.

That night in bed, Emma relived the entire story told by Auntie Go. José, the three-year-old, youngest brother of Lia, was eating dinner and laughing as usual when he suddenly became quiet. No one paid attention at first. Six children at the table were often noisy and boisterous. By the time Lia's mother turned around, she could see that José had turned beet red. She jumped up and began pounding the little boy on the back. Lia opened his mouth and tried to dislodge what had become stuck, but it was no use. They turned José over and held him upside down, slapping his back and coaxing him to spit it out. "José, *minha menino,*" Lia's mother yelled over and over. "Spit it out!" First red. Then blue. José began to turn gray and his arms twitched. His legs jerked. His eyes rolled back. Lia's mother screamed. By the time Auntie Go arrived, José lay quietly in his mother's arms as if he were asleep.

The next afternoon Emma and her family sat in the Barbosa living room, along with other friends and relatives who had come to pay their respect. The drawn damask curtains and heavy wood furniture made the room dark and solemn. Emma breathed in the painfully sweet scent of fresh flowers. Lia's mother was upstairs resting, leaving Lia to stoically accept the tearful kisses, and basket after basket of fruits and vegetables. Her three younger brothers and sister sat quietly with aunts and uncles.

Emma watched her somber friend move politely from one person to the next. Just as Lia approached them, Emma heard Mahmee whisper, "The poor girl, she has to do her mother's job," to Auntie Go.

A soft, quick, mechanical "Thank you for coming" emerged from Lia.

She moved in a dull, heavy manner, like someone Emma had never met. Lia's wild hair was combed tightly against her head, and she wore an ill-fitting, long-sleeved white blouse, rolled up at the sleeves, and black skirt. Emma kept her gaze focused on Lia, hoping to gain her new friend's attention for just a moment. But in her face Emma saw the same dazed look of disbelief that she'd seen just after the occupation, when so many in Hong Kong had lost someone they loved.

For weeks after, the Barbosa house seemed lifeless, as if Lia and her family had all vanished into its dark rooms. Emma longed to hear the singing voices and the high squeal of laughter that used to draw her to the window, but each day she was greeted with an empty, silent yard.

The only time Emma caught a glimpse of Lia was when she left for school in the mornings. Lia looked pale and drawn as she shepherded her sister and brothers out of the house for the short walk to the Portuguese Catholic school they attended. Before Emma could speak, Lia brushed her aside with a wave of her hand, leaving Emma to watch as Lia disappeared down the dirt road with her sister and brothers. She never looked back.

Emma and Joan walked in the opposite direction to Poi Do, the Chinese girls' school that many of Emma's Hong Kong friends also attended. It was nothing more than a few neighboring houses, whose upstairs and downstairs rooms were transformed into a temporary school. Many of the teachers were the same ones Emma and Joan had had in Hong Kong before the occupation. Sometimes, when Emma sat in the classroom and listened to the familiar whisper of voices around her, she shuddered to think she might still be in Hong Kong. But when she left the confines of Poi Do and stepped out into the soft air smelling faintly of the sea, she breathed a sigh of relief. She walked quickly down the uneven pavement toward home, hoping to catch a glimpse of Lia.

One month later, Emma was surprised to find Lia waiting for her when she arrived home from school. Lia looked thinner and older, as if she had just pulled through some great illness. Her wild hair flew in all directions as she stood by one of the large palm trees. Two old bicycles leaned against the tree.

"Our month of mourning is over," Lia said shyly. Then before Emma could say anything, she asked, "Would you like to go bicycle riding?"

"Yes," Emma answered, happy she hadn't followed Joan and Foon to the market. "Just let me change my clothes."

Emma ran into the house, dropped her knapsack on the hall table, then slipped out of her dress and into a pair of overalls. From her bedroom window she peeked outside to make sure Lia was still waiting for her. When she glimpsed her friend's dark hair, Emma swallowed her happiness and ran outside.

"I'm sorry about José," Emma said as they pushed their bikes out to the main road. She gripped the handlebars tighter as she spoke the little boy's name.

Lia stopped and closed the gate behind them. She smoothed her hair away from her face and took her time answering. "*Mamae* thinks it was the *fantasma*," she said, turning to Emma.

"What?"

"It's a ghost. *Mamae* thinks a ghost killed José." Lia swung her leg over the bicycle seat, which creaked a long sigh as she settled onto it.

Emma hesitated. "There's a ghost in your house?"

Lia nodded. "First, it took my *papai*, now José. The house is very old and the spirit refuses to leave."

Emma straddled her bike, letting it lean against her leg. "Why haven't you moved if your house is haunted?"

"It was left to us by my *mamae*'s great-aunt Carmelita. We wouldn't have anywhere else to go. It's her ghost that refuses to leave."

"But why would she kill her own family?"

"*Mamae* says her great-aunt Carmelita always acted strange around my *papai*. She would stare at him for the longest time, then whisper how he had only married my *mamae* for the house."

"But what about José? He was just a little boy."

"José was the spitting image of my *papai* as a boy. My *mamae* thinks Carmelita simply disliked him for that reason and no longer wanted José in her house."

"She must have been an awful person!" Emma said, lowering her voice. A sudden shiver moved through her body. She turned back to look at the old, rambling Barbosa house. Other than needing a new coat of paint, it appeared ordinary and harmless.

"I never knew her," Lia said, pushing down on the pedal of her bike. "She died the year I was born." She turned back as she began gliding away. "Come on, I'll race you down to Avenida Amizade!"

Emma paused a minute to digest the story about Lia's great-great-aunt Carmelita. Emma wasn't sure if it was true or not, but she supposed Lia's mother had to find some excuse to live with José's senseless death. Besides, the idea of a ghost roaming the dark rooms of the Barbosa house captivated Emma's imagination. She looked ahead and saw Lia already creating a distance between them. A sudden, cold wind brushed the back of Emma's head, and the sweet, rotting smell of flowers filled the air, even though the first spring blossoms had yet to bloom. Emma glanced back into the empty yard where the two looming palm trees stood guard, then quickly jumped onto her bicycle and began pedaling as fast as she could.

Emma and Lia rode their bikes to the Avenida Amizade. Down by the harbor, they watched entire lives pass before them. Vendors lived behind crates and boxes, hustling everything from noodles in watery soup to thick ceramic teacups. They cried out in high, strained voices, hoping someone might stop long enough to listen. The ferries moaned and inched their way into the narrow docks to unload passengers. Emma was surprised to see refugees still coming. She easily recognized which families came from Hong Kong— their concerned, slightly dazed faces standing out among the others. She wanted to take their hands and lead them through the wonderful maze of Macao streets, but knew that they, like her own family, would soon find their way.

Emma had brought along some money Auntie Go had given her, so they bought coconut candy from a vendor who was kind to them. The thin, old man gave them an additional piece for free. "For the pretty one, and for the smart one," he said, holding the candy out between the two of them. Emma and Lia shared the extra piece of candy equally, never doubting who was who. All that mattered was that it afforded them the extra energy to ride up to Monte Hill. Perched on top was the stone facade of St. Paul's Catholic Church. A plaque commemorated all that remained of the magnificent baroque church built by the Portuguese in the 1600s. The rest of the chapel, having survived two hundred years of wars and pirates, was destroyed by a fire. But the facade remained as a symbol of strength and resilience. Emma and Lia immediately claimed it as their own, imagining as they passed through its large front doors that they were entering a glorious nave with a high, wood-beamed ceiling and tall, stained-glass windows. And for a moment, they could have been anywhere, done anything, forgotten everyone.

That night at dinner, as every night, Emma's family came together like a flock of birds around the dining room table. With the soft clicking of chopsticks against bowls, each told the story of her day.

Mah-mee and Auntie Go had had lunch with a distant cousin on Ba ba's side. They had never met before and both sides were under the careful scrutiny of watchful eyes.

"She looks nothing like the Lew side of the family. Much bigger-framed," Mah-mee said. She palmed her rice bowl with her left hand as the chopsticks in her other moved through the air like magic wands.

"Could have come from her other side of the family," Auntie Go said.

Joan looked up and asked, "Where did you eat?"

"Mandalays," Mah-mee answered.

"What did you eat?" Joan continued.

"Sticky rice . . . dim sum . . . nothing special," Auntie Go answered.

Emma listened, thankful that cooking had replaced Joan's passion for the movies. Mah-mee held out a thin sliver of pork between her chopsticks, waving it through the air as she spoke before it landed safely in Emma's bowl.

Then Mah-mee turned her attention toward Joan. "I told this cousin you'll be graduating from Poi Do soon. She has a son studying to be a solicitor. Not married yet."

Joan coughed, then sipped her tea, half-hiding her face behind her cup.

"I was out with Lia this afternoon," Emma said, quickly changing the subject. She had waited anxiously to tell them about Lia's great-great-aunt Carmelita.

"Umh . . ." Mah-mee responded, pushing rice into her mouth. The click-click of her chopsticks filled the air.

"How is her mother feeling?" Joan asked, smiling at Emma.

"Lia's mother thinks the ghost of her great-aunt Carmelita killed José!"

"Aii-ya!" Mah-mee exclaimed. "Is she filling your head with stories again?" She put down her bowl and scraped back her chair.

"It sounds like it could be a movie. What did Carmelita look like?" Joan asked.

"She died before Lia was born, but she never liked Lia's father, and José looked just like him!" Emma explained.

Auntie Go began to say something, but held back her words.

"Ghosts like to linger in old houses," Foon suddenly interrupted, clearing an empty bowl from the table. Her tongue flicked across her gold tooth. "Others say so all the time. Mostly playful. They take things, move them around."

"Foon, you're scaring the girls," Mah-mee snapped.

Foon gathered up the rest of the bowls, stacking them neatly on her tray. Only then did she answer: "Better they know. Silence would scare them more."

Every so often Emma discovered subtle changes in the faces of her family. After just two years in Macao, they had all grown older. Auntie Go had gained then lost weight worrying about her knitting business and working in the garden behind the house, while Joan grew steadily more self-assured with each new dish she mastered under Foon's supervision. Even Mah-mee had changed. Emma saw thread-fine lines around her eyes and lips every time she smiled. But the only change for the better that Emma noticed in herself at fourteen was that she'd nearly caught up in height with Joan.

During their first year's stay in Macao, Emma had rarely seen her father. "Ba ba's too busy with his business," Mah-mee would say, the few times Emma asked. Emma knew that Ten Thousand Profits had all but failed with the Japanese invasion and wondered what he did day after day in their Hong Kong flat. Joan said he was guarding their family heirlooms. Emma couldn't imagine him wasting away his days playing mah-jongg and having long lunches. Without work, she somehow thought he would blow away like dust.

The few times Emma saw Ba ba, he seemed to have lost weight, his hair a tinge grayer. She began to note how he'd changed in a journal she kept, as if by writing it down she could prevent his shrinking away. Still, when she entered their small, stucco house and smelled her father's sharp, flowery cologne, Emma knew that for at least a little while they would be a family again.

From her father, they heard firsthand accounts of Hong Kong. "Chaos reigns everywhere," Ba ba said, sipping from his tea. "Most of the city still stands in ruins from the bombing. Everything good has been confiscated. The Japanese have done little to remedy the food and fuel shortage. If it weren't for the black market run by the triads, we would have nothing."

Emma's mouth felt dry and bitter listening, while Mah-mee and Auntie Go whispered quietly to him, and Joan stayed silent, her dark eyes dazed with a faraway look.

The stories Emma had heard from her grandmother about her father as a young boy didn't make him seem to differ much from her father as a man. His head had always been filled with numbers and sums. Calculations didn't fool him, as they sometimes fooled Emma in her math classes. He thought in numbers the way she thought in color or words. "You've grown a half inch taller," he would say, or, "Bring me two feet of that string."

Emma often thought about what brought her quiet father and beautiful mother together. Watching them closely held no answers. Two people couldn't be more opposite in nature. Her father's calmness could settle an entire room, whereas her mother's passionate temperament was catlike and might flare at any time. In her father's eyes, they must have added up to the right equation, like two fractions equaling a whole number.

During their second year in Macao, Ba ba began visiting them every few months. At the end of May, he came back for Joan's graduation from Poi Do. In the cramped front room of their temporary school, Emma and her family sat on uncomfortable metal chairs waiting for the program to begin. Sitting quietly next to Auntie Go, even Foon attended, her hands wrapped around a jar of kumquat soup she'd specially brewed for Joan.

As they waited, Emma leaned over and asked her father, "Ba ba, what do you do all by yourself in Hong Kong?" The palms of her hands felt hot and sticky.

Her father took off his glasses and smiled. He'd always been slight and trim, and his hair had begun turning gray before he was thirty. "I take care of our flat and wait for all of you to return."

"Aren't you lonely?"

"No more so than when I'm away from you in Japan."

"But you had your work there."

"My work now is in keeping what little we have."

"You won't return to Japan, will you? I mean, when the Japanese leave Hong Kong?" Emma had heard on the radio how the Japanese were losing ground all over the Pacific.

"That remains to be seen," he answered calmly. "The Japanese aren't all bad. They're just people like us. It's their leaders who . . . Now, we have to be quiet, moi-moi. Look, there's your sister."

Emma nodded and looked up at the makeshift stage. Mrs. Chen, the principal, had stepped up to speak, followed by the graduates, dressed in yellow robes that Joan, at first, refused to wear. "They're ugly," she had complained. Emma smiled, wiping her sweaty palms against her cotton dress. Beyond the buzz of whispering voices, Joan stood calm and self-possessed. Her presence filled the stage. In the white haze of lights, Emma saw that even in her ugly yellow robe, Joan was stunning.

Emma's father's last visit to Macao was in June of 1945. She was going to go bike riding with Lia when she heard Foon's excited voice welcoming him. "Lew *seen-san*, welcome, welcome."

It was a warm, humid day, and Emma was happy her father had come to visit. He looked tired, but smiled warmly when she hugged him.

"Moi-moi, you can start packing soon," Ba ba said.

"What?"

"To return to Hong Kong."

Emma stood perfectly still, as if turned to stone. She had come to love Macao as her own, adapting to its lazy heat, thick as a blanket. But most of all, she couldn't bear the thought of leaving Lia.

"When?" Emma asked when she recovered her voice.

"Come, let's go tell the others." Ba ba led her back into the house.

As they sat around the dining room table, her father smiled and continued to tell them all his news.

"The Japanese can't go on much longer. Hong Kong is simply becoming too much of a nuisance to them. They never could Nipponize us. Even the *Hong Kong News,* their own propaganda sheet, can't hide the fact that Hitler is being defeated in Europe, just as they are losing grasp of the Pacific." Ba ba looked over at Emma and Joan. "You'll be sleeping in your own beds sooner than you think."

"When will we return?" Joan spoke up first.

"In a few months at most," Ba ba answered.

"May I be excused? I'd like to tell Foon," Joan said, glancing at Emma. Joan stood up, ran her fingers through her shoulder-length hair, then disappeared through the kitchen door.

Emma tried to smile. Given all the rumors and news bulletins, she knew her father was right. The war had turned, and the Japanese no longer had the resources to keep going. In the bathroom, Emma splashed cold water on her face and decided to go tell Lia. She looked in the mirror, surprised to see someone older and sadder staring back at her.

By mid-August, the bombings at Hiroshima and Nagasaki had brought a final end to the war. The Lew family listened to the radio in stunned silence. Finally, Auntie Go shook her head and said aloud, "All those poor children." Emma tried to imagine how it must feel to be enveloped in that hot flash of light, to feel your flesh melt away. The absolute horror of it chilled Emma to the marrow.

Outside, another life prevailed. In this wet summer season, when storms typically raged through Macao, the day remained dry, and the sea unusually calm. In the stillness, Emma and Lia rode their bikes down to the harbor and then up to St. Paul's together for the last time. Emma tried to commit everything to memory, the dying sweetness of Auntie Go's garden of flowers, the salt-fish air, the solid facade of the church gleaming in the sunlight. It made her feel light and strong to see it standing there against all odds, yet the finality of leaving frightened her. After she said good-bye to Lia, nothing would be the same. Emma didn't know what to expect after

Macao, but she knew deep down that she hungered for something more than Hong Kong.

"And what do we see when we enter through these doors?" Lia's smooth voice filled the air.

"A large, wood-beamed ceiling," Emma was quick to answer.

"And what else?"

"Stained-glass windows of every color. Reds, blues, greens, and yellows. And on the altar sits a gold chalice, and above it, a large wooden cross."

Lia closed her eyes against the sun. "Yes. Yes, I can see it all."

Daydream —
1942–45

AUNTIE GO

Over the years, whenever Auntie Go's thoughts drifted back to her childhood summer in Macao, the memories seemed to move in slow motion. The quick, frantic pace of Hong Kong gave way to a lazy dance of tropical heat, sweet coconut milk, simmering black beans, the high, shrill call of Portuguese voices, the damp, moldy smell down by the creek, a child's contagious laughter, the cool water, the dull thumping . . . thumping . . . thumping . . .

Since escaping to Macao from the terrors of Japanese-occupied Hong Kong, Auntie Go had felt that faraway summer more strongly than ever. Her first month back on Macao, Go found herself dreaming of events long forgotten, the faces and voices of her parents returning with such clarity they'd startle her awake.

Most mornings she rose early, careful not to wake her cousin Kum Ling, and walked along Macao's tree-lined streets, watching the Macanese women and servants rushing back from the market. Occasionally, she would see Foon from a distance, scurrying home with fruits and vegetables, one bag clutched in each hand. If Foon saw Auntie Go, she never let on, respectful of her privacy, even in public, for that was what these morning walks meant to Go. It was the privilege of being by herself, of simply smelling summer's sweet tropical perfumes emanating from the fruits and flowers that grew in abundance everywhere.

And along with each scent, a memory flowed through her of the young girl who had come to Macao so many summers ago. Although her nieces were living proof of all the years that had gone by, Go's recollection of that summer intensified with every day that passed.

After twenty-five years, Auntie Go once again shared a small room with Kum Ling. And each night, as they lay in bed listening to the gentle sway of the palm trees, Go could almost feel her cousin's thoughts move away from her husband, daughters, and the Japanese occupation, drifting back to the stifling afternoon of which they had never spoken.

Auntie Go waited patiently, the memory heavy in her heart. Then on one particularly warm and airless night, a restless rustling of sheets moved through the room. Auntie Go turned onto her side, the faint, transulucent threads of her mosquito net barely visible. Suddenly, Kum Ling's low whisper startled the distance between their beds: "Do you remember?"

"Of course."

"Do you ever wish you hadn't spent the summer with us?"

Go stayed quiet for a moment. "It was my choice," she answered, taking full responsibility. She heard her cousin's slow breathing from the bed next to hers, felt the thick darkness around them.

"I should have made him stop, when the rest of us did. He would have listened to me. But he was having such a good time, I didn't think . . ." Kum Ling stopped.

"No one could have known. We were no older than moi-moi is now. Just children," Go said. Outside she heard the soft hum of the crickets.

"But I was the oldest, I should have known better," Kum Ling said, her voice small and strained.

Auntie Go stayed silent. She had grown up with Kum Ling, who had always been outspoken and fearless since she was a child. Now Go was struck by her cousin's soft words of defeat. It felt strange to refer to the past without really addressing it. Still, it was the first time they had spoken of that summer to each other. For twenty-five years, the silence had grown louder in Go's head. So many times she had longed to take Kum Ling's hand and recall the past, finally bringing it out in the open, so they could put the ghost of her brother to rest. In Macao again, the memory seemed always hovering around them, and though they'd never really talked about Sai-lo's death, neither could they erase it.

"We were just children," Go repeated, her fingers reaching out as if to meet Kum Ling's, touching gauzy net instead.

Auntie Go was the sole child of Kum Ling's mother's younger sister. Their mothers were the second and third daughters of their grandfather's second concubine. Go couldn't fathom how they could have all lived together within one compound—her grandfather, his five wives, and his seventeen children. Her mother was happy to move away after marrying Go's father, who owned a store that sold rice and barley. Perhaps that was why Go's mother always cherished her solitude and could often be found in their courtyard, knitting by herself, a serene smile pressed between her lips. "Silence is the greatest gift your ba ba has given me," she often said throughout the years.

Auntie Go wondered if her mother had ever wished the same for her—a husband to lavish her with such special gifts. If so, Go's mother had kept such thoughts secret, never once saying them aloud for fear they might hurt Go or stir the fates. Go learned from her how silence could sometimes be a kindness.

Auntie Go had just turned twelve when her mother said Go had been invited to visit Macao with her aunt and uncle, Kum Ling, and her two brothers for a month's summer holiday. Go balanced her decision for days, wanting to see Macao, yet not wanting to leave her parents.

As small girls, the cousins had been as close as sisters. Kum Ling, older by two years, was the prettier of the two, but Auntie Go was blessed with height and intelligence. In fact, by the time she was twelve, Go was as tall as many men. And while Go's mother blamed it on all the good soups she'd made her daughter as a child, Go secretly relished one of the few things she had over her cousin— Kum Ling would always have to look up to her.

But despite Go's height, Kum Ling always had the last word when they argued. After all, she had had the distinction of having two younger brothers. And by nature Go was shy, loved by her parents for her patience and diligence. As a girl, she spoke little, often teased by Kum Ling's little brothers for having lost her tongue.

"I can't hear you up there," Sai-lo taunted her.

"Did you say something?" Tong added, teasing.

It only made Go quieter. "I . . ." she said.

"I . . . what?" they pursued.

"Leave her alone," Kum Ling demanded, her pale arms crossed over her chest.

"Leave her alone," they echoed. But no sooner had the words left their mouths, then they would run off, obeying Kum Ling in their own way.

What they couldn't understand was that, like her mother, Go found great comfort in silence. Auntie Go learned what her mother had told her: "Some words are meant to be kept inside; if you let them out, they might wound someone deeply. Or fly away forever."

In spite of that, Auntie Go learned as she grew older that some words needed to be let out, or else they simmered inside, waiting to boil. Now she found herself wanting to translate their childhood nightmare into words that would fly away forever.

This is what I remember, Go thought to herself as she walked down the narrow, stone streets every morning.

She remembered the hot, sticky heat of that afternoon, and how it had drenched their skin by the time she and Kum Ling had made their way across the yard with her two younger cousins, Tong and Sai-lo. They were supposed to be playing in the backyard, but often wandered off through the tall *kuku* trees to a more adventurous spot down by a running creek. Go lagged behind. The newness of her sudden height had left her feeling awkward in her own body. Even waking up that morning, she felt a dull ache pulling against her bones and wondered when all her growing would stop.

Go heard Kum Ling call to her from the creek, then the cracking voice of Tong. "This way!" he yelled.

"I'm coming," she answered, in no hurry to catch up. Go felt the July sun beating down on her back and neck, like a heavy hand pushing her forward. She didn't like the mosquitoes, nor the damp, moist smell of the earth and trees down by the water. Most of all, after almost two weeks surrounded by her boisterous cousins, Go relished some time to herself.

As she made her way down the slope to where her cousins played on the embankment, Go was thankful for the tall pine trees that grew by the creek. In their cool shade, Sai-lo was laughing and pointing upward to a large tree whose thick branches hung over the creek. "There! There!" he yelled. At nine, he was still the baby of the family. He looked over at his eleven-year-old brother, Tong, who smiled and nodded his head.

Kum Ling stood next to her brothers, hands on her hips, looking up at the old tree.

"What are you doing?" Go asked.

"You'll see," Tong answered.

He lifted his loose shirt to show her the tight coil of rope wrapped around his thin body. He handed the end of it to Sai-lo, who began to run around him in circles, unwinding the rope from his brother's body.

Go laughed, hardly believing that Tong had worn the heavy rope around his body in such heat. When the rope lay on the ground like a sleeping snake, they all looked upward to find the best branch from which to swing. All around them buzzed a thick cloud of mosquitoes, which Go tried in vain to swat away.

They all took turns trying to throw the rope up and over a thick branch jutting out over the water. Go's height gave her the advantage, and the rope cleared the branch with a quick whip and snap.

"Go did it!" Sai-lo's high voice called out happily.

She stood among them, suddenly unaware of the damp smell and mosquitoes, accepted for the first time by all her cousins.

"I want to go first!" Sai-lo said.

Tong tied the two ends of the rope together, then stripped off his shirt. "Not until I test it out," he said, slipping his foot into the loop. With all his weight he stepped down once, twice, to make sure the rope was strong enough to hold them all.

"Be careful," Kum Ling said.

Tong pulled on it again. Then he drew the rope back as far as it would go up the slope of the hill, stepped into the loop, and swung off the embankment, splashing into the creek not ten feet below them.

All afternoon they took turns swinging from the rope into the creek, climbing and falling in perfect rhythm. Go was hesitant at first, but was finally persuaded by Kum Ling and Tong to give it a try.

"Don't be afraid, the water won't hurt you," they urged.

"I'm not afraid," she said, keeping her voice strong and steady, leaving out any trace of the fear she felt.

When she let go of the rope and her long limbs fell into the cool water, Go thrilled, victorious over the heat and fear. She couldn't wait to try it again.

Auntie Go still remembered it as an afternoon of perfect harmony. She, Kum Ling, and Tong finally lay exhausted on the slope of the creek in their wet clothes, laughing and trying to figure out how to get back into the house and into dry clothes without being caught by Go's aunt and uncle.

It was a short, sudden scream that changed everything—more of a cry caught in the throat, which you might hear from an animal in pain. Their heads jerked upward just in time to see Sai-lo falling, his foot slipping from the rope, his arms extended at his side, flapping up and down as if he might really fly, then falling hard and heavy onto the bank. A second later, Go's nine-year-old cousin lay motionless on the embankment, halfway in the creek, his neck twisted cruelly to one side. Tong scrambled down the slope, while Kum Ling stood up and began to cry, softly at first, then wild and frantic. Go followed Tong as fast as she could, sliding down the embankment, the mosquitoes as loud in her ears as Kum Ling's cries.

The silence that came afterward lingered for days, long after the hot, pink pain of the mosquito bites had faded. Grief and shock made Go and Kum Ling want to sleep, though, hours later, they'd wake up just as tired as before. During those lucid moments, she heard something thumping against the wall in the next room. "You'll hurt yourself," her aunt pleaded with Tong. The sound stopped only for short intervals, then the rhythmic thumping began again, at last lulling her to sleep.

Years later, Sai-lo's death had become a quiet memory, a thin shadow that remained in the back of the mind.

"A child should never die before his parents," Kum Ling once told Auntie Go. Her brother had been dead for years, and Joan was just a baby they were watching in amazement.

"No, it's too cruel," Auntie Go added.

Joan slept, her lips still sucking in a dream.

"I would die too," Kum Ling said, smoothing the pink blanket across the beautiful baby she'd finally brought into the world after so many disappointments.

"Don't speak of such bad omens," Go whispered, hoping the gods hadn't heard them. It was so delicate—this thin line between life and death.

Auntie Go's parents died in 1933, within ten months of each other. Go had just turned twenty-eight and was working in her father's store. His death was sudden, from a heart attack that struck without warning. Her mother's cancer moved slowly, giving her time to take care of business, and to speak more words to Go than she'd ever said in a lifetime.

One night, at dinner, her mother stared a long time at her before saying anything.

"What is it? Are you in pain?" Go asked, worried.

Her mother smiled. "I hate to leave you alone," she finally said.

Go felt a lump in her throat. "But I won't be . . . there's Kum Ling and the girls," was all she managed to say, though she thought, *Part of me will go with you.*

Her mother looked up at her. "You're different from them. Stronger. So tall and independent like a stalk of bamboo. But still not meant to grow alone." Her mother dished more bitter mustard greens into her bowl. "Never mind me. I'm just talking too much. Getting old."

Go seized every word her mother said. They were so few, so precious, that she held on to each one like a jewel.

In Macao they all began to heal. Away from Hong Kong and the constant terrors the Japanese soldiers had instilled in them, Emma no longer had nightmares, while Go and Kum Ling gradually grew less suspect of every sound they heard. Even Foon appeared less anxious, smiling wide enough to show the glint of her gold tooth.

But most of all, Auntie Go delighted in seeing Joan gradually emerge from her shell, as she worked each day in the kitchen with Foon. In the kitchen, Joan began to thrive again. She had steadfastly refused to speak about what had happened the night she returned home late and frightened. From then on, the silence that Joan had chosen was deep and profound. After that night, Auntie Go realized there were many ways to lose a child.

When they'd first arrived in Macao, Kum Ling wanted to put a stop to what she saw as Joan's "cooking foolishness." Auntie Go bit her tongue for as long as she could, but one day she pulled her cousin into the small room they shared and closed the door behind them, shutting them in together with the smell of Shalimar and Revlon powder. Again they disagreed. Again they had words.

"She shouldn't be in the kitchen," Kum Ling said, "like a servant, slicing black mushrooms! Lotus roots! Green onions! It isn't right. I should put an end to it. I'm only glad Hing isn't here to see his daughter!"

Auntie Go walked to the window of their bedroom. She knew Hing wouldn't mind one bit. She hated it when her cousin acted like something, or someone, was beneath them, an irritating affectation that Kum Ling had acquired through the social ties she had made.

"It's good for her," Auntie Go said, controlling her voice.

"In what way?" Kum Ling snapped.

Go turned back toward her cousin. In the sunlight, she could see faint lines along Kum Ling's forehead. "It's a skill she can always use, both for her family and for herself." Then in words soft and measured, yet insistent, Go added, "You must keep silent about this, Kum Ling. Joan needs something right now. It can't hurt."

Gazing back at Auntie Go, Kum Ling's eyes turned moist and luminous. "I suppose you're right," she said at last. "It's just a passing phase."

In the days to follow, there were a few long sighs from Kum Ling, and the impatient shaking of her head, but she remained silent, while Joan continued to cook in the kitchen with Foon.

Very slowly the Joan they all knew returned to them. One afternoon, when Kum Ling was at the Miramar Hotel playing mahjongg and Emma was next door at Lia's, Auntie Go heard voices coming from Joan's room. The door was ajar, so she peeked in.

Joan was seated in front of her mirror, speaking passionately to her reflection.

Auntie Go knocked lightly. "What are you doing?"

Joan eyed her in the mirror, smiled. "Just seeing how the expressions on my face change when I say different lines. Watch this: *I hate you!*" she said at the mirror. "See how my eyebrows went up and my nose flared?"

Auntie Go smiled. "Do it again."

"I hate you! I've always hated you."

"You're right," Auntie Go agreed, sitting next to Joan.

Joan leaned closer to the mirror. "It's amazing how much a face can show."

"Or not show." Auntie Go caught Joan's dark eyes in the mirror, held on to them.

"Or not show," Joan repeated, pulling her gaze away.

During their days in Macao, while Kum Ling occupied herself with afternoon mah-jongg games, Auntie Go spent her time reading and caring for the little garden in back of the house. It was no bigger than a small square patch of dirt, overgrown with shrubbery, yet Auntie Go was grateful to give it her attention. It bloomed under her hands, springing up like Joan and Emma. She couldn't believe how quickly her nieces were growing. Soon, marriage and their own families would take them away. Go had given up worrying about the knitting business she'd left behind. Its loss lessened as their days in Macao lengthened. She knew the Japanese had no intention of leaving her business intact. They would pilfer all they wanted, then destroy everything else. But even when these dark thoughts gathered, Go pushed them away, refusing to let hopelessness overwhelm her. She could do nothing from so far but prepare herself for the worst.

Meanwhile, she spent every day on her hands and knees, digging deep into the dark soil, pulling out weeds and dead shrubs by their roots. By spring, she was determined to have the garden blooming again.

On one cool morning in March, Auntie Go went to work early on her spring planting. She wasn't expecting any company when she heard Emma's light footsteps come from around the house. Under her arm she carried a small sketch pad she'd begun drawing in lately. Go was just happy that Emma had found an artistic outlet for her emotions. Sometimes, Go feared all Joan's dramatics over-shadowed her younger niece.

"I thought you were going bike riding." Go smiled, lifting her hand up against the morning sun.

"Later. Lia has to go to church with her family now." Emma dropped the sketch pad and fell to her knees next to Go. "What are you doing?"

"Getting ready to plant."

"Can I help you?"

Auntie Go smiled. "Of course you can. Here, start digging." She handed Emma a trowel.

"Can I ask you something?" Emma picked up the trowel, tested its edge.

"Of course, anything."

"What was Mah-mee's younger brother like? I found a family photo with him in it, but all Mah-mee told me was that he died here in Macao when he was a young boy."

Startled, Auntie Go crouched next to Emma and began digging a hole in the dirt, avoiding Emma's gaze. A sudden cold breeze chilled her neck.

"It was an accident down by a creek where we used to play. Senseless," she finally answered matter-of-factly.

"Were you and Mah-mee there?" Emma glanced over at Auntie Go while keeping her hands busy digging.

"Yes, we were." Auntie Go rose up onto her knees. She pushed the fallen strands of hair away from her eyes. "So was Uncle Tong. We were all there swimming."

"And he drowned?"

"He fell from a rope we were using to swing into the creek." Auntie Go felt a strange sense of release, as if someone else would now help her carry the burden. "He broke his neck."

Emma gripped the trowel tighter. "Why doesn't Mah-mee ever talk about him? Wouldn't it be better to keep his spirit alive?"

Auntie Go smiled. She realized again that Emma, at thirteen, wasn't much older than she had been then, though she seemed so much wiser. "For the longest time we only knew how to keep the horror of it silent. I suppose we hoped if we didn't say anything, it might all just go away. We were all very young when we witnessed it. By the time we grew up, it was all buried too deep inside of us."

"And now that you've returned to Macao?" Emma asked as she began digging again. "Do you ever think about him?"

Auntie Go nodded. "All the time. He adored your uncle Tong. He was a precocious little boy, with boundless energy. You would have liked him."

"It's sad to think that he never had a chance to grow up."

"Yes. It would have been nice to see what kind of man he'd have been." Auntie Go smiled, then looked up. The bright light of the sun stung her eyes, and for a moment everything fell into shadows. "He might have been someone who used his hands—an architect, builder, or engineer." Then Auntie Go bent over again and ran her fingers through the dirt. "We've kept silent much too long. Perhaps it's time to set Sai-lo's spirit free."

"Somehow, I think you just have." Emma smiled. Then she sat up. "When this garden is in full bloom I'll draw a picture of it for you."

Auntie Go put her dirt-stained hand on top of Emma's and smiled. "I'd like nothing more."

That night, Auntie Go dreamed of Sai-lo once more. She saw his foot slip from the rope again, but instead of falling, he floated upward, laughing and buoyant in the heavy summer air.

chapter 5

Wildfire

and

Spring

Wind —

1946

JOAN

Joan's bedroom door creaked open. She turned around to see her fifteen-year-old sister come in. "You could knock first," Joan said, turning back to her mirror.

"Sorry," Emma said, plopping down on Joan's bed. "Where are you going?"

"Out," Joan answered, glancing up to see her sister staring at her.

It made Joan feel hot and uncomfortable now, not like when Emma was a little girl of nine watching her get ready to go out to collect their father's debts. Then, Emma's eyes were filled with anxiousness and admiration, and all Joan wanted was to protect her. Since they'd returned to Hong Kong last year, she couldn't tell what Emma was thinking, and her curious gaze only made her nervous.

"Where?" Emma asked.

Joan twisted open a jar of cream. "The Gloucester Hotel," she answered, looking away.

As she dressed for her afternoon out, it gave Joan strength to think of Gene Tierney in *Laura*. Joan hoped to have the same air of mystery that kept men wanting to find out who Laura really was. *Keep them guessing*, she thought to herself. But lately, Joan was tired of the acting and had just been going through the motions of dating, carrying with her an indifference she couldn't at times hide. Usually she ended her evenings by flagging down a taxi and saying to her date, "You aren't coming, are you?"

Sometimes Joan wondered how she would ever keep up with all her mother expected of her: the endless array of prearranged dates, the quick scrutiny of another new "auntie" in Mah-mee's mah-jongg group, and their boring conversation leading up to a perfect marriage into a good family.

Last week Mah-mee had come home with another marriage prospect. "Mrs. Chun's son is coming back from America. Do you remember him? I think you met him when you were about six or seven. And now he's graduating from Harvard! The Chuns are one of the first Chinese families to live on the Peak. Before the war, they wouldn't allow Chinese to buy there."

Joan smiled, remaining silent, listening to Mah-mee's words running on like a travelogue before a movie. All the finest features were listed. She shuddered to think what Mrs. Chun and all the others had said about her. *She's a beauty like her mother . . . think what beautiful children . . . they say she studied poetry with Professor Ying. . . .* Joan knew that Mah-mee's weekly mah-jongg games centered on which family had money, and whose son was going to be a doctor, as if that guaranteed his being in love, or making a good husband. And while Joan never shared her mother's social ambitions, she at least humored Mah-mee by going out and being seen.

Sometimes one of Mah-mee's prearranged movie dates turned out to be particularly distasteful—such as the opinionated, overweight nephew of Mah-mee's mah-jongg friend Auntie Lai. That evening, Joan took Emma along with them to see *Another Thin Man*.

"Sit here," Joan said sweetly, placing Emma strategically between them in one of the plush, red-cushioned seats.

"But . . ." the nephew protested.

"Her eyes are bad," Joan quickly added, pushing Emma down. "She'll see the screen much better from here."

The nephew slumped in his chair and began sucking loudly on dried plums. Joan felt Emma's elbow nudge her in the side, and it was all they could do to keep from giggling.

Afterward, when Joan and Emma returned home, Joan kept a straight face as she mimicked Myrna Loy from the movie they'd just seen. "And bing! Another murder!" she said, covering her heart and falling onto the bed. Emma laughed out loud.

At twenty, Joan was bored by talk of marriage, although she knew Mah-mee was nervous about her future. Since returning from Macao, several boys from good families had dated her. But after a few months, each became just another friend to see a movie or have tea with. Not one would she consider marrying. Most were spoiled and childish, all hands and hot breath. None of them swept her off her feet, as she'd seen in the movies.

Joan typically spent her afternoons having tea with friends at the Hong King Hotel, or sitting in movie theatres where she dreamed of being an actress in Hollywood. Romantic adventures played through her mind like music. She envisioned herself as the clever, beautiful female lead alongside Errol Flynn or Tyrone

Power, enveloped by flowers, perfume, and wine. It struck her at odd moments that this was how it felt to be in love, and her legs grew weak at the thought as she tasted the richness of it in her mouth.

Joan pushed the jars of cream and bottles of perfume back in place. In the mirror, Emma's gaze followed her every move as she plucked her eyebrows, shaping them into perfect arcs, then wiped the corner of her eye with a tissue and blotted her deep red lipstick.

"Do you like this shade?" Joan asked, opening a tube of eye shadow.

Emma shrugged. "It's fine."

Joan stroked a pale blue-gray streak across her lids with the tip of her little finger. She brushed her dark hair. It was long and luxurious, hanging just below her shoulder blades. She studied her sister's reflection and wondered how she'd look with a little eye shadow. With her pageboy haircut and no makeup, Emma looked much younger than fifteen. Still, she had a wonderful fair complexion. Joan pulled back her own hair, twisting it into a chignon. No, she decided, makeup would only make Emma's features look rounder and plainer, as if she were the older sister. Which was how she behaved, sometimes.

Joan remembered how Emma had worried and fussed over her on the ferry from Macao back to Hong Kong. It was less than a year ago, September of 1945, after the Japanese surrender. Joan had pretended everything was fine, but inside, her stomach was in knots, uncertain what to expect. When they entered the silent harbor and Joan glimpsed the shadowy outlines of buildings against the gray sky, her fears were not eased.

Hong Kong was in shambles. Damage from the bombs appeared even worse than Joan remembered. The harbor was eerily asleep, filled with the remains of sunken ships, reduced to pieces of scrap metal. Not one sampan moved on the dark waters. Joan tried not to breathe the lifeless air as they stepped onto the dock. She looked up toward Victoria Peak in the dead silence and wanted to cry. The large buildings she once thought so stately and grand looked old and tired, stark in the rubble. Mah-mee, Auntie Go, and Emma also remained quiet. Only Foon raised her head and muttered, "Too many ghosts, too many ghosts."

Joan pushed the last bottle against her mirror and stood up. She swallowed hard and felt a dull ache move through her stomach. The gnawing pains had begun to worry her, but they usually subsided if she ate something or paused for a moment. When she felt better again, Joan turned toward Emma and smiled. "I'm ready to go."

Emma looked up at her. Joan saw again a quick flash of the admiring little sister Emma had once been. "Don't you ever get tired of it?"

"Tired of what?" Joan asked, looking for her purse.

"Doing the same thing. Just going to tea or the movies week after week."

Joan hesitated, felt a rush of heat rise up in her. She hadn't thought of her life as repetitious. It was simply the path she was supposed to follow until she married. Mah-mee had done much the same. "No, why?"

Emma leaned forward. "There's just so much more to do and see in the world."

Joan's eyes pulled away from her sister's gaze. "I've seen enough, thanks. The war and Macao have satisfied my wanderlust. I'm just glad we survived, and that our lives are back to normal again."

"Normal doesn't have to be boring," Emma said, getting up from the bed. "I want to see it all. Paris, New York, San Francisco . . ."

"Well, I like it right here in Hong Kong," Joan said, even as she thought, *What am I supposed to do? I'm waiting, waiting for someone or something.* "What did I do with my handbag?" She glanced quickly around the room.

"Aren't you curious about how other people live?"

Joan laughed. "I can barely keep track of my own life!" She located her handbag on the bedside table. "One day I know you'll see it all, moi-moi." She forced a smile. "But until then, I'll pick you up after your piano lesson." Joan moved quickly past Emma and patted her gently on the cheek on the way out.

"Where are you going?" Mah-mee's high voice suddenly rang out in the hallway.

Joan paused, startled. "I thought you'd already left."

"I'm running late," Mah-mee said, staring into the bathroom mirror.

"I'm going to meet some friends. Then I thought I'd pick up Emma from her piano lesson later," Joan answered carefully. She knew Mah-mee was delighted with Emma's gift for music.

Mah-mee nodded.

Joan braced herself for a waterfall of questions, another one of their "little talks." Whom are you meeting? Where are you going? Lately, Mah-mee often called Joan aside, speaking to her in a low confident voice, like Mah-mee's serious discussions with Ba ba or Auntie Go.

But now, Mah-mee remained quiet, distracted. "Your ba ba will be home early this evening, so I want you both here for dinner on time." Dabbing more Shalimar onto her neck, Mah-mee waved Joan closer. "Here, use some of this. A man remembers a young woman by the perfume she wears. You are lucky, you have the skin of Tai Pao. Your great-grandmother was known for her flawless skin."

"Mine isn't so smooth." Joan's fingers swept lightly across the small sprinkling of blemishes on her forehead.

"Just temporary. You'll soon grow out of it. And when you meet the right young man, you'll blossom all over again."

Joan glanced into the bathroom mirror and caught the determination of her mother's stare, then felt her stomach grind again as she looked quickly away.

When Joan heard the taxi arrive, she ran down the stone steps, opened the car door, and slid in. "The Gloucester Hotel," she said quickly to the pale, thin driver. It was a relief just to be out of the house where she could breathe once more. She sat back in the seat and rolled down the window. April had hardly begun, but already the air felt sticky and humid. When the car started moving, Joan loosened the collar of her silk cheungsam, then leaned toward the warm wind, letting it embrace her.

She stared hard when the taxi drove past Robinson Road, where the Japanese sentry post had stood. "Right there," she whispered to herself. All that remained now was the small, square concrete foundation, all of the wood having been stripped for fuel. Joan shuddered, remembering the fear she'd felt during the occupation every time she passed a checkpoint. Her stomach tightened. As the taxi sped away, she couldn't help turning back to make sure it was really gone.

At times, the blackness of night still haunted her with vivid nightmares of the Japanese soldier's clammy touch. She'd thought of it less and less during the past year, but occasionally she could still feel him grab her arms, push her back against the wall, and begin to claw at her clothes. It was something she had not been able to tell anybody, especially not her sister. Joan remembered Emma's face that night, wide-eyed and glassy with fear, her anxious questions floating through the dark damp of the room.

Joan didn't know what she would have done if she hadn't left so soon for Macao and learned to cook. It was almost as if Foon had read her mind and thrown her the one lifeline she had to offer—her cooking skills. Keeping her mind and hands busy, Joan slowly began to heal. Each dish she learned to prepare became a journey she needed to complete. When one was accomplished, Foon would have another dish for her to tackle—sliced pork with pickled vegetables, beef with lotus roots, steamed bok choy with oyster sauce. Sometimes the steam made Joan's eyes water, until tears rolled down her cheeks and salted the chicken or soup she prepared. It was the only time she allowed herself to cry.

Occasionally, Joan still stole into the kitchen to help Foon stuff a bitter melon or cook a soy sauce chicken, but it wasn't something Mah-mee ever liked her to do. "It's a servant's job," her mother said, though Joan couldn't see much difference between cooking and having had to collect money.

The taxi turned onto Queen's Road. Joan checked her watch. She felt a burning sensation in her stomach, but swallowed the sour taste that had risen to her mouth. It was just before two o'clock. First, she had to meet her date in front of the Gloucester Hotel—another blind date, set up by a friend whose brother had returned from studying in England. If they didn't waste too much time with small talk, they might still be able to catch the matinee showing of *Double Indemnity,* with Barbara Stanwyck, at the King's Theatre. Afterward, she planned to politely excuse herself and walk over to pick up Emma at her piano lesson. Then they could go on for tea and still have time to do some shopping.

Joan stared out the taxi window, still surprised that in less than eight months the British government was fully restored, and the streets were again bursting with people and automobiles. A new sense of enterprise filled the air, which she knew Ba ba was determined to share in. Mah-mee had quickly reestablished ties with all their old family friends, while Ba ba hoped for a thriving business again, this time, he said, dealing with Koreans and Vietnamese who had made their way to Hong Kong after the war.

Best of all, Hong Kong was again filled with merchandise. Every day, shipments of goods poured in from all over the world. From the Lane Crawford department store in Central to the shops and vendors of Lee Yuen East and West Streets, Joan loved the bustling street crowds and vendors who sold everything from blankets to perfume. Voices rang out in high, whining cries: "Stockin's! Cee-garettes!" It was hard to believe that just a few years earlier, during the occupation, an old wool blanket was worth ten times the most expensive bottle of Chanel No. 5. Now, women and men alike bargained at stalls for the abundance of goods that changed hands daily.

It was like magic to Joan, who loved shopping, almost as much as going to the movies. Ever since her bill-collecting days, she'd felt a kind of hunger, as if the less money she had, the more she wanted to spend.

Just after they had returned from Macao, Joan discovered a small shop in Central that carried nothing but "sample" shoes at such good prices she went to Auntie Go to borrow money.

"It's a once-in-a-lifetime sale," Joan pleaded, standing in the middle of Auntie Go's almost empty flat. The Japanese had taken everything not nailed down, and then some. Auntie Go was so busy getting her knitting factory going again, she had neglected to refurnish her flat.

"Do those shoes mean that much to you?" Auntie Go asked.

"Yes." Joan knew it was ridiculous, but she couldn't help herself. "I can't tell you why, but they do."

Auntie Go watched Joan for a long time, then sighed and relented. "Spend it wisely, and don't tell your mah-mee."

Joan bought fourteen pairs. They ranged from flats to heels, in leather and patent leather, with straps and buckles, in an array of colors. That night Joan went home and gave four pairs to Emma.

"Where did you get them?" Emma said, beaming.

"From a shop in the Prince Building. I borrowed the money from Auntie Go."

"That means she'll never see it again." Emma laughed and flopped down on Joan's bed.

"But look what I've bought you." Joan handed Emma one of the boxes.

Downstairs from the courtyard, the servants' voices floated through the window like a high, whining song. A feeling of closeness and contentment, like a childhood secret, spread through Joan as she watched Emma happily try on pair after pair, then place them lovingly back into their boxes, wrapping them tightly with the milky white tissue paper.

Joan paced back and forth in front of the Gloucester Hotel, her anger growing with the heat. This endless assortment of pre-arranged dates was going nowhere. And now Joseph Wong was already more than half an hour late. The Sikh doorman with his cloth-wrapped head followed her every move as she sidestepped people and checked her watch every few minutes. Then Joan stopped, breathed in some of the warm, heavy air, and turned to leave. If she hurried, she could still make it to the King's Theatre on time.

"Miss Lew! Joan Lew!" A low, smooth-sounding voice rang out in the air.

Joan hesitated, then glanced back to see a tall, dark figure plowing through the crowd toward her. She looked at her watch again, thought of the string of fruitless dates she'd had, and quickly picked up her pace. After all, Kate Hepburn would never put up with someone who couldn't keep an appointment. She strode guilt-lessly down the street without turning back. In the near distance, she heard her name called again and again, the faint, sweet music of it slowly lost among the crowds.

After seeing *Double Indemnity*, Joan picked up Emma for after-noon tea. The Hong Kong Hotel was teeming with people. Joan left Emma to wait in line and went to see if any tables were free, only to return shaking her head. The room vibrated with voices. Silver-ware clinked against china as waiters moved swiftly through the packed room carrying silver trays laden with teapots, cakes, and layered trays of cucumber and chicken sandwiches. A good two hours could slip away each day at afternoon tea. Just as in the movies, money could be made or lost, marriages saved or broken, lives changed, all in a few hours. Joan always thought it one of the more interesting habits the Chinese had picked up from the British.

"How was your date?" Emma suddenly asked.

"I don't know. I went to the movies by myself." Joan looked across the room. She was surprised that she hadn't yet run into anyone she knew. Usually, some acquaintance materialized out of the crowd.

Emma stood there with her mouth wide open. "He stood you up?" she finally whispered.

Joan nodded her head and smiled. "At first. And then when he finally arrived, I stood him up."

Emma smiled, but before she was able to say anything else, a group of Joan's friends surged toward them. Maria Wong, whose brother Joan was to have met, reached them first. She had never been a particularly close friend, but their mothers knew each other casually, so Maria had insisted that Joan meet Joseph. Joan braced herself against the onslaught as Maria leaned close to her and whispered just loud enough for everyone around them to hear. "Joan Lew, you're terrible leaving Joseph waiting at the Glouces-ter. He came back and said you practically ran away from him!"

Joan took a deep breath as a small pain rippled through her stom-ach. She searched for her old money-collecting voice. "Joseph needs to get his story straight," she answered curtly in her best im-itation of Bette Davis. "I was the one who did all the waiting."

"I'm sure it was just some kind of misunderstanding." Maria laughed. "Perhaps you just missed each other. I know you'll like my brother once you're introduced. Enough with all these blind dates, I'll introduce you myself!"

"It really isn't necessary. I don't think it's meant to be." Joan couldn't imagine having to see Maria more than occasionally.

"Give him another chance. I know it was just some big mis-take."

"Oh, look, there's a table ready for us across the room!" Joan said, pulling Emma along with her. "I'm sure we'll see one another again soon." Joan crossed the room briskly, raising her hand in the slightest wave to the crowd behind her.

Joan smelled the garlic Foon was cooking even before she and Emma set foot in the house. She assumed Foon was making sticky rice and sliced beef with ginger, two of her father's favorite dishes. He was so rarely home from his business travels that she knew Foon would go out of her way. The tall doors leading out to the ter-race were open. She and Emma stood still a moment and listened. Except for the dull thuds of Foon's chopping coming from the kitchen, and the more distant singsong voices of their neighbors' servants in the courtyard below, the house was quiet. The door to their parents' room was closed. If Mah-mee had returned and was resting, then Joan could still spend some time in the kitchen with Foon without her mother knowing. While Emma went downstairs to visit their neighbors, Joan changed into a cotton cheungsam and slipped quietly into the kitchen.

"Your moi-moi?" Foon asked without looking up.

"She's downstairs at the Tongs. Do you need any help?"

"Everything's done. Waiting for your mah-mee to return from her mah-jongg game."

"Ba ba's resting?"

Foon nodded. "Came home two hours ago." She lifted a large bowl and placed it on the stone slab she used as her working space.

Right after returning from Macao, Foon had reverted to her old methods of bargaining and bartering to put food on the table. Those first few months after the Japanese surrender seemed harder for the Lew family than the early days of the occupation. Like so many others, Auntie Go's house had been stripped of everything not nailed down. Ba ba had sold or bartered away their paintings, vases, and jewelry for provisions or cash. Though the enemy was gone, so was much of the food and fuel supply. The war had paralyzed everyone. At first, aid from abroad was slow to arrive, but more and more refugees seeking food and shelter flowed from China into the ravaged city. People wandered slowly, burdened by heavy loads, heading nowhere. Foon told Joan and Emma of the thousands who formed long lines outside government rice kitchens, waiting for anything that might keep them alive for another day.

Joan saw how the war years had aged her old amah. Her gold tooth seemed to have dulled. Her black hair had streaks of gray that she no longer tried to pull out. Foon had slipped into middle age right before their eyes. Joan wanted to wrap her arms around her small, dark figure.

Every day, even during the hard times, Joan was constantly amazed at all the delicacies that came out of Foon's primitive kitchen. It seemed all Foon's color was saved for her food. Joan glanced down at the dull red, sliced beef marinating in a bowl, next to the bitter Chinese mustard greens ready to be cooked. Foon's old cleaver lay on its side, waiting for her nimble fingers to pick it up and slice the Chinese mushrooms floating like black caps in a bowl of water. Joan knew that everything would be stir-fried at the last minute, though Foon sometimes cleaned and peeled, sliced and chopped, a good part of the afternoon away. There always seemed to be some kind of strange-looking root, or cluster of leaves, soaking or boiling in a pot waiting to become one of Foon's famous soups or teas.

"Can I slice those?" Joan asked, gesturing toward the mushrooms.

Foon looked up at her and smiled, her gold tooth glinting. When Joan was a little girl, she had first heard the story of Foon's gold tooth from Mah-mee, though Joan never knew whether to believe it. Mah-mee had told her Foon had once been the fourth wife of a wealthy farmer. He married her at fourteen for her cooking skills and showered her with gifts, including her gold tooth. Hated by his other wives, Foon was hustled out of bed one night, bound and gagged, and taken by men hired by the farmer's other wives to Hong Kong. It was the last time she ever saw her husband, or the life she had known. To support herself, Foon became a servant and cooked in several households until she entered Joan's grandfather's house, where she'd remained ever since.

Once, when they were alone in the kitchen of their Macao house, Joan had gathered enough courage to ask Foon how she came to have a gold tooth.

"Paid for it," Foon answered, chopping away.

"How?" Joan didn't look up.

"Just as always," was all Foon would say.

Joan assumed she meant by her cooking skills, but kept quiet, hoping the steamy aromas of the food they were preparing might loosen her old servant's tongue.

"Aii-ya, you get nothing in this life without paying for it," Foon suddenly continued. "I always paid my share. I have the tooth to prove it!"

Joan realized it was the first time Foon had actually spoken complete sentences to her.

"I know," Joan whispered.

Foon picked up her cleaver and began chopping bamboo shoots, creating a rhythm in which her words hummed. "My ba ba was a poor farmer in Fukien. Never enough for the family to eat. Ma ma was a good cook. She taught me how. Used mostly herbs and roots. Gathered from the land. Ma ma could make stones into tasty soup." Foon laughed aloud. "But never enough. One by one, Ba ba sold his children. I was a girl bride. Too young to know anything. The husband was already a gray, old man. I cook and clean. At night I warm his bed and waited. Two years later, he no longer got out of bed. Another year, he no longer breathe. I took little money he left. Bought gold tooth. Earned it."

Foon stopped. She looked up at Joan and smiled so that just a sliver of gold shone between her lips. At that moment Joan knew the real story and felt closer to Foon than she'd ever been. She watched as Foon scraped the round circles of bamboo shoots off the counter and into a clay bowl.

By the time Mah-mee returned from her mah-jongg game, Joan had sliced the black mushrooms into thin crescent moons to be fried with the beef. As she stepped out of the kitchen, she heard her parents' low voices floating from their room on a wave of her mother's Shalimar. Then the door to their room swung open and they walked toward Joan, smiling.

Joan had always thought her mother and father were a handsome couple, the Chinese equivalent of Ronald Colman and Hedy Lamarr. As a young girl, Mah-mee's large eyes and flawless skin had been famous throughout Hong Kong. Joan had been told that her father, at eighteen, had taken one look at thirteen-year-old Kum Ling and known he would marry her. Three years later their wedding was arranged. Both came from good families.

Joan still thought it was one of the most romantic stories she'd ever heard, even if she knew they had since grown apart. Even before the war, and their move to Macao, Ba ba had spent more and more time away on business, while Mah-mee stayed in Hong Kong and became immersed in her mah-jongg games and finding Joan a suitable husband through her society friends.

Joan swallowed, pulled at her collar, and straightened her cheungsam. Her father's hair had turned almost completely gray in the last three months; his eyes drooped a bit in tiredness. Ever since he'd begun trying to establish business relations with the Koreans and Vietnamese, Joan could feel him slowly lose the vitality he once had. She wanted to run to Ba ba, put her arms tightly around him in a hug. Instead, Joan quickly kissed his cheek, smelled his flowery cologne, as he lifted his right hand and touched her lightly on the back.

"Where's moi-moi?" Mah-mee asked.

"Downstairs. I was just about to call her. Foon wants to know if you're ready for dinner," Joan said.

After an afternoon of mah-jongg, Mah-mee had broken even and was in good spirits. Wearing black silk trousers and a tunic, she massaged her neck with one hand. "I'm more tired than hungry. Auntie Lai had her cook prepare a large tea this afternoon. You go ahead, I'll be right in. Your ba ba is famished."

Joan turned around and followed her father to the dining room, happy that her mother hadn't mentioned the cooking smells clinging to her clothes, nor asked about her afternoon with Joseph Wong.

* * *

When the doorbell rang the next morning just before noon, Emma was first to the door. A hint of surprise was in her voice when she called out Joan's name. At the door, Joan saw what was so startling to Emma. On the threshold stood the smallest old woman she'd ever seen, supported by a servant, holding a large box of chocolates. The old woman was a head shorter than Joan, no larger than a nine-year-old child. Under the weight of the box, she balanced on two tulip feet, once bound, now deformed. All Joan could think was, *Who would send such a frail, old lady to deliver such a big box?*

"Excuse me, Missee Lew, but this is for you." The old woman leaned forward. "From Mr. Wong."

Joan quickly reached for the box, taking the weight from the old woman. Emma stood watching, her hand still clutching the door-knob.

"Thank you. Please come in," Joan said, stepping aside. The box felt heavy and solid perched against her hip.

The old woman shook her head in refusal. The servant stepped aside as she bowed several times before turning around to leave, amazingly agile on her bulbed feet.

The card read:

> *I promise it will never happen again. Please forgive me.*
>
> > *Joseph Wong*

Emma leaned over Joan's shoulder and read the card. Emma smelled of Camay soap and coconut candy. "Will you forgive him?" she asked.

Joan felt the small hairs on the back of her neck rise. "I haven't decided."

* * *

Three days later Joan was in her bedroom, taking her time to get dressed even as Emma rushed her along. As soon as the doorbell rang, Emma ran out to take a good look at Joseph Wong.

Ever since he'd called to arrange a date with Joan, Emma had been the one to pace and anxiously await his arrival. He had insisted on picking Joan up at home so there would be no more confusion. "I won't make the same mistake again," he had told Joan on the telephone, his voice as smooth as cream.

"He's as handsome as a movie star!" Emma said, breathless, rushing back into the bedroom. She sat down on Joan's bed and excitedly spilled out a full description.

Joan darkened her mole, then felt the back of her chignon to make sure all the pins were in place before standing up and following Emma into the living room.

Joan heard Mah-mee's eager voice. "How is your mother?"

"Very well, thank you."

"I must call her to play mah-jongg. It has been much too long."

"She would be happy to hear from you." His voice was deep and calm.

Joan could already imagine her mother's words and laughter tinged with happiness. At last, a young man worthy of her older daughter! Joan cleared her throat, licked her red lips, and hoped for the best.

She saw the back of his head first. He was facing away from her, sitting on the couch, as she entered the living room. When her mother looked up at her, Joseph Wong rose and turned, bowed his head slightly, and extended his hand. He was tall, with deep-set dark eyes, and a straight nose. Emma was right: dressed in a dark pin-striped suit, he was as good-looking as a movie star.

"Miss Lew," he said.

Joan shook his hand. "Mr. Wong. It's nice to meet you. Finally."

His hand felt warm in hers; the scent of his musky cologne made her dizzy.

Joan tried to remain calm and not stare. The collar of her cheungsam felt tight and she prayed she wouldn't perspire through the red silk. It was something she'd never seen happen in the movies of Ann Sheridan or Rosalind Russell. But as they turned to leave the house, Joan thought how even Robert Taylor seemed to pale compared to this young man walking beside her.

After her first date with Joseph Wong, the last traces of anxiety Joan had harbored so long were replaced by warmth and relief. At last she'd come to the end of her mother's long search. Since their return from Macao, things had been difficult between them. Arguments usually erupted out of small, annoying habits—a door left ajar; the clicking of Mah-mee's long nails against the table; Joan forgetting to put her mother's cosmetics back in place. It seemed the smallest thing could turn into a war of words, followed by days of deadly silence.

Joseph Wong brought a cease-fire. He possessed a sense of style and excitement that Joan longed for. He drove a green Bentley coupe convertible that roared up the hills, and he often let Emma ride in back on his rumble seat. Joan knew Emma loved him almost as much as she did. He nicknamed her Rosebud the day they saw *Citizen Kane* together, which made her laugh. He often brought Emma books and other small gifts, such as charms for her bracelet: a little gold piano, a tiny dancing ballerina.

After Joan met Joseph, her stomach pains calmed. The fears eased. With him, she felt safer than she had since before the war. Joan tried to curb her happiness, fearing that something too obvious could easily be taken away.

A month after they began dating, Joseph picked up Joan for dinner at Jimmy's Kitchen. The restaurant was dim and quiet, most of the diners having already gone by the time they finished dinner. Candles flickered a muted light as Joseph talked about his mother and two sisters, but said little about his father, a well-known Hong Kong businessman, whom Mah-mee had said died just before the war.

"Tell me something about your father," Joan said.

Joseph drummed his fingers on the table, sat back in his chair. "There's not much to tell. He was a hard-driving businessman who built a thriving company from nothing. Growing up, we rarely saw him. He died several years ago of a heart attack." Joseph stopped, sipped from his cup of coffee, then combed back his thick black hair with his fingers.

Joan looked away from his dark eyes, even features, and quickly took a drink of water. "I'm sorry," she mumbled.

Joan knew that by the time Joseph's father had died, the Wong family had long been established in the restaurant business, with a proliferation of dim sum and seafood places on Hong Kong Island and in Kowloon. Joseph now ran the business from his office located in the Swire Building.

"Don't be. He died in his girlfriend's apartment," he snickered. "Didn't even have the decency to expire on neutral territory."

Joan's hands played with her napkin, folding and unfolding it in her lap.

"Being the only son," Joseph continued, "I was sent abroad to school, groomed to take over the family restaurant business. While I was away, my mother kept the business afloat. She's a remarkable woman. And that's the whole story."

Joan had met Mrs. Wong just once, two weeks after Joan had begun dating Joseph. Unlike Mah-mee, Mrs. Wong wore little makeup, allowed her hair to go gray, and was quiet and calm. She spoke in low tones and was nice to Joan from the moment they sat down to tea at the Hong Kong Hotel. Joan's palms felt sweaty as she smiled, afraid of saying or doing the wrong thing. "She likes you," Joseph had whispered when he brought Joan home. She hoped it was true. Joan breathed in the slightly sweet air. The car was warm and closed as he leaned over and kissed her, moving his hand upward and placing it on her left breast.

Joan grew weak at the memory. "Ready to go?" Joseph asked. He stood up, held his hand out toward her as she reached for it.

Within three months, Joan and Joseph were the couple everyone watched as they glided into the Repulse Bay Hotel for tea, or the King's or Queen's Theatre to catch the latest Hollywood movie. Their movie-star good looks, and his family's restaurant business, were enough to stimulate rumors and stares. Joan also knew gossip was contagious in Hong Kong, spread quickly by those who had too much time and money. Joan began to understand the value of family connections. Even though her own family was no longer considered wealthy, her mother remained an important member of Hong Kong's elite, reinforced by her thrice weekly mah-jongg games.

By early June, Joan knew Mah-mee prayed that the Wong and Lew families might soon join together. Every morning at the breakfast table, Mah-mee casually spoke of things she had learned from her own marriage. "When you're married, it will be up to you to keep the house running smoothly. The right servants are essential. Why, what would we ever do without Foon?" Joan kept quiet, knowing that it was too soon to speak of such things. But in the back of her mind, she was almost certain that marriage would come. Her family loved Joseph, and he was generous and good to Joan. Only Foon kept her distance, watching from the safe confines of her kitchen. Mah-mee was ecstatic, but bit her tongue against saying too much to her mah-jongg friends. Still, whispers drifted through Hong Kong Island of an upcoming union between the Lew and Wong families.

By August, the heat was unbearable. The humidity left tears flowing down the walls and a sour smell on the damp bathroom towels. An occasional tropical storm came their way, which left the wet heat clinging to their bodies. Emma wrote letters to Lia, read books, or practiced the piano. Joan, when she wasn't out with Joseph, sat by the phone waiting for him to call.

During the last few weeks of sticky heat, Joan felt their relationship take a new turn. She could hardly believe they had been together for six months. Joan had never felt such closeness as when Joseph took her hand in the movies or kissed her over and over again at the end of an evening, whispering when his hands strayed too far that he loved her. When Joan wasn't with him, time felt interminable. And when they were together, time ceased to be. It was love as Joan had always imagined it, the kind of love that flashed and sparked, that flickered in the movies she had watched for so long.

The heat waned by September, broken by a sudden tropical downpour that usually signified the beginning of their typhoon season. Joan knew the signs all too well. The sky thickened, low and heavy, wrapping everything in an eerie, hot silence. Then the sky opened up and the warm drops fell with a vengeance, followed by days and nights of wind. Each year Joan held her breath, hoping the winds wouldn't be violent, remembering the time their windows had been blown out and Emma's 78 rpm recordings of Chopin and Bach had been smashed against a wall across the room. But this year, the winds never picked up, adding to Joan's good spirits.

"Where's Joseph taking you tonight?" Emma asked, her voice filled with excitement as they ate breakfast. The sky had cleared again and brightened the room.

Joan looked over at her and smiled. It was the young Emma again, eager and open-faced, who had once watched Joan get ready to go out and collect. "To the Jockey Club for dinner."

"Then dancing?"

Joan laughed. "Maybe."

Emma was quiet.

"What's wrong?"

"I was just thinking, when you and Joseph get married and I move away from Hong Kong, we won't be able to see each other very much."

Joan stood up from the table. "Well, I'm not getting married tomorrow, and you're certainly not moving anywhere for a while!" She leaned over and kissed her sister lightly on the head.

The Royal Hong Kong Jockey Club was once again operating at full capacity. The restaurant had remained open through much of the Japanese regime, and the slim stable of horses that had survived the Japanese bombing raids was once again at full strength and running races each Saturday. All the other nights of the week, the Chinese and British dined and drank at the Jockey Club, entertaining family and guests in lavish style. As with any other business enterprise in Hong Kong, a restaurant or two was an integral part. Since Joan had begun cooking with Foon, and now dating Joseph, she understood how food was fundamental to the Chinese in every aspect of life.

Almost always, when she and Joseph entered the room, voices quietly buzzed for a moment, then everything seemed to move in slow motion. No matter how many times it had happened to them, Joan trembled with the sensation of holding a roomful of people under her spell, just like in the movies.

Joseph was quiet during dinner. He sipped his shark's-fin soup in silence. Joan worried that he was coming down with something. He was usually smiling and talkative. She thought he looked sullen and pale, which confirmed her belief that driving a convertible was bad for his health. During the summer it was too hot, and in winter, one could easily catch a chill.

"Are you feeling all right?"

Joseph looked up at her and smiled. "I'm fine."

"You're awfully quiet tonight."

"I have a lot on my mind," he mumbled. "We're thinking of opening a new restaurant."

"Where? Hong Kong or Kowloon side?"

"I'm not quite sure yet," he answered, then scooped rice from his bowl into his mouth. Joan continued to pick at the abalone and mushrooms, feeling his distraction grow as the evening wore on. When the band began to play "Moonlight Serenade," Joseph stood up, and for a moment, she thought he might ask her to dance.

Instead, he coughed hoarsely. "Maybe I am a little under the weather. Would you mind if we left early?"

Joan felt her heart beat faster. Her stomach began to churn as she chanted in her head for Joseph's well-being, *Let him be all right. Let him be all right.* She felt his hand touch her bare arm, and his warmth spread quickly through her. She grabbed her purse and couldn't get out of the Jockey Club fast enough.

Joan had known from the very beginning something was wrong. It was obvious Joseph was not feeling well. Foon would have seen it right away when he didn't eat with his usual enthusiasm.

The next day Joan sat and worried. When she didn't hear from Joseph all morning, she thought about calling him at home, or at his office. Just as she made up her mind to call, Joseph telephoned. Joan held the receiver tight against her ear. "I'm fine," he said. "Just a little sore throat. Nothing that staying home a day or two won't cure. Don't worry, I'll call you tomorrow morning."

When Joan replaced the receiver, she could still feel the warmth of Joseph's voice. She walked back to her bedroom and closed the door, trying to keep him with her as long as she could.

95

* * *

That afternoon Joan couldn't sit still any longer. "Do you want to go shopping?" Joan asked Emma. "Or, maybe we can go visit Auntie Go at the factory."

Mah-mee was already out playing mah-jongg, Ba ba was at a meeting, and Foon was nowhere to be found. Joan felt anxious. She was tired of pacing around her room and needed to find something to take her mind off Joseph.

"Sure," Emma answered, a wide smile spreading across her face. Emma jumped up from where she lay on the sofa and hurried into her room to change.

Joan felt guilty. Ever since she had begun seeing Joseph, she'd hardly paid any attention to her sister. Now, it seemed Emma was all alone and waiting for Joan's company again. Emma hadn't found another friend in Hong Kong as close to her as Lia had been. They had been inseparable in Macao, and Joan knew they still kept in close touch through letters. "Lia may be visiting soon," Joan faintly recalled Emma saying the other evening, just as Joan was leaving the flat to meet Joseph.

Just this morning, Joan had seen her mother staring at Emma while they were eating breakfast. After a long pause, Mah-mee said in a low, serious tone, "A little makeup is just the thing you need to give you some character."

Joan sighed, hoping Mah-mee's matchmaking wouldn't now be focused on Emma. Emma had so many other talents that went beyond makeup. Joan felt a sharp twinge move through her stomach, but was quickly relieved by the thought of Joseph's dark eyes, and the way his voice floated across the room to her.

An October heat wave left Central hot and airless, as if everything had come to a standstill. Joan and Emma walked out of a small dress shop into the stale, breathless heat. Joan was debating if she should buy a green silk blouse she'd just seen when she glanced across the street and saw Joseph. He was laughing and holding on tightly to the hand of another woman. Her face looked faintly familiar. They were coming out of the King's Theatre, which was still showing *The Lost Weekend*, a movie he and Joan had just seen together last weekend. She stared so hard her eyes watered and blurred. She couldn't move. The air had been knocked out of her. She could feel Emma pulling her away, saying something with words so soft she could barely hear them. All night, the echo of those whispers rang in her ears, until she finally made them out. Afterward, Emma's words, "It can't be him. It can't be him," reverberated just as loudly in her mind.

The next day a warm, driving rain clicked against the windows. The phone rang continuously, but Joan refused to speak to Joseph. Emma came into the dark, messy room, bringing with her the heavy sweet smell of roses.

"He says it was just a friend of his sister's," Emma said softly. "She doesn't mean a thing."

Joan looked up at Emma. Her sister's hands were clasped tightly around the roses, holding them out to her. Joan shook her head at the offering. She coughed, her throat dry and sore. "What does he want? Forgiveness?"

"He made a mistake," Emma pleaded. She cradled the roses in her arms.

"I can't . . ."

"You could try."

Joan searched for the right words to tell her sister how betrayed she felt, how unjust it was when she had followed all the rules, but tears came instead, followed by a soft moan rising from deep down in her throat.

*   *   *

It had been almost a week since Joan had seen Joseph. She rose slowly from bed and dragged herself over to her mirror. Her face was puffy and pale. She had lost weight. Foon made her drink soups brewed from lean pork and astragalus roots to strengthen her blood. She had cried and cried, until the tears no longer came.

Joan felt sick to her stomach again, a sharp, burning pain that stabbed like a knife. She bit her lip till it passed. The doctor had said it was a tiny hole in her stomach lining, a small ulcer that would heal in no time with rest and the right foods. Joan swallowed and rubbed her temples slowly, until she felt the tightness behind her eyes relax. She looked into the mirror again, wondering if the cold, dark hole in her heart would heal and disappear as easily.

Rosebud —

1946—47

EMMA

Emma sat in her room, two hours after seeing Joseph in Central, carefully removing from her bracelet the three gold charms he had given her. The latest one was the rosebud he had given her last week on her sixteenth birthday. "So you'll always remember me," he had said. Now she'd never hear him calling her Rosebud again. She could still feel the warmth of his hand as he took her wrist and gently attached the gold bud.

She pulled down the sleeve of her pink cotton cheungsam, glanced up, and caught her reflection in the mirror. Her features appeared thinner, complemented by her shorter, shoulder-length hair-cut. When Emma heard Mah-mee return from playing mah-jongg at Auntie Kao's house, she set the bracelet down and hurried to find her mother in the living room.

"Moi-moi, I just read the note you left. I didn't think you two would be back from Central yet," Mah-mee said, dropping her jacket on the sofa.

"We saw Joseph," Emma started, her hands clasped behind her back.

"Then he's feeling better. That's good to hear. Auntie Lai says there's a bad virus going around."

Emma swallowed, her mouth dry and bitter. "He was holding hands with another girl."

Mah-mee's eyes grew wide, the lines deepening on her fore-head. "Another girl?" Mah-mee whispered under her breath. "Are you sure?"

Emma nodded.

"The dirty devil!" Mah-mee snapped.

A warm slant of sunlight filtered through the windows as Mah-mee paced the length of the living room, her head lowered in thought, arms crossed on her chest. She paused for a moment, ab-sently smoothing back a strand of hair. She mumbled something Emma couldn't hear, then walked out of the living room and down the hall to knock lightly on Joan's door. Without waiting for an answer, she opened it and disappeared inside, closing the door be-hind her.

Emma hesitated, then followed and listened against Joan's door. Much to her relief, Mah-mee's voice remained calm.

"Just talk to him. He may have a perfectly reasonable explana-tion."

"I can't."

"But why? I don't understand. Perhaps she was just a friend."

"She was more than just a friend!" Joan snapped back. "Joseph lied to me about being sick so he could chase after her! The picture seems clear enough!"

Emma stepped away from the door, expecting Mah-mee to explode.

But there was only the faintest pause before Mah-mee said, "You might as well know now, this isn't a world that's simple for women. Sometimes you must swallow your pride and move on."

"I'll move on then." Joan's voice sounded flat, indifferent.

Still, Mah-mee's voice remained even. "Do you think it has been easy for me? For any of us? We accept what we must and make the best of it. All foolishness aside, a husband always returns to his wife and family."

"Maybe you can accept that sort of philandering, but I can't!"

Emma waited for Mah-mee to say something, but there was only silence, then her mother's quick footsteps. Emma ran back to sit on the sofa just as Mah-mee emerged from Joan's room, marched straight into her own room, and slammed the door behind her.

Emma leaned back against the sofa, wondering where Ba ba was, and when he would return from his business trip.

After dinner, Emma stepped into Joan's dark, airless room, closing the door behind her. "It's me," she whispered.

"Go away." Joan's voice was sluggish.

Emma clicked on the lamp beside the bed. Joan lay in her slip on the disheveled bed, her arm raised against the bright light. "Joseph called again."

"Tell him to go cheat on someone else!" Joan groaned.

"Why won't you just talk to him?" Emma pleaded. "He deserves another chance."

Joan lowered her arm. Her eyes were red and swollen. "Why?"

"Because everybody makes mistakes."

"That wasn't a mistake, moi-moi." Joan raised her voice. "He knew exactly what he was doing! Now he has to accept the consequences!"

"Well, if you ever made a mistake, I bet Joseph would forgive you. He wouldn't just let you suffer!"

Joan sat up against her headboard. "I have made mistakes. I have suffered!"

Emma's blood rushed to her head. "You're so spoiled because everybody thinks you're beautiful, but you're just being stubborn, acting like you're Garbo!"

Joan sat there stiff and pale with her arms crossed. "What do you know, you're only a child, you can't possibly understand, you're probably in love with Joseph yourself. Well, you can have him and good riddance to you both!"

Emma's eyes stung. "When did you become so cold? Where did the old Joan go?" She turned and ran from the room before Joan could answer.

Alone in her room, Emma began drawing furiously on a pad of paper. The dark lines ran into each other in a blur. Her breath came in spastic jerks. Tears ran down her jaw and dripped onto her white sheet of drawing paper. She was sick of trying to understand all of love's contradictions and tired of trying to understand Joan. All she wanted was to turn the clock back, to see her vivacious sister, lipsticked and perfumed once again, ready to collect on all debts owed.

But wasn't Emma herself partly to blame? If only she'd made an excuse today when Joan invited her to go shopping. Too much homework! Have to practice piano! A chapter in *Jane Eyre* to read! But, no, she jumped at the chance to run down to Central, only to have as the result . . . The memory felt like a dull, throbbing ache.

Emma ripped the paper from the pad and tore it in half, then again into fourths. It scared her to think that you couldn't really know someone, not even your own sister, if she didn't want you to.

At the end of the week, the doorbell rang again. Emma glanced at her watch, then ran out of her room to answer it. Every day at noon for the past ten days, Joseph had sent a servant and his old aunt balancing on tulip feet with gifts for Joan. Boxes of candy piled up in the kitchen. By the end of the fifth day, Joan stumbled out of bed, gathered up all the sickenly sweet roses that filled the flat, and threw them down into the courtyard. Emma knew the greater distance Joan created between them, the faster Joseph would fade away.

"For Missee Lew," the old aunt said, handing Emma a small box.

Emma smiled, holding the gift, and watching the old aunt sway, then lean back against the servant. Emma would never forget the story Joseph had told her of how his aunt had come from Hankow to live with his family after the 1911 revolution. With the fall of the Manchu dynasty, his aunt's bound feet were a constant reminder of her gentry roots. Left with no acceptable opportunities, she was sent to Hong Kong to live with Joseph's family long before he was born. She had helped raise Joseph and his sisters and would do anything to ensure their happiness.

"Thank you. Please, won't you come in?" Emma asked.

But today like every day Joseph's old aunt smiled and shook her head. Then she turned around and, with the help of the servant, made her way slowly back down the steps.

Emma knocked softly on Joan's door before entering, still shy and hesitant since their argument. She carried the small box wrapped in cheerful red-and-gold paper along with the latest *Movie Mirror* magazine. The room was dark and musty, smelling of stale perfume. She pulled apart the drapes and pushed open the window, filling the room with harsh sunlight and outside voices. Then she turned and held out the box. "Another gift from Joseph."

Joan lay still, her dark hair spread out weblike against her pillow. "I don't want it," she whispered. "Just leave me alone. My stomach's bothering me."

Emma hesitated, then placed the gift on the bedside table. She sat down with a bounce on her sister's bed and flipped through the movie magazine on her lap. "I picked up this issue for you at the store this morning. They say Lana Turner is a smash in *The Postman Always Rings Twice*. Real steamy kitchen-table scene. There's also a new Li Lihua film out called *Phony Phoenixes*. And guess what! Gary Cooper told the House Un-American Activities Committee that he's turning down scripts that have anything to do with Communist ideas."

A slight smile crossed Joan's lips. It was a good start, and Emma refused to let her sister slip away from her. "It's a nice day. Do you want to go for a walk?"

"Not today." Joan turned away.

Emma kept up her one-sided conversation. "Auntie Go's coming over with the latest Paris sweater designs to show you. Oh, and Foon needs to know if you want thousand-year-old eggs in your jook."

Joan turned on her side and pulled her pillow down, hugging it close. "Just tell them I don't need anything right now, except to rest. And think."

"It's been two weeks," Emma said, pleading. "We miss you."

Joan, her eyes moist and shiny, stared at Emma for a moment. Then Joan closed her eyes against the white November light.

* * *

By December, Emma's spirits were lifted by Lia's visit from Macao. She was to arrive two days after Christmas. They'd been planning it for months, and even her sister's despair couldn't dampen Emma's excitement. As the date grew closer, Emma could hardly sleep. The night before Lia's arrival, Emma sat late into the night at the dining room table and carefully made a list of all the places she wanted to take Lia—the Peninsula Hotel, Repulse Bay, Stanley Village, the beach at Shek O, the tram ride up Victoria Peak.

"Drink this, or you'll be too tired for your friend," Foon said, appearing from the kitchen. She placed a bowl of dark, foul-smelling tea on the table.

"What is it?" Emma looked up and wrinkled her nose.

"Tea. Made from white flower and snake-tongue grass. Help you sleep." Foon waited by her side.

Emma knew better than to argue with Foon. Even Joan gave up and drank whatever she was told, although it seemed that her sister's ulcer was taking forever to heal. Emma put her pen down and lifted the bowl in both hands. The tea smelled like dirt and licorice and tasted even worse. She held her breath and in three gulps drank it down, then handed the empty bowl back to her old servant.

"Good for you," Foon said, returning to her kitchen.

The next morning, after a good night's sleep, Emma caught a taxi down to the Hong Kong harbor to wait for Lia's ferry. The sun was out and the wind mild, but all around her harbor life revolved like a storm. Large boats and sampans skillfully swept past one another. Ships from all over the world tilted and swayed. Emma strained to see where they were from as she pushed through waves of travelers toward the ferry building. Spittle spattered the ground, and the smell of urine and cigarettes swirled in the air. Just outside

the ferry building, rickshaws formed a snakelike line to await disembarking passengers, while vendors of candy and firecrackers
hawked their wares.

Emma leaned against the gate until she heard the deep wail of the
horn announcing the ferry's arrival.

"It's here!" she said aloud, though no one in the surging crowd
paid any attention to her. As the gates opened, Emma looked
around, suddenly anxious. She stared at the disembarking passengers. What if she didn't recognize Lia? After all, they hadn't seen
each other in over a year. But just as the thought filled her mind, she
looked up to see her tea-colored friend with the wild hair coming
straight toward her.

"Lia!" Emma yelled above the noise.

Lia smiled widely, erasing their last year apart, dispelling the
sadness of Joan's break up, Emma's loneliness, and all the days
she'd dreamed of being far away.

In the taxi on the way home, Emma could almost smell the tropical scent of flowers and coconut. Sitting close to Lia, she sensed the
strength in her friend's strong shoulders, dark against her pale yellow sundress. They had both grown taller in the past year; Lia's
breasts and hips were full, while Emma remained thin and wiry.

"How are you?" Emma asked, suddenly shy.

"I'm well. But you've been sad. I can tell from your letters. Even
if you don't say." Lia paused to look at the tall buildings in Central.
"So big."

"My sister hasn't been well," Emma said at first, then quickly
changed the subject to something lighter. "There's so much I want
to show you. We won't have time to sleep!"

"I can go back to Macao to sleep." Lia laughed.

"And how is your *mamae*?"

Lia sat forward as they began winding their way up the hill, past
another new building cocooned in bamboo scaffolding. Then she

looked back at Emma. "She's well. No more visits from her great-aunt Carmelita."

They both laughed out loud, and Emma brightened with each musical word that Lia spoke.

Lia's visit passed so quickly, Emma wished she could stop time. They went someplace new each day—Repulse Bay, Stanley Village, and Shek O. On the fourth day they saw *The Best Years of Our Lives* at the King's Theatre, then had tea at the Peninsula. On the last day, they rose early to catch the Victoria Peak tram so as not to miss the morning light. Emma also hoped it would make their final day together last longer.

The large peak tram squeaked as it made its way back down the steep mountain. The cables vibrated while Emma and Lia waited on the platform.

"Will your sister be better soon?" Lia asked.

Emma shuffled from one foot to the other. Beneath her feet she felt the platform shake as the tram approached. "It's not just because of the ulcer that you haven't seen much of her. She also broke up with someone she was close to."

Lia shook her head. "Brokenhearted."

"Even if she won't admit it. I don't understand her sometimes."

The tram came to a full stop in front of them. The door slid open and a few people disembarked. Emma and Lia hurried in to take their seats.

"There's no understanding love," Lia continued. "It's like a great weight when it's with you, and also when it leaves you."

"Sounds like you've been in love," Emma teased.

Lia blushed. "I've seen enough of my relatives to know. Joan will be better soon, I bet."

The tram began its ascent toward the peak, and Lia became quiet, watching intently as they rose above Hong Kong, her mouth open slightly. All Emma could think of was how fast the days had passed, and how empty she would feel when Lia returned to Macao.

At the top of the tram line was a restaurant and a small gift shop. Emma led Lia away to the circular path around the peak.

"When we were young, Mah-mee and Ba ba brought us here for walks," Emma said over her shoulder. Lia followed her along the path. "I remember once when I was about seven, and there was a thick mist up here. Like we were wrapped in a white blanket. Mah-mee had warned us, 'Don't go far, you can't see your five fingers right in front of you.' So I held out my arms like a blind person and started running, following the fingers that I could barely make out in front of me. Before I knew it, I was lost. I started crying. I couldn't see anything but a cool white haze. I'd never felt so completely alone before. And then I saw something coming towards me. It was just a shadow at first, and it scared me, but when it came closer, I saw it was my sister, reaching out for me. Somehow Joan had found me in all that fog."

Lia laughed. "I couldn't lose my brothers and sister if I tried."

As they walked farther, the shrubbery grew thicker. Jasmine and wild indigo, daphne, rhododendrons, and shiny wax trees lined their path. The air was so much sweeter and fresher than down in the city. Emma breathed in the rich fragrances and couldn't get enough. They continued walking until they came to a sudden gap in the shrubbery that opened up to them like a window. Down below lay all of Hong Kong, breathtaking in the morning light. And beyond, ferries crossed the shimmering harbor to Kowloon.

Emma remembered the game they used to play in Macao and turned to Lia. "And what do we see down below?"

Lia raised her hand against the glaring light. "I see the entire world below us."

*   *   *

In early January, a week after New Year's Day, Joan surprised everyone by getting up one morning in time for breakfast. Lia had been gone a week, and Emma was still feeling miserable. She dropped her sweet bun in her plate when Joan sat down across from her. Mah-mee, still in her robe, pulled it tighter as if someone she didn't know had suddenly arrived.

"*Tso sun,*" Joan said, almost cheerful.

"Good morning," Emma said, surprised.

Joan was fully dressed in cotton slacks and an off-white tunic. Her hair was combed back into a ponytail, revealing a calm, if tired, face.

"How are you feeling?" Mah-mee asked.

"Better. My stomach isn't burning anymore. I think the fire's finally out."

Mah-mee smiled and called for Foon, who peeked out the door, then hurried from the kitchen carrying a bowl of plain jook. "Good. Don't have to walk so far," she said, placing the bowl in front of Joan.

"Can't I have something else for a change?" Joan asked Foon.

"One more week," Foon answered, disappearing back into the kitchen.

Emma leaned over and gave Joan the rest of her sweet bun, spread generously with butter and marmalade.

After breakfast, Joan looked across the table and said, "Let's go out for a walk."

"What?" Emma wasn't sure she'd heard right.

Joan smiled. "It's a good day for a walk."

Emma looked at Mah-mee, who simply said, "Don't walk too far."

Without a word, Emma scraped her chair back and ran to her room for a coat.

The beginning of January had brought cooler weather. The sky was a flat, dull gray—low and heavy. Joan walked slowly at first, but soon Emma heard her inhale large mouthfuls of air, releasing each slowly. Emma waited for Joan to lead the conversation.

"I woke up this morning feeling better," Joan explained. "It's a new year and I just didn't want to be alone anymore."

Emma walked slowly beside her sister down Conduit Road as they passed Auntie Go's flat. Emma felt warm and happy. "I'm glad."

"Mah-mee must be devastated by my breakup with Joseph." Joan's voice filled the chilly air. "She must wish I had been a son . . . then she wouldn't have to worry about me having to marry someone like Joseph."

"She's strong." The two words came out of Emma's mouth without any thought, even before she realized the truth of what she was saying.

"Stronger than I am."

"Stronger than both of us. It isn't the end of the world you know. You can have anyone you want."

Joan smiled. "I'm not sure I want anyone else."

Emma stopped just in front of her sister. "Then why can't you forgive him? It isn't too late."

"I don't know." Joan stepped aside and walked on. "It's just that I felt so sad and angry at first, and now I feel totally empty. Nothing."

"Maybe you just need more time."

"I can't imagine it'll make any difference." Joan picked up the pace. "The grief and anger are gone. There's nothing left."

Emma wanted to ask, "What about love?" but held her tongue. Perhaps in the end, all the love, sadness, grief, and anger were one and the same.

* * *

They had just turned down Robinson Road when Joan suddenly stepped to the curb and waved for a taxi. "Let's visit Auntie Go," she said, swinging open the taxi door and stepping in.

Emma hesitated. "Mah-mee said not to walk too far. You've just gotten better."

"Come on," Joan insisted. "Don't be a spoilsport. Besides, we're taking a taxi, aren't we? Anyway, I feel fine, and Auntie Go will be so happy to see me up and around again."

Emma couldn't argue. She didn't want to. It'd been so many months since Joan had been her old self. Emma was afraid that the smallest thing might send Joan back to her dark, closed room. Emma jumped into the taxi and slammed the door shut behind her.

The Wanchai District was bustling with people, crowded with bars, girlie shows, and small shops. Neon signs, which glowed and blinked madly after dark, seemed asleep and harmless in the day-light. Mah-mee wasn't happy that Auntie Go worked in such a dis-reputable area, but Emma once heard her aunt snap back, "At least prostitutes and pimps are honest about what they do! Not like the businessmen and bankers wearing dark suits and sly smiles." Emma remembered that Mah-mee didn't speak to Auntie Go for a couple of days after that fight.

Morning traffic inched along. Sidewalk vendors with high, piercing voices screamed out words; horns blared; young and old alike crowded the sidewalks. In the taxi, Emma glanced at Joan, who seemed to be taking it all in peacefully, as if viewing it for the first time. Even pale and tired, Joan appeared a lovely mystery to Emma.

The Western Wind Knitting Company was in a narrow, two-story building that had been almost completely destroyed by the

Japanese. Right after the war, Emma had returned with Mah-mee and Joan to help Auntie Go clean it up. Emma would never forget the glassy stare of fear in her aunt's eyes.

"It's going to be all right," Mah-mee had said.

But when Auntie Go pushed open the door, the large downstairs room was hollow and empty. "It's all gone," she whispered.

Joan wandered off to the other end of the room. "I found some yarn!" she said, holding up a blue spool.

"It's a start," Emma added optimistically.

Auntie Go had stood in the middle of the room as if frozen. Only now was she getting the ravaged factory back into full production. Downstairs in the large open room was the smell of hot metal, dusty air, the rhythmic hum of the knitting machines, which played like music. Emma loved the beautiful patterns they created. She stood and watched, hypnotized, as little by little, right before her eyes, flowers or animals gradually came into being. Wool and cotton cardigan and crew-neck sweaters hung from racks, waiting to be packed and shipped all over the world. Upstairs was Auntie Go's office, and room for storing yarns and patterns. Emma quickly ran up the wooden stairs, followed more slowly by Joan.

Emma knocked three times on Auntie Go's office door, then waited for a distracted, slightly irritated "Come in" before she pushed open the door, letting in the quick swishing sounds of the machines from downstairs.

"We've come to visit you," Emma sang out.

Auntie Go looked up and smiled. "We?"

"Me too," Joan said, stepping into the office, her arms outstretched.

Auntie Go stood up and hugged Joan first. Her aunt was almost half a head taller. "It's so good to see you up and feeling better."

Emma looked around the room—a standard desk and chair, two chairs for clients, a small table, and on it, a tray holding a pot of tea and a thermos. Framed reproductions of paintings by Monet and Degas leaned against one wall. Everything simple and effi-cient.

"And you, moi-moi." Auntie Go hugged Emma. "What brings you two down here?"

"It was my idea," Joan volunteered before Emma could say any-thing. "I've been thinking . . . wondering if maybe you would like some help here. I could help you with office work."

For a moment, both Emma and Auntie Go were surprised into silence. In the near distance, Emma heard the hollow whoosh of the knitting machines.

"I'd love you to come work with me." Auntie Go spoke care-fully, leaning back against the edge of her desk. "Perhaps in a cou-ple of weeks when you're stronger and your mah-mee and ba ba agree to it."

"They will," Joan said almost too quickly. "I'll see to it."

Emma listened to the dull surge of the machines, absorbing the newness of the idea. She wondered if this was what Joan meant by telling Mah-mee she'd move on, rather than forgive Joseph. Then Emma wondered, *doesn't a person deserve more than just one chance?* But she simply smiled and nodded, saying nothing.

"Let's get something to eat and discuss this further," Auntie Go said. "You two must be famished."

"The Hong Kong Hotel?" Emma asked.

Auntie Go smiled. "Of course, we have to celebrate Joan's re-covery!"

Emma opened the door again, letting in the noise of the ma-chines below.

Alone in her room that evening, Emma smiled remembering Joan's hearty appetite at lunch. She had eaten three steamed pork buns and two plates of rice noodles. Auntie Go wouldn't allow her to eat any more, fearing she might be sick again. Then she would have to face the wrath of Mah-mee and Foon. But as they left the restaurant, Emma knew her sister had revived. She saw it in her quick, fluid movements, the spark of light in her eyes that Emma had almost forgotten.

Now Emma sat at her desk and took out the pearl-inlaid, black lacquer jewelry box Ba ba had given her. She swung open the two doors and pulled out the bottom drawer. Buried beneath her gold bracelets and a jade pendant were the three gold charms Joseph had given her last year. She picked them out one by one—first the piano, then the ballerina, and finally the rosebud. She felt their lightness in the palm of her hand.

The Way of Love — 1948

AUNTIE GO

Kum Ling suddenly sat back and asked her mah-jongg group, "What am I to do? Joan isn't bad looking, but she has hands which men seem to slip through. And her head is always in the clouds."

"Don't worry," the nasal-high voice of Auntie Hong piped in. "Joan has plenty of time. She's only twenty-two. Why push her?"

"Aii-ya! These precious years can't be wasted," Kum Ling said.

In the pause between their chattering voices, Auntie Go sat quietly while her cousin and mah-jongg partners lifted the covers and sipped from their steaming cups of tea. They nibbled on a small banquet of peanuts, dried plums, Chinese beef jerky, and shrimp chips, which Foon had left on small tables beside each woman.

Auntie Go was Lew Kum Ling's first cousin and the only true blood relative included in her cousin's weekly mah-jongg games. Now in her midforties, Kum Ling's beauty and style, as well as her husband Lew Hing's business connections, made her an invaluable asset to any social event. She played mah-jongg with the wives of the wealthiest bankers and businessmen in Hong Kong and was often included in their social events. Auntie Go knew Kum Ling's solid social connections were what her cousin dearly wanted for her daughters.

"It's a different world now, a girl can wait longer before settling down," continued Auntie Kao, tugging at the collar of her sleeveless cheungsam. "In our day, if you weren't married by sixteen, seventeen, you were too old for a good match. Nowadays, it isn't the same, times have changed. The war . . ." Her voice trailed off.

"Look at my sister's daughter Mei, not married until her late twenties, and now expecting her third child. And the first baby a son!" Heavyset Auntie Hong snatched a piece of beef jerky and sucked on it thoughtfully. "You can't change fate, better to sit back and relax."

Kum Ling's face remained expressionless. Auntie Go could tell she was seething underneath by the way she made a throaty sound in response.

Auntie Go knew Kum Ling's friends were just as old-fashioned as her cousin. Their words were meant to pacify Kum Ling, to help her save face, even though their feelings about marriage were the same. And like Kum Ling, none of them could really understand why a young woman as beautiful as Joan hadn't yet found her match.

Auntie Go waited a little longer. She bit her tongue rather than voice any thoughts that might upset her cousin and disrupt their mah-jongg game.

After all these years, Auntie Go knew there was always something to keep her apart from the others. First, there was the fact that she had never married. The years had softened this distinction and she was accepted into Kum Ling's circle of *tai tais*, though she still cringed at the same words now directed toward Joan.

Then, there was the fact that she'd started her own knitting business, entering in her late twenties "a world she had no right to," as Kum Ling once warned her. She knew her cousin was just worrying about her, but the words had incensed her all the same. Only in recent years had Auntie Go realized it had been fear more than desire that made her risk everything she owned. She refused to be pitied, refused to become a stone always carted around by others.

And it was Auntie Go to whom Joan first turned, a few weeks after her breakup with the Wong boy. Go had been working long hours at the knitting factory and had returned home late one evening to find Joan waiting for her. Joan was the last person Auntie Go had expected to see.

"Joan, what are you doing here? It's almost midnight." Go unlocked her front door and offered her frail-looking niece a chair. "Sit, sit. Does your mah-mee know you're here?"

Joan shook her head. In the dim light, Joan appeared even paler and thinner than when Auntie Go had seen her the evening before. Her cotton cheungsam and matching jacket hung loosely on her body. Joan hesitated a moment, then sat down. "I don't want them to know I'm here," she said anxiously. "I needed to talk to you."

"Of course," Auntie Go said, pulling another chair closer to Joan. "I'm so sorry about everything that has happened."

It was the first time she had mentioned the Wong boy, electing to give Joan some distance. Besides, she had her hands full trying to keep her business afloat.

"I don't understand why . . ." Joan began, her voice halting.

Auntie Go quickly continued, "Sometimes there aren't any reasons for what people do, or don't do. Maybe he wasn't ready for such a big commitment."

"Then why did he tell me he loved me?" Joan asked, trembling.

Auntie Go took hold of Joan's hands. They felt smooth and small in her own. "I believe he does love you, but love isn't a guarantee against hurt."

For a moment Joan stared at her without speaking. Auntie Go could see the tears forming in the corners of her eyes.

"Is that how it was for you?"

Auntie Go let go of Joan's hands and sat back in her chair. "What do you mean?"

Joan shifted in her chair, then leaned closer. "I heard Mah-mee once say you had lost someone you loved."

Auntie Go paused in thought. The memory seemed so long ago. "I was nineteen and in love." She smiled wistfully. "He was a teacher, the youngest son of a family friend, whose kindness made up for any lack of material wealth. We were making marriage plans when he became ill. Within months, what I now know was cancer had spread throughout his body. Just over a year later, he was gone. . . ." Go's voice trailed.

Afterward, there were other suitors, many of them, but never anyone she wanted to create a life with. Go knew other girls would have settled with any one of them, simply for the sake of being married, but it wasn't a lie she could swallow without choking.

Auntie Go looked up at her niece. "It did hurt me very much."

"What am I supposed to do now?" Joan whispered.

"You go on. The road has just begun for you."

Joan dropped her head and began to cry softly. Auntie Go wrapped her arms around her niece and folded away her own memories. Then much later, when Joan had calmed, they stepped out into the warm night air tasting faintly of litchi as Go steered her home.

Only with Joan and Emma did Auntie Go's words flow with ease. They held a special place in her heart. From the time of their births, Auntie Go was like a second mother to them. Sometimes, in the quiet of her mind, Go felt her barrenness. It echoed through her, like the empty rooms of her house that would never be filled. But over the years, her sorrow lessened as she watched her nieces grow into such fine young women.

Auntie Go looked up and stared into the faces of her cousin and friends across the mah-jongg table. She listened, as if each slippery tongue directed at Joan were also addressed to her. So many years had passed, but the words still stung with the same power. Auntie Go held her breath, but couldn't swallow the words that would defend her niece and put these women in their place.

"And what if she never marries? Would it be such a crime?" Auntie Go exhaled in one hurried breath. She avoided her cousin's eyes, Go's hands quickly turning the ivory mah-jongg tiles facedown in the middle of the table. "Joan is a capable girl who can do many things."

The voices stopped. Auntie Kao sighed, while Auntie Hong crunched down on shrimp chips. Go knew she had slipped again. She tried not to make her thoughts too evident. There'd been too many occasions when her views and her cousin's had clashed. Then, their conversations would end either in an argument or a hard, cold silence. Joan's working at the knitting factory had been a sore subject between them. But Kum Ling refrained from saying too much, knowing Joan was happy working part-time there.

Auntie Go prepared for the worst.

"Not everyone is as industrious as you," her cousin snapped back amid the noisy clatter of the tiles being mixed together.

"That seems to be the way you always like to see it. I'd like to think anyone can do what I've done."

Auntie Go heard Kum Ling mumble something under her breath that sounded like, "We should all remain single without a family of our own."

Then it became so quiet, all Go could hear was the crackling sound of the thick ivory tiles, etched with patterns of bamboo, circles, and Chinese characters, being mixed and stacked into four neat double rows in the middle of the table. One after another, each woman reached out to take her tiles, thirteen in all, standing them upright in front of their places like soldiers.

Go smiled when Auntie Kao reached out to pick first from the remaining rows, slyly grabbing two tiles rather than one. Glancing quickly at them, Kao kept the more advantageous of the two, then threw one back from her original thirteen, slipping the extra tile into the discard pile along with it.

Auntie Go picked, rubbed the etched circle pattern on the tile, then threw it back.

"No good, no good," Auntie Kao mumbled as she studied the tiles in front of her. If the others had seen her cheat, they also kept quiet. Auntie Kao came from a wealthy and powerful family that had always taken care of her indiscretions. She was well-known throughout Hong Kong for "borrowing" things that didn't belong to her. Ever since she was a small child, objects of her fancy had disappeared from houses and stores alike. Her family and husband arranged for the merchants and friends to send a bill for the missing items. Nevertheless, Auntie Kao had a reputation for donating generously to charitable causes and was invited to every important social function.

Auntie Hong cleared her throat and changed the subject to a relative whose son had abruptly denounced his mother and father and joined the Communist Party. "Can you imagine," Auntie Hong gossiped, "he had the nerve to steal his mother's jewelry and give it to the Party as an example of the family's decadence!"

"They don't know any better. They're brainwashed," replied

Auntie Kao. "The entire country will be following Mao pretty soon."

"Young people nowadays, they only care about themselves," snapped Kum Ling, tapping a tile on the table before throwing it back into the pile.

"They're certainly not the same as our generation." Auntie Hong shook her head, then reached for another tile.

Auntie Go leaned back at ease in her chair as she watched Kum Ling sigh and slowly sip her tea, already distant, nodding absently at whatever was said.

Auntie Go had inherited everything upon the death of her parents. Her father's store was sold, and though it didn't bring in a great deal of money, it would take care of her if she lived wisely. At that most financially secure time in her life, Auntie Go decided to take her biggest gamble. From a friend of her father's, Go had heard of a small sweater knitting factory for sale. She'd little knowledge of the knitting business, but had always been fascinated just watching her mother produce sweaters and socks by the simple clicking together of two needles. Having been trained in accounting at her father's store, she decided to risk her savings on it. The day she told Kum Ling what she had done, her cousin simply shook her head and said, "Well, I suppose you can always stay with us after Joan and Emma are married."

Auntie Go bought the Western Wind Knitting Company using her father's name. Already having a head for sums, Go learned to walk through the business step by step. Though the hours were long, and learning to run the machines was a maze of dead ends, Auntie Go was determined to master her factory and create a life of her own. She hired experienced knitters and held on to a small list of existing merchant and exporter clients. Specializing in sweaters made from wool, cotton, and silk, Go was beginning to turn a profit when the war intruded and brought her growing business to a deafening silence.

When Go returned from Macao in 1945, she was grateful that Kum Ling and the girls insisted on returning to the Western Wind with her. Though she had prepared herself for what she might see, Go's hands shook as she squeaked open the door and stepped into the cold, only to have her heart sink at the destruction she found. What wasn't bolted down had been taken away by the Japanese. The largest room, where the machines once hummed, stood skeletal, stripped of everything, from her knitting machines to the stools and light fixtures. The bits and pieces that were left had been totally destroyed.

"The devils," Go whispered as she stood in the middle of the empty room wanting to cry, willing herself not to, the tears burning behind her eyes.

"It's not so bad," Emma said, keeping her voice happy and optimistic.

"There's nothing left," Kum Ling said, her hand still covering her mouth, holding in her surprise.

Joan stood at the far side of the room, fingering a spool of blue yarn she'd found. "It's like an empty tomb," she said.

"Don't say such things," Kum Ling said. "It's bad luck!"

Auntie Go nodded. "She's right. Dead and buried. So I'll just have to start again from the beginning," she said, the words choking in her throat.

The next month, Auntie Go sold some of her jewelry and managed to scrounge enough parts through the black market to get first one machine running, then a few more. Accounts began flowing slowly in from England, France, and even New York and San Francisco. Go knew if she could produce up-to-date styles at a reasonable price, her business would grow. Three difficult years later,

Auntie Go was riding the wave of prosperity that had flooded Hong Kong after the war.

Since the war, Auntie Go had seen more new places than she had ever dreamed of, traveling to Europe and the United States. Sadly, each trip also took her farther away from Kum Ling. The success of the business was becoming a growing barrier between them. At the same time, her cousin's husband, Lew Hing, had lost money exporting his silks and art to a growing market in Korea and Vietnam. Several large shipments of Hing's goods had not been paid for after arriving in the hands of foreign merchants.

On one rare evening when Auntie Go left work early, she was delighted to find Lew Hing home from Tokyo. The family had just finished dinner and Kum Ling had been called away to the phone. Joan and Emma had excused themselves, leaving Go at the table with Lew Hing. He looked thin and tired sitting in his chair at the head of the table. Over the years, it had been vacant more often than it was filled with his presence.

"Will you be traveling again soon?" Auntie Go asked, leaning over and choosing a pear from a bowl Foon had placed in the middle of the table.

Lew Hing cleared his throat, his eyes watching her hands as she began peeling the pear. "Things have been difficult with these new business partners."

Auntie Go continued to peel, the white flesh cool in her hand. "Perhaps you might consider helping me at the Western Wind."

"I'm much too old to learn a new trade." Lew Hing forced a smile. "Besides, these setbacks are just temporary. I don't expect them to last."

"The offer is always open," Go said, dropping the spiral of pear skin onto her plate.

Lew Hing scraped his chair back, and for a moment, Go thought he was rising to leave, but he reached for a pear and sat back down.

"Thank you, Go," he said softly.

Auntie Go had no idea Kum Ling would be made uncomfortable by her offer. The following day Kum Ling seemed awkward and unusually quiet around her. *What's wrong?* Go wanted to ask, then thought the better of it. A few months later, Lew Hing returned to Japan in hopes of resurrecting his import-export business. His refusal to join her company was a subject she and Kum Ling stayed as far away from as they could.

As different as they were, only Go knew that Kum Ling's own life had been one of ups and downs. Her once wealthy father had lost most of his money in bad investments. Go knew it was her cousin's good fortune to have been betrothed early on to the Lew family. It was love at first sight on Lew Hing's part. Kum Ling was no more than a girl of thirteen, helping to carry home vegetables from the market, when he first saw her. A marriage broker appeared a week later on behalf of the Lew family. Her parents had to sell most of their possessions to secure Kum Ling a decent dowry before she turned sixteen, if she was to marry Lew Hing. In turn, Kum Ling's new husband worked hard and was good to his new wife. But although Lew Hing's import-export business flourished, the first few years of her marriage brought Kum Ling unexpected grief. She miscarried twice, becoming anxious and despondent at the loss of two sons. "Be happy you have your health. The rest will follow in time," Go had said to console her cousin.

Two years after her second miscarriage, Kum Ling had Joan, followed by another miscarriage, and finally, after a great many complications, Emma. From then on, Kum Ling led the involved life of a Hong Kong *tai tai*, balancing lunches and mah-jongg games with business and social obligations. Kum Ling lit up a room with her delicate beauty, while Go marveled at how well she orchestrated every event, easily fitting into Hong Kong's top society.

But recently, as Lew Hing's business ventures failed, and Joan remained unmarried, Kum Ling began again to mumble that her daughters were poor answers to her prayers for sons to carry on the Lew family name. To Go, however, Joan and Emma were sweet voices that helped to fill her own emptiness.

Of course, Auntie Go knew that the girls' fates would be determined by their strengths and weaknesses. Whereas Joan was gifted with Kum Ling's beauty, she could also be an impulsive daydreamer. And while Emma was quick and intelligent, she often worried too much. Auntie Go could only hope that both of them would find balance in their lives.

During the past year Auntie Go prayed to the gods that Joan might find some solid ground again. Her part-time work at the knitting factory seemed to have helped. Go despaired as much as Kum Ling over Joan's breakup with the Wong boy, if not for the same reasons. Auntie Go hated to see how Joan suffered in silence, while Kum Ling's motherly concerns were also intensified by the missed opportunity of such a prodigious union.

After the mah-jongg game, Auntie Go returned to her flat, thankful for the silence. The clacking of the tiles and the chatter of voices had given her a headache. She poured herself a cup of tea and sat down, grateful that the servants were still out at the market. Go looked around her spare living room, still not completely furnished since the Japanese had appropriated everything not bolted down. For the most part, there wasn't anything that couldn't be replaced, except for the mother-of-pearl cabinet left to her by her parents. The empty place where it stood still felt like an open wound. Go had hidden and carried all the important things with her to Macao—the family photos and her mother's jewelry.

Distant voices woke Auntie Go from her thoughts. She heard her servant Ming's voice echo up the stone steps and was delighted when Emma followed Ming through the front door.

"Moi-moi," Auntie Go said, opening her arms to greet her niece. At seventeen, Emma was too old to be addressed as "little sister," but old habits were hard to break. "How was your day?"

"I think I did well on my English exam," Emma answered, her dark eyes widening with anxiousness. "It's important for my college applications."

"Good, good." Auntie Go looked up to see her niece shifting her weight from one foot to the other, her arms tightly clutching a load of books. "And what else do you have to tell me?"

Emma hesitated, sat down on the chair across from Go, then let her words pour out. "What do you think about my going to a university in America?"

Auntie Go smiled. "Does it matter what I think?"

"Of course it does. I need someone to tell Mah-mee for me."

Auntie Go looked closely at her younger niece and saw how she had grown in the past few years. Emma would never be as beautiful as Joan was, but Auntie Go saw a quiet strength in her dark eyes that had been there since the day she was born. It was something the winds would never blow away with time, and in the long days of life, she knew that it was a priceless trait.

"I think you should talk to your mah-mee by yourself. You don't need to involve me," Auntie Go answered, remembering the sharp words that she had had with Kum Ling just that afternoon.

"You've been to America. You can tell Mah-mee there's nothing for her to worry about."

Auntie Go sighed. "It's one thing to visit. It's another thing to live there."

"It won't be for at least another year or more, and I'll be over eighteen. Lots of girls go to study overseas."

"But why so far? You can do your first two years here, then think about going."

Emma's dark eyes pleaded with Auntie Go. "Have you ever felt that if you don't do something as soon as you can, you're never going to do it? Well, that's how I feel about going to school overseas."

Auntie Go thought about the buying of the Western Wind. She knew deep down that for her own selfish reasons she wanted Emma to wait two years. Go hated to think of her so far away from the family.

"All right," Auntie Go gave in, "I'll speak to her."

Emma leaned over and hugged her. Auntie Go breathed in deeply, smelling the faint scent of mothballs on Emma's winter coat.

Auntie Go let a few weeks go by before she dared to bring up the subject of Emma's leaving. She knew it was important to go slowly with her cousin, plant the seed and let it grow, until it ripened into Kum Ling's own idea. The right time presented itself one evening after her cousin had won big at mah-jongg. Joan and Emma had gone out to the movies, Lew Hing was working in Japan, and spring had brought warmer, softer weather.

"The girls should be home soon," Kum Ling said, sitting on the sofa and unbuttoning the collar of her cheungsam.

Though she had put on some weight during the past few years, Go thought Kum Ling still looked remarkably beautiful.

"Joan seems much happier," Auntie Go said.

"Yes." For a change, Kum Ling added nothing to lead the subject in another direction.

"Perhaps she's finally over the Wong boy."

Kum Ling smiled thoughtfully. "It's about time she met someone else."

"Yes. Does she intend to go to Lingnan, or Hong Kong University?" Go knew very well her older niece had long ago given up any intention of continuing her studies.

"She wouldn't be able to get in," Kum Ling answered matter-of-factly. "She doesn't have the diligence of moi-moi."

Auntie Go paused and sipped her tea. "Emma could go anywhere. She has always had the desire to learn."

"Now, Emma could get into Hong Kong University!"

"Or go to school elsewhere," Auntie Go added, putting down her cup of tea.

"Where elsewhere? There are plenty of schools close by. Anyway, elsewhere costs money."

Auntie Go carefully chose her next words. "You know your daughters seem like my own. It would give me great honor to help them with their education. It's true an education extends outside the classroom. It might do moi-moi good to go elsewhere, get out of the shadow cast by Joan."

"In our generation, you simply stayed home with your family until you married. When did it become so complicated?"

"It's a different world now." Auntie Go paused and waited. They both knew Joan could still prove herself socially, whereas Emma could succeed academically. Go watched her cousin sip her tea, turning the words over in thought.

"Maybe," Kum Ling finally said. "We'll see what time brings."

Auntie Go smiled. She laid her hand lightly on Kum Ling's arm for a moment, pleased that her cousin didn't pull away.

That night Auntie Go slept lightly, dreaming her parents were alive again. Every so often they came to her, making sure she was all right, reassuring her on decisions she'd made. Go thought they looked younger, their hair no longer gray, their movements no longer stiff and frail. "But will she be all right alone in a foreign land?" she heard herself asking them about Emma. Her parents mouthed the word *yes*. "And have I done the right thing getting involved?" Auntie Go stared hard and waited for a response. It felt like an eternity before her mother rose above her, smiled gently, then nodded her head.

The

Voyage —

1950

EMMA

In the darkness of her room, Emma lay wide awake, breathing in and out slowly to calm herself. In two days she would fly on Pan American Airlines to Tokyo, where Ba ba would meet her at the airport. She'd spend the night with him before boarding the *President Coolidge* and sailing for America. After Tokyo, the ship would dock briefly in Honolulu, then sail on to its final destination—San Francisco.

Emma had finally realized her dream, thanks to Auntie Go and Ba ba, who convinced Mah-mee that Emma should study abroad over the year. The sharp, flat declarations of "No" or "Not yet" of their early debates slowly gave way to more fluid ones such as "Maybe" and "We'll see." There had been several discussions every time Ba ba came home from Japan. One evening, Emma came home unexpectedly to find her mother and father arguing. She closed the front door quietly, then tiptoed into the living room and stood soundless behind the black lacquer screen, listening to her name startle the air as if they were talking about someone else.

"Emma's ready to leave. And more importantly, it's what she wants," Ba ba said resolutely.

Emma heard Mah-mee snicker. "How does she really know what she wants? A young girl can change her mind many times before she settles on something!"

"Joan, yes. Not Emma." Ba ba cleared his throat. "She has always known what she wanted."

Emma watched her mother lean forward on the sofa as if she were ready to strike. "But it isn't necessary for her to go so far. She can go to Hong Kong University for the first two years."

"Do you remember when Emma was just a little girl?" Ba ba's voice suddenly dominated the room. "You were visiting me in Tokyo with the girls, and Emma was fascinated with all the places on the small globe in my office. Do you remember? She began to cry when it was time for us to go have dinner, until I finally allowed her to take the globe with us. How can we stop her now, Kum Ling? She has grown into a young lady, and still she carries all the places on that globe with her."

The room became quiet as her parents sat looking away from each other. Emma leaned back against the wall and swallowed, astonished her father had remembered. She had only a vague memory of the globe in his office. It was blue, with raised brown continents, and it had felt much lighter in her hands than she'd expected. She remembered carrying it around all that summer like a plastic ball.

"You would send her so far away then?" Mah-mee accused, her voice piercing the silence.

Ba ba weighed his words carefully before he answered. "Sooner or later, she will be going anyway."

On a windy Saturday in mid-February, just after lunch, their stomachs full of Foon's duck and thousand-year-old-eggs jook, Mah-mee sat up straight in her chair and said, "Moi-moi, Ba ba and I discussed it when he was home for the New Year. Now that you are nineteen years old, we think it would be good for you to go abroad and get an education."

Emma glanced first at her mother, in hopes that what she had heard wasn't her imagination, then at Auntie Go in gratitude, and finally at Joan, who smiled at the news, leaned over, and whispered, "Bon voyage, moi-moi!"

"Thank you," Emma gasped, taking hold of her sister's hand and squeezing it tightly. She hugged both Mah-mee and Auntie Go until they were breathless.

Then came the exciting search to find the right colleges to apply to. Emma treaded carefully, to avoid a battle of wills. All the marketplace bargaining skills she had learned from watching Foon over the years would finally be put to use.

"Why not England?" Mah-mee asked. "Hong Kong is a colony, and there is no language problem like in Europe."

Emma shrugged her shoulders. She already knew enough about the English culture. "What about the United States?"

"New York is too far away," Mah-mee said emphatically.

"California isn't so far," Emma said, thinking of all she'd read about Hollywood and the Golden Gate Bridge.

Mah-mee fell silent. Her tongue flicked across her upper lip before she pressed her mouth tight in thought. "It is closer," she finally said.

To satisfy Mah-mee's requirements for safety and Emma's for location, it was decided Emma would apply to private schools in California. She immediately chose the cities of San Francisco and Los Angeles, steeped as she was in all the mysterious, alluring books she'd read—*The Maltese Falcon* by Dashiell Hammett, and *The Last Tycoon* by F. Scott Fitzgerald. Emma repeated the name of each city every night, the exotic words filling her mouth, humming through her head like a chant. She hoped it would somehow bring her luck. And it did. Two months later, Emma opened a fat envelope from Lone Mountain, a small Catholic girl's college in San Francisco. She had been accepted with a full academic scholarship.

Emma realized that she would be alone, at nineteen, for the first time in her life, and just the thought made her stomach feel unsettled. For a few days after she'd learned she was really going, Emma's legs felt wobbly, as if she were already bracing herself against the sea. Each morning, she planted her feet squarely on the floor and took a deep breath against the swaying.

Besides her family, Emma would miss a few good friends from school, and of course, Lia in Macao. But there was no serious boyfriend to keep her in Hong Kong. She had grown tall and slender like Joan, but had not made the leap to ravishing beauty. She was no longer the bud that would eventually blossom into a beautiful flower. Her nose was a little too large, her lips too thin. And all the makeup in the world wouldn't change that. She had accepted the truth that she would never be as beautiful as her mother and sister. But what Emma secretly wished was that Mah-mee would see who she was, instead of seeking new ways to re-create her.

Emma blossomed in her own way. In her last year of high school, she had remained at the top of her class, kept up with her piano recitals, and often entertained classmates with her poetry and drawings. Going to America was the culmination of hard work and a persistent dream she had built from the books she'd read and the movies she'd seen. Leaving the protected confines of Hong Kong would lead Emma in new directions, down a path she'd never traveled. But she yearned to see the unknown faces, the empty rooms she could slowly fill herself.

Still, Emma had never dreamed she'd leave home before Joan— Joan, the beautiful Lew daughter, the one primed since her youth for a good marriage, as ever, the main topic of their mother's mahjongg games. However plain Emma was, she'd never been reduced to that and felt sad overhearing such conversations. Fortunately, Mah-mee wouldn't begin to worry about finding her a husband until Joan had settled down. It was painful to think that her sister had been so badly deceived after loving someone as much as Joan loved Joseph. But worse was the thought that the voyage to America made Emma the beneficiary of Joan's failure in love.

After Joan's breakup with Joseph, Mah-mee had returned to matchmaking with a vengeance. Emma couldn't understand why Joan consented to date a string of listless boyfriends who grew progressively worse.

First, there was the son of a rich recluse, the father having made a fortune during the war selling his own patented Chinese medicine. It was said to cure everything from a toothache to malaria. Mahmee had arranged for Joan to meet the son through the sister of the recluse. All the young man's invitations were delivered by his chauffeur, who came to the house in a full brass-buttoned uniform to ask formally, "Would Miss Joan Lew join Mr. Lum at eight o'clock tomorrow evening for dinner?" Emma could hardly prevent herself from laughing out loud every time she saw the massive, black 1947 Mercury parked outside. This continued for about a month, until Joan grew tired of the young man's pretentious games and the uniformed messages quickly disappeared.

Then there was the thin, short son of a family friend. He would have given his right arm to marry Joan, though most of the time she treated him like a distant relative. His small, slight frame made him seem more like a boy than a man, as did his chronic stuttering. "Is J-J-Joan h-h-home?" he would ask when Emma answered the door. Emma would usher him into the living room, hoping his tongue would untie before Joan appeared. But he only grew more nervous at the sight of her, and his whole body seemed to stutter involuntarily. After three months' effort, he never again rang the bell nor shyly bowed his head as he walked past Emma into the house.

In the last year, only one boyfriend, an architect, showed any character. He was funny and intelligent in the same way that Joseph was handsome and charming. In Emma's eyes, he was the sole prospect with any real possibilities after Joseph, until they found out he had earlier applied for a visa to leave Hong Kong and Joan for America.

Emma knew Joan had had some feelings for the architect by the careful way she applied the deliberate lines and curves that darkened her eyes and eyebrows when she dressed for their dates. A few months later, when the architect left without a word, Emma found Joan in her room staring out the window.

"Are you all right?" Emma tentatively asked.

Joan turned around with a tired smile. "Yes, I'm fine."

"I don't know what to say."

"Better to find out sooner than later," Joan said quietly. "Maybe my luck's getting better." She tried to laugh, but it came out high and false.

Still, Emma was thankful he didn't leave the same kind of devastation Joseph had. She watched Joan closely, somehow sensing her sister was better prepared this time, protected against another blow. Maybe it was different after the first time. As with an open wound, Joan had healed tougher.

As dawn approached, a gray light filtered into Emma's room. She dozed on and off, then sat up suddenly wide awake, listening to the wind snap against her window. She heard Foon moving about beyond the closed door in the pale morning hour, breathing life into the cold kitchen. Emma's eyes teared at the thought of missing these echoes and whispers of her childhood—the soft clink of the wok on the fire, the high whine of the fruit vendor selling oranges and bananas from worn baskets balanced on a pole across his neck and shoulders. She'd even miss the pungent odor of salted fish drying in courtyards, dangling from lines like the leather soles of shoes. Until that very moment, she'd taken the habits of her daily life for granted. Everything in America would be new and strange to her. She longed to ride the cable cars up and down the steep hills she'd read about, and to hear the deep moan of foghorns blaring soulful warnings to ships entering the Golden Gate. Still, Emma felt anxious. She tried to ignore it, remembering Mah-mee's reassurance: "When you've seen enough, and your mouth waters for Foon's cooking, you can always come home."

Emma tapped lightly on Joan's door across the hall and heard a surprisingly wide-awake "Come in!" Joan's room was bright with lamplight. "You're up early," Emma said, stepping over the cashmere cardigan, silk cheungsam, black slip, and half dozen movie magazines that cluttered the floor. The sweet scent of Revlon powder and Joan's favorite perfume, My Sin, hung over it all.

"I couldn't sleep." Joan lay in bed, propped up by three green brocade pillows, flipping through a *Movie Mirror* magazine. "Oh! Bette Davis has a new movie out called *All About Eve*. No one plays a home wrecker better than Bette Davis, except maybe Li Lihua. It's all in their eyes!"

"What's it about?" Joan's regained passion for the movies delighted Emma. Even in this severe light, Joan looked just like a movie star herself, dressed in the cream-colored silk pajamas she'd bought at Lane Crawford's.

"Eve, apparently!" Joan laughed.

She raised herself up from her pillows, threw her magazine aside. "I've been thinking. . . ." She adapted a casual pose, though Emma saw her upper lip quiver. "I mean . . . what would you say if I told you I wanted to act?"

"Act?" Emma swallowed a small stone of surprise and sat down on Joan's bed. At twenty-four, Joan had never expressed a wish for any kind of career, except part-time work at Auntie Go's knitting factory. "Gosh, you really want to act?"

Joan smiled. "Maybe if I became an actress, I could follow you to California someday."

Emma looked away and didn't know what to say. Sometimes decisions came so easily for her sister—too easily—while Emma worried about everything. Still, there was nothing more natural than for Joan to act. She'd been doing it all her life.

"How would you go about it?" Emma asked, always practical, then remembered their aunt's knitting company. "And what about Auntie Go? She's hoping you'll take over."

Joan hugged one of the brocade pillows, half hiding her face. "Part-time never meant lifetime. Auntie Go knows my heart's not in it. And I've been at the library researching the Hong Kong movie industry," she said, her voice growing in excitement.

"You, at the library! You must really want to act." Emma laughed.

Joan threw the pillow at her. "I bet you didn't know this." Joan rose to her knees and flung her arms out like an opera singer. "Ever since the Japanese invasion of Shanghai in 1937," she said, her voice dark and dramatic, "Chinese directors and actors have gradually made their way from Shanghai to Hong Kong. In the past few years, Hong Kong has become the major moviemaking mecca of both Mandarin- and Cantonese-speaking movies."

"I guess you *have* been to the library," Emma teased.

Joan crossed her eyes. "And God knows I've seen enough movies! But lately, I've been seeing beyond just what's up there on the screen. Each gesture, each look, can tell you something different. It's like a whole new world to me!"

Emma smiled. Joan certainly had enough beauty and drama to fill up the big screen. "One day you'll be as big as Joan Crawford!"

Joan leaned forward and threw her arms around Emma. "I'm really going to miss you, moi-moi."

Emma pulled back. Her hopes never came without doubts. "Will you be all right?"

Joan gave her another squeeze. "You don't have to worry about me. I'll be fine. I promise," she said, falling back into her pillows.

Joan talked happily of her new aspiration, while Emma balanced on the bedside, trying to memorize Joan's unblemished profile as she shared in her sister's joy. Soon shivers of excitement overtook her in the cold morning air. Then, without a pause in the soft ring of her words, Joan raised her green silk comforter and Emma crawled in.

Emma cried as she peered from the small window of the airplane and waved good-bye to Mah-mee, Auntie Go, and Joan. Foon had refused to accompany them to the airport, mumbling, "Not a bird. Not right to be in the air so long."

At the dinner table the night before, Emma knew how sad they were by their sudden loss of words. Even Mah-mee fell silent, and Auntie Go seemed to be watching Emma's every move. She was grateful when Joan finally spoke up. Joan had read in one of her movie magazines about a new American television show called *The Lone Ranger.*

"It stars a mysterious, masked cowboy who rides around on a horse helping people."

Emma had listened, wishing the masked man would guide her safely to America.

Emma fastened her seat belt, her throat dry and scratchy. She felt a jet of cool air coming from one of the many nozzles overhead. Outside her window, propellers roared to life and spun in a noisy blur. She breathed in and out, thrilled, yet frightened, and took a quick look around her. The plane resembled a large, hollow tube with seats on both sides of a narrow aisle. Tall American women in pressed navy-blue uniforms and crisp white blouses smiled at everyone as they helped passengers stow away their belongings. Emma glanced quickly around at the rows of faces. Half the passengers were Japanese or British businessmen, so formal and polite with one another that she could scarcely believe they'd been at war just five years ago. Emma leaned back, grateful that the seat next to her was empty. She looked past it out the window as the plane jerked and moved slowly forward. The harbor glimmered on either side of the runway, as if the plane were gliding across the glassy water, crowded now with ships from all over the world. She remembered again the awful stillness when they'd returned from Macao. All she'd wanted to do then was to turn around and go back to Lia.

In her purse was the letter she had received from Lia a few weeks ago, the music of her voice in each word. . . . *I take the bus every Friday to our neighbor island, Taipa. It's where Antonio, my boyfriend, lives while he works on his papai's fishing boat. You would like him. Makes me laugh all the time. Makes life lighter. Which reminds me to tell you I've decided to study nursing. I've been taking care of my sister and my brothers' scrapes and cuts all these years anyway. Why not*

*make it a career? Blood and bones have never frightened me. It's the
things I can't see! . . .*

Emma had written back that she was finally leaving for California, the words on the paper sliding from her pen feeling foreign and
complicated. Now Emma missed Lia all over again.

When the plane suddenly lifted off the ground, Emma's stomach sank. She closed her eyes and repeated a prayer she'd learned
in sixth grade at St. Cecilia's, before advancing to the Chinese middle school. *O my God, I am heartily sorry for having offended thee, and
I detest all my sins. . . .*

After five hours in the air, Emma was anesthetized by the low
hum vibrating through the droning plane. But when it began to de-
scend toward Tokyo, all her fears reawakened. She felt hot and
sweaty at the thought of the big plane landing. Emma leaned back,
praying that Ba ba would be there waiting for her. She checked her
passport case again for his address and the money Mah-mee had
given her. The plane dipped lower and lower. Emma panicked and
closed her eyes tight. Her heart beat wildly when the plane bucked,
but at last she felt the wheels bounce once and bump along the
ground. Her feet pushed hard against the seat in front of her until
the plane came to a full stop.

Emma was relieved to see Ba ba at the gate. He looked old
and tired and seemed to have shrunk in the months since she'd
seen him.

"Ba ba, I'm so glad to see you," Emma said, hugging his thin
body.

"How was your flight?" he asked, taking her suitcase.

"Frightening."

"You sound like your mother." Ba ba smiled. "She doesn't believe me, but it does get easier. How are Mah-mee, Go, and Joan?"

"They're all fine."

"Come, let's get the rest of your luggage."

They waited at the baggage claim for Emma's trunk, the same one Mah-mee had used on countless trips between Hong Kong and Japan. Emma loved every scratch and dent marring its brown leather surface. As it rumbled up the conveyor belt, Emma began to worry. Had she packed everything she needed? Would a woolen coat and three cashmere sweaters keep her warm in San Francisco? Did she bring enough shoes? Emma finally relaxed when Ba ba laughed and said, "Moi-moi, you can always buy or send for whatever you've forgotten."

He led her out to a waiting car, and they drove through heavy traffic to his small apartment. Tokyo was large and almost as crowded as Hong Kong. It amazed Emma to think that all these strangers had been her enemy just a few years back. Now they walked down the streets in colorful kimonos and Western clothing, apparently shy and harmless.

It was still warm for late September. Emma rolled down the window. The sounds and smells of Tokyo were so different from Hong Kong—lighter and fresher. Ba ba leaned over and showed her some rose-purple flowers growing by the roadside. "Those are called lespedeza. They're a type of bush clover, known here as one of the seven flowers of autumn." Before Emma asked what the other six flowers were, he pointed at the butterfly petals falling like snowflakes, blanketing the ground. They seemed to muffle the car horns, the cries of babies, the shrieking voices. Ba ba smiled. In that instant, Emma began to understand why Ba ba preferred to do business in Japan.

That evening Ba ba took Emma to a small Japanese restaurant on the Ginza for dinner. She had changed into a midcalf, yellow linen cheungsam. As they sipped tea and ate quietly together, Emma tried to remember how many years had passed since she'd been out alone with her father at a restaurant. She had grown up in the company of her mother, aunt, and sister. Her father was only a shadow who materialized for short visits. His sweet, flowery cologne reached across the table, familiar as ever, but his lean body had softened with age. Now Emma looked away, aware that it wasn't polite to stare. How could she have grown up without knowing him better? Suddenly she yearned to expand her childhood vision of him. As she picked at her rice and vegetables, she was filled with a sad, urgent need to take some small part of her father with her to America.

"Is everything all right?" He had a calm, melodious voice, which Joan had been lucky enough to have inherited. Emma's carried the high, excited edge of Mah-mee's.

"Yes," Emma answered, looking up from her food.

"Is there anything else you'd like?"

Emma smiled shyly. "Will you come to California and visit?"

Ba ba smiled. "If my work permits. Don't worry moi-moi, I don't think you will have any trouble settling in. It's what you've always wanted."

Emma sipped some green tea, watched his kind, tired eyes. A small lump caught in the middle of her throat as she let her fingers lightly touch the sleeve of his linen jacket.

"I'll still miss you," she said at last.

Ba ba poured more green tea into her clay cup. "So will I. Just as always."

The *President Coolidge* jerked several times, then slowly eased away from the harbor, letting out a deep, hollow moan that Emma felt throughout her body. Just before she boarded—amidst a blaring, staticky version of "Auld Lang Syne"—Ba ba had hugged her tightly, slipped her an envelope, and said, "Take care, moi-moi, and don't open this until the ship sets sail."

Emma could still detect his flowery cologne above the rank harbor smells. She cried, even as she willed herself not to, grasping the envelope as tightly as if it were her father's hand. Emma squeezed her way through the crowd on the deck and leaned heavily against the rail, watching until Ba ba and the last dim outlines of Tokyo were no longer in sight.

Emma turned around, engulfed by the lingering crowds. Her romantic notions of long strolls on empty decks would never be realized, she thought. As it was, she could barely make her way through all the people to her cabin below. Loud voices and strange faces came at her from all directions. She'd never seen so many Americans in one place before. This must be what it would be like in California! She was entirely on her own! Emma felt dizzy. Ba ba was already so far away, and there was no Mah-mee, Auntie Go, or Joan to rescue her. She pushed through the crowds until she reached the lobby and felt she could breathe again.

Emma's cabin was half the size of her room at home, and her bags and trunk were the only familiar things in it. She sat on the hard single bed and took a deep breath until another deep wail of the ship's horn startled her to her feet. The floor vibrated beneath her as she pushed open her small porthole. They were under way, the ship already dancing from side to side as it pushed through rough seas out of Tokyo Bay.

Emma looked down at the envelope still clutched in her hand. Her fingers clumsily opened it to find two one-hundred-dollar bills in American money. Emma wished she could give Ba ba another hug. Instead, she replaced the crisp bills in the envelope, then hid them at the bottom of her purse.

Suddenly Emma's stomach churned. She sat down on the bed and inhaled deeply. The nausea lessened as she breathed slowly out. It was just all the excitement, she told herself, taking another breath, then releasing it. She kicked off her shoes and lay down on her small bed. As she waited for the feeling to pass, she recited over and over again the comforting old dry chant: *wheat, sesame, barley, beans, rice.* Foon would be proud to know that Emma was sailing to America with the five great grains of Chinese cooking.

That night at dinnertime, Emma struggled into a beige lace cheungsam. She dragged herself through a maze of identical hallways until a sign pointed her to the dining room's tall doors. Her stomach still churned, but she hoped that eating something might settle it.

The wide, bright room hummed with passengers halfway into the second dinner seating. It felt hot and noisy and smelled like Foon's steamed pork. Tall and rigid, the maître d' scanned his list for a seat. Emma stared across the tables crowded with foreign faces and felt sick to her stomach again. She was just about to flee to her cabin when a smiling, uniformed man stepped forward.

"Is everything all right?" he asked, his voice calm and friendly.

"I'm trying to find the young lady a seat. She's not on my list," the maître d' answered.

"Well, you can stop searching. She can sit with me." The man turned to Emma. "Let me introduce myself. I'm Ron Stuart, the ship's purser."

Emma glanced up at his face. She guessed he was in his midthirties, though she knew white ghosts often looked older than they really were. He wasn't handsome, but he had kind blue eyes and a boyish grin. She steadied herself, took another deep breath, and said, "I'm Emma Lew."

"Well, Miss Lew, would you do me the honor of joining me at my table?"

Emma hesitated. "I . . ."

"I'm sitting with some people you might enjoy meeting. Please, you would be doing me a great favor," he said, smiling kindly.

She could already tell his eyes were his best feature. "I just need something to settle my stomach."

"I know just the thing. Some chicken broth and crackers, along with good company," he said, stepping aside to allow her to walk first. "My table's right over there."

No one at home had ever thought to tell Emma how to handle such a problem. She knew Joan would know exactly what to do and say. "Just think of Lauren Bacall," Joan had once told her. "She meets any situation head-on." But this kind of predicament was new to Emma. She looked around the vibrating room, doubting she'd be able to handle any more new faces staring at her. She managed a shy smile, then took a step in the direction of the purser's table.

Purser First Class Ron Stuart became Emma's guardian angel aboard the *President Coolidge*. He had a wife and two young daughters at home in Seattle and didn't ask Emma silly questions as did other good-intentioned Americans, such as "How can you speak English so well?" or "Have you ever eaten a steak before?" Most evenings, when Emma was well enough to sit for dinner, it was with Ron and two other students from Hong Kong who were on their way to Holy Names College in Oakland, across the bay from San Francisco. Other nights, when she couldn't keep anything down, Ron stopped by her cabin to bring something to keep up her strength. His chicken-soup-and-crackers theory had failed miserably. Now he brought plain toast and tea.

Aside from his friendship, Emma feared her memory of the journey would be dominated by seasickness. She couldn't imagine ever feeling well again, free of the queasiness that plagued her day and night. But, after nine days of rough waters, the sea calmed and Emma's stomach settled along with it.

When the *President Coolidge* docked in Honolulu, Emma was enormously grateful she'd made it that far. They would remain in Hawaii for two days while some of the ship's passengers disembarked and others boarded to sail on to San Francisco.

When Emma first set foot on land again, she felt the earth still swaying beneath her feet. She stood very still and closed her eyes until the dizziness passed.

After nine days of seasickness, Honolulu was heaven-sent. It reminded her of Macao, with its warm tropical air smelling of flowers, and the slow, easy pace. The Hawaiians were friendly and helpful. She saw hints of Lia everywhere in the dark-haired, smiling faces of the Polynesian girls. Yet, standing in the soft ocean breeze and feeling well again, Emma felt her first real stab of loneliness since leaving Tokyo.

On the final evening in Honolulu, Ron took Emma and the other two Hong Kong students to the Royal Hawaiian Hotel. He told them it had been called the Pink Palace of the Pacific since 1927, for its unusual color and Spanish cupolas. Emma loved the lobby, with its high Moorish ceiling. The large open room bustled with Americans, flower leis and cameras hanging from their necks. Outside the hotel, it was warm and humid in the surrounding fragrant tropical gardens, filled with bird-of-paradise, red hibiscus, and sweet-smelling ginger flowers. The beach was just steps away. Emma heard the deep rhythmic beating of drums nearby.

Ron led them to a large, grassy area, where beautiful young women in grass skirts demonstrated the hula. They mesmerized Emma with graceful, swaying hands and hips, telling a story with each movement. Their hands shaped through the air, gesturing and beckoning, leading Emma through the tale of love and loss, then gently carrying her to its end. She couldn't wait to write Joan and Lia about this wonderful island.

Emma realized why Ron had told her to wear a loose dress, as after the hula demonstration they sat cross-legged on the grass. "It's what the Hawaiians call a luau," he explained as she adjusted to the awkwardness of sitting on the ground. An entire pig roasted in a large pit in the ground. It smelled delicious, like the roast pork with crispy skin she'd always eaten in Hong Kong. Emma's stomach rumbled at the thought of biting into a thick, juicy piece, though she quickly learned that a sticky, gray paste called poi tasted exactly the way it looked—bland and gritty as wet cement. Emma took one taste and pretended to eat the gray paste, then spit it discreetly into her napkin. She did eat bowl after bowl of rice, as well as the fragrant and sweet mangoes and papaya, glad that Mah-mee and Foon weren't around to see how much weight she'd lost from being seasick.

On the last leg of Emma's journey to San Francisco, Ron said she had acquired her "sea legs," since she no longer suffered from seasickness. And though it would be hard to leave the kindness and security he'd offered, Emma already felt the anxious stirring of her new life as they stood on deck and steamed under the Golden Gate Bridge. She leaned forward, gripping the rail, slightly apart from the rest of the crowd. The cool, crisp sea air stung her face as Emma's first glimpse of the serene, elegant city left her speechless. San Francisco was just as beautiful as she had imagined it to be. She breathed in deeply, tasting the salty sea, her heart beating faster as the ship pushed closer to the dock. She loved the way the pastel-colored buildings caught the early-autumn light, revealing themselves one above another, stair-stepped up the sides of the hills. Then, beyond the rhythmic surging of the ship, and the buzz of other voices, Emma faintly heard Ron say, "It's a sight that never fails to amaze me."

Not quite three weeks after leaving Hong Kong, Emma changed into a cotton cheungsam and finally set foot on Pier 19 in San Francisco. The late-afternoon sun felt much cooler than she expected. By the time she said a tearful good-bye to Ron and the other students, then found her luggage waiting on the dock, Emma felt scared and alone. Sister Madeleine from the college had promised in her last letter to have someone waiting for her, but no one appeared. The air smelled salty and metallic. The sunlight had given way to shade. Emma waited as the passengers disembarked and the crowd dissipated. What would become of her? Alone on the pier, she listened for the voices of Mah-mee and Auntie Go telling her what to do, but they seemed lost across the ocean. Emma took a deep breath and thought of Joan's advice: What would Lauren Bacall do? She decided to take a taxi to Lone Mountain College.

A sympathetic cabdriver, himself an immigrant from Russia, was kind and helpful. "You're a smart one, taking taxi. These docks is no good at night," he said, his thick, bushy mustache moving up and down as he talked. "Don't worry, Sergei is getting you to your school nice and safe."

Emma watched as he loaded her luggage into the trunk, then opened the rear door and waited for her to step in. He was short and heavyset, yet light and quick on his feet. His hair was longer than any other man's she'd ever seen before, hanging in uneven strands below the back collar of his plaid shirt. She wrapped her sweater closer against the cold wind, happy to be in the safe confines of the cab.

Sergei turned around and looked over his shoulder. "We'll take scenic route. I want to be first one to show you this great city!"

Emma suddenly felt warm. "No, I have to . . ."

"Don't worry. No extra cost for you. Sit back! Enjoy!" He winked and started the car with a great roar of the engine.

Emma's fear quickly disappeared as Sergei drove along the Embarcadero toward the bright lights of a place he called Fisherman's Wharf. Emma fixed her gaze out the window at the large buildings and the big cars parked along the wide, open streets—so clean and uncluttered.

"This is where you can eat best crabs in all the world!" Sergei boasted.

When the cab turned down a narrow street toward the harbor, Emma had a full view of the small fishing boats docked in the crowded marina, and she smiled at the hopeful names painted on their bows— *The Lucky Star, Mary's Dream, The Full Catch, A Pot of Gold*. She sat forward and rolled down her window, inhaling the distinct aromas of fresh fish and crabs. In the narrow street, Emma could almost reach out the window to touch the crabs that scrabbled over each other in boxes, waiting to be boiled in a large black pot.

From the crowded wharf, Sergei turned onto a street he called Columbus. "Like the explorer," he said, slowing down as he peeked at her in his rearview mirror. "And this is North Beach, where all the I-ta-lians live and eat."

Emma quickly looked away from the mirror. "From Italy?"

He nodded. "At one time."

"And where do all the Russians live and eat?"

"Wherever we can," Sergei answered with a laugh.

"What street is that?" Emma asked, looking at all the glittering lights that ran up and down the block.

"That's Broadway. Home of the sailor bars. No place for nice young lady like you," Sergei said quickly, his eyes avoiding the mirror.

He drove several blocks, then turned right. "This is Washington Street. Just remember, the first American president." Then he made another right turn onto Grant Avenue. "We are now in heart of Chinatown!" His thick eyebrows flashed upward as he again caught her eyes in the mirror.

Emma's pulse raced. Chinatown appeared much smaller than she had expected. Restaurants and storefronts painted red, green, and gold were crowded together into several blocks. She turned from window to window, soaking in all she could, seeking echoes of the life she'd left behind. Preoccupied faces she might have seen in Wanchai, or down in Causeway Bay, rushed down the bustling Grant Avenue. Names of streets flashed by—Jackson, Pacific, and back to Broadway. As if he knew what she was thinking, Sergei circled and drove through Chinatown again. Emma smiled, finding comfort in the Chinese characters written on signs and windows: The Forbidden City Nightclub, Golden Harvest, Kuo Wah Restaurant, The Great Wall of China . . . As different as this was from Hong Kong, San Francisco's Chinatown held the most familiar sights she'd seen in weeks.

Emma leaned forward and whispered to Sergei, "You are very kind."

He quickly turned back with a smile, his warm cigarette breath touching her cheek. "I know how it feels. When I first come here from Moscow eleven years ago, I didn't know if I should go left or right! Now you know Columbus, Washington, Grant . . . so you are one step ahead of Sergei. Now, I better get you to school before they wonder what happened to you!"

They drove up the winding hill and through the iron gates of Lone Mountain College. In the gray, murky light of early evening, the large stucco buildings loomed immense and intimidating. Sergei helped Emma with her luggage, then waited with her as a flustered nun hurried out to greet her.

"I'm Sister Madeleine. We've been so worried about you!" She smiled kindly, her wimple squeezing her cheeks pink. "I'm so sorry, my child. You were supposed to be picked up by another one of our Chinese students. I don't know what could have happened to her. I do hope she's all right," Sister Madeleine mumbled, her long black robe billowing in the wind.

Emma returned a shy smile.

As Sergei drove slowly away, he stuck his head out the window and winked at her. Emma wanted to call out for him to wait. He was the only person she remotely knew in San Francisco, and she suddenly felt too tired to do anything but follow the tall, sturdy Sister Madeleine.

Emma tightly gripped the handle of her suitcase, while Sister Madeleine's singsong voice filled the calm air with rules and regulations. Emma tried hard to pay attention to what the sister was saying: "We have about three hundred girls living here. . . . I'm sure you'll make new friends in no time. . . . We eat at six . . . simple but nourishing . . . no visitors after ten o'clock on weekdays . . . eleven-thirty on weekends. . . ."

But her instruction fell hard and flat against the words that turned over and over in Emma's head.

Columbus, like the explorer. Washington, Jackson, and Grant, like the presidents. Broadway and Pacific . . . Pacific, the vast ocean that now separates me from Hong Kong . . .

The Woman from Swan River — 1951–53

JOAN

Joan ran up the stone steps to the Lew flat, late as usual. Her head still swam from the vivid scenes in *The Woman from Swan River*, the latest film by C. K. Chin. Joan had read that the Hong Kong Cantonese movie industry was dominated by Chin and his Tiger Claw Film Company. It was said that he could churn out a movie in a matter of weeks. In the past year alone, he had released over twenty films to an increasingly appreciative Hong Kong audience. But seeing *The Woman from Swan River* convinced Joan that Chin was someone who might give Chinese filmmaking new credibility.

Unlike Hollywood productions, his films were still grainy and amateurish, but lately were heavily influenced by the Shanghai filmmakers who had migrated to Hong Kong. Joan saw how Hong Kong films had grown in scope and insight.

"There you are!" Mah-mee said as Joan closed the door behind her. Her mother was sitting in the living room with Auntie Go.

"Sorry I'm late," Joan said, breathless, putting down her purse. "I just saw the most wonderful movie."

"I thought that must be it." Mah-mee held up a blue airmail envelope. "A letter from Emma came today."

Joan took the letter from her mother. Since Emma left Hong Kong for San Francisco almost three months ago, her letters had arrived almost every week. The wrinkled blue sheets felt light in Joan's hand.

"What did you see?" Auntie Go asked, the pages of her fashion magazine slapping shut, sliding from her lap.

"*The Woman from Swan River,* with Ming Li."

"I think I just read about that movie." Auntie Go's eyes widened with recognition. "The Chin movie about the woman who forsakes her family and village to seek a better life in some city."

"That's it," Joan said, falling onto the sofa next to Auntie Go. "You have to see it! Ming Li's just perfect in the role. The haunting expression in her eyes could tell a hundred stories. And it's not one of those typical family dramas like those churned out by other studios. There's so much more to her. There's hope, even in her shame and disillusionment!" Joan said in one excited breath.

"Certainly not like real life," Mah-mee added, clearing her throat and pointing at the blue sheets. "Hurry, read moi-moi's letter."

Joan leaned back on the sofa, glanced down at the familiar fine strokes of Emma's handwriting, and wished the letter hadn't come today of all days. Joan wanted to hold on to the images of Ming Li for as long as she could.

Joan had never imagined she would miss Emma so much. Now at times she couldn't help but envy her sister's new life. She realized lately that, different as they were, a measure of her own identity was that of Emma's older sister; the sudden realization frightened her. She dragged herself from day to day with no direction, while the hard facts became more and more evident—she was twenty-five, still unmarried, and without a profession.

She looked up and smiled at Mah-mee and Auntie Go, who had already read the letter and now anxiously waited for her to join them in conversation, first repeating everything Emma had told them, then scrutinizing between the lines at all she hadn't said.

Ever since Emma left for America, Joan had had trouble sleeping, her restlessness punctuated by early-morning dreams of running toward someone or something she never reached. Once, her dream led her to a large warehouse where a yellow-red light flickered from underneath the door. Joan entered to see Emma and an enraptured audience staring at a movie screen where someone who looked just like Joan in a fur coat sat sandwiched between Celeste Holm and Hugh Marlowe in *All About Eve*.

Then, within weeks of Emma's leaving, Joan began experiencing a dull ache in the middle of her stomach. She thought it might be her ulcer returning, though it wasn't the same sour, burning sensation. This ache throbbed quieter and deeper, like a seed she had swallowed from the dried plums she loved to suck on—solid and annoying. She wondered if fear and loneliness could be physical ailments that settled and grew in her stomach.

Through these weeks, Joan tried to eat and behave as she always did, hoping not to worry Mah-mee and Auntie Go any more than she already had. With Emma away, Joan and Mah-mee had grown even further apart. They stood on opposite sides of a rushing river that Emma had always bridged. With her sister in America, Joan struggled to find her way across.

Without saying a word, Foon began brewing Joan a foul-smelling tea. Each evening for a week, Joan found a bowl of bitter-root, black tea waiting for her on the table by her bed. "Drink," Foon said. "Cures all. Even makes hair grow on a bald dog!"

As Joan read her sister's letter, Emma's voice behind the words grew stronger: *I'm taking all the basic requirements—Math, Science, English, American History. But it's Art that I love the most! It's a universal language that I don't have to sit for hours trying to understand. I'm taking a wonderful drawing class that allows me to express myself in ways I never thought possible. How can lines from a pencil or piece of charcoal suddenly come alive? And you won't believe this, but the other day when I walked into my drawing class, a naked man was sitting there, waiting for us to draw him!*

"And what's all this about art and a naked man?" Mah-mee asked, as if she were reading along with Joan.

"It's called life drawing." Auntie Go laughed. "How are you going to draw something without seeing it? Just think of da Vinci, or Michelangelo."

"Well, I'm beginning to understand what she loves about art," Mah-mee continued.

"Don't worry. It's how every great artist gets started," Auntie Go said.

"Staring at naked men? Hah!" Mah-mee said. "I know what *that* gets started! You better worry too."

Joan had to smile. The push-and-pull pattern of conversation between her mother and her aunt had been that way for as long as she could remember. She read on.

Of course, I was too embarrassed to get much drawing done, not wanting to stare at him. But imagine! He just sat there, like he was in his own room and there weren't thirty gawking students just waiting for him to move a muscle. I suppose he's a starving artist himself, and has to earn money some way or another!

A starving artist. Joan stopped reading. Just like *The Woman from Swan River*. Imagine the courage it took to die for art! For something you believed in! Was she strong enough? Joan knew from the moment *Swan River* ended and the light filled the theatre again that she wanted to work with C. K. Chin. She would gladly sacrifice—work hard and suffer! Even starve!—for the chance. She was glad Emma hadn't mentioned her acting ambitions in her letters. Joan could still feel the weight of Emma sitting on her bed that morning before her departure, the smell of My Sin in the air, the edge of fear in Emma's voice. Joan knew how much Emma worried about her.

But Joan also knew the dreams she'd been having were a sign, a "voice from heaven," as Mah-mee would say. Joan unbuttoned the top frog on the collar of her cheungsam, then took a deep breath before raising her voice. "I have an announcement to make."

Mah-mee and Auntie Go stopped bickering, surprised into silence.

"I want to become an actress," Joan continued before they said anything. "I'd like to be in the movies." She folded Emma's letter against her knee and creased it with her thumb.

"What are you talking about?" Mah-mee responded.

Auntie Go remained silent.

Joan swallowed. "It's something I've given a great deal of thought to. I think I would be good at acting. It's not as if I haven't been doing it all my life!"

Mah-mee leaned forward, placing her palms flat on the polished surface of the teak coffee table, and sighed. Joan thought Mah-mee might get angry, but instead, she looked at Joan for a long time, then said softly, "What kind of life is that? All make-believe."

"It's real to me." Joan felt the blood rush to her head. How had it taken her so long to realize something so simple?

"Don't you think you're too old to begin now?" Mah-mee finally said.

Joan felt stung. "I'm twenty-five. It may be too old for marriage, but not for acting. Ming Li is in her late twenties." Joan had also read that Ming Li was just one of the twenty or thirty actresses C. K. Chin hired on contract and trained for his movies, but she didn't mention that to Mah-mee.

"You know that wasn't what I meant," Mah-mee flared. "You think it's all glamour and movie magazines, but it's a difficult life with a lot of hard work. Tell me, what do you really know about it? What will people say?"

"I've always loved the movies. And I don't care what people think!"

Auntie Go stood up and grabbed her sweater and handbag from the chair. "I believe a person should always have the chance to follow her dreams," she said, turning to leave.

"You would," Mah-mee mumbled.

Joan took another deep breath, let it out slowly. For the first time in months, the dull ache in her stomach had lessened. She felt lighter now and less foolish than she had when she told Emma her secret desire.

"I'll see you tomorrow," Auntie Go said. Her steps rang out across the hardwood floor, until Joan heard the soft click of the front door closing.

Mah-mee looked away from Joan and stalked off down the hall. The room, which had just been filled with voices, suddenly felt big and hollow.

Joan opened Emma's letter again and read to the bottom of the page: *San Francisco is the most beautiful city! There's so much open space here, Golden Gate Park is as big as Central and Wanchai put together. I spend half the time getting lost, and the other half finding my way again.*

From that evening on, Joan immersed herself in every film she could, not just for the stories, which ranged from political and family dramas to historical and horror films, but for how subtle expressions and movements of the actors added texture and depth. Gradually the dull pain in her stomach disappeared as her ambition grew.

Though not yet noon it was already hot as Joan walked down Nathan Road in Kowloon. She turned the corner and stopped in front of the Tiger Claw Film Company. On two large wooden gates TIGER CLAW appeared in faded red characters. Joan paused long enough to see what lay behind the gates, which were slightly ajar. The studio consisted of several large stucco buildings surrounded by tall walls—plain and unobtrusive. She was so close, she could see costumed actors walking from one set to another. Joan stood melting in the blistering heat. Perspiration ran down her neck, damp linen clinging against her back.

She looked over at the small wooden cubicle by the doors, then straightened her green cheungsam and walked casually past the guard and back toward Nathan Road.

Joan imagined hundreds of young women must try to call on Chin, using every excuse possible: *Didn't he leave my name at the gate? Mr. Chin's expecting me. . . . I'm due on the set at any minute. . . . I'm his long-lost daughter. . . .* Joan swallowed the sour taste that rose to her mouth. She would have to find another way in.

Most of Chin's actresses were handpicked and trained on the job, while she couldn't even get through the front gate. The major movie studios in Hong Kong were all like tight-knit Chinese families—unwilling to accept new blood, but once embraced, there was no turning back.

Still, acting didn't seem anywhere near as daunting as convincing Mah-mee of her desire to act. Although after months of watching movies and reading everything she could find about Chin and his studio, Joan was beginning to doubt whether she had what it took to get into the Tiger Claw family.

The next morning at breakfast, Joan drank down her coffee, swallowed her pride, and asked nonchalantly, "Do you think Auntie Kao knows C. K. Chin?"

She watched as Mah-mee spooned some marmalade onto her plate. "She might. Auntie Kao knows everyone through her family connections."

Joan handed her mother a piece of toast. "Do you think she might introduce me to him?"

"When will you stop all this nonsense about being an actress?" Mah-mee said, her eyebrows arching upward. She sounded more exhausted than angry and put her spoon down with a quick clink on the side of her plate.

"It's what I want. Why can't you see that?"

Mah-mee sat back in her chair, her dark eyes focused on Joan. "I just don't want to see you disappointed."

"Are you sure it's me you don't want to see disappointed?"

Mah-mee remained quiet for a moment. "Wouldn't it be nice if we both weren't disappointed?"

Joan tried hard to smile and keep her voice steady. "Then you'll just have to trust me." Her eyes felt puffy from sleep. She ran her fingers through the dark strands of her shoulder-length hair.

Mah-mee watched Joan over the rim of her cup for the longest time, neither of them looking away. Then she lowered the cup slowly, depositing it back on its saucer. "I'll talk to Auntie Kao," she said, lowering her gaze. "I'll see what I can do."

Joan leaned back and smiled. Mah-mee looked older and tired in the harsh morning light, yet even without makeup she was still beautiful. Joan thought it was a pity Mah-mee had never been an actress. She would have been perfect for the screen.

One morning less than a week later, Joan came into the dining room to find her mother up early and waiting for her. Mah-mee sipped her tea, the remains of her breakfast—orange skins, toast crumbs, and marmalade—still on her plate. A blue airmail letter lay unfolded on the table before her.

"*Tso sun,*" Mah-mee said.

"Good morning." Joan sat down and poured herself some coffee, its rich aroma waking her. She needed something stronger than Mah-mee's English tea to get up and going each morning. Joan glanced down at the letter to see Ba ba's small, even handwriting.

Outside, she heard the high, whining voice of the fruit man. She knew that Foon would handpick the best of the season from his baskets for her and Mah-mee.

"*Or-anges!*"

Mah-mee sat back and watched Joan closely. "Your ba ba is happy you've found something you want to pursue with such passion." She tapped the thin pages in front of her. "I also spoke with Auntie Kao. She told me last night Uncle Kao has spoken to Chin, and that you can have a bit-part position at his studio if you want it."

"*Man-goes!*"

Joan stopped drinking and looked up at her mother. "Are you

sure?" she asked, holding her cup in midair. "Of course I want it!"

"*Ba-na-nas!*"

Mah-mee smiled and poured herself some more tea. "Now you will see if this is really what you want."

For the first time in years, Joan rushed over to hug Mah-mee, her warmth smelling of lavender soap and oranges. When Joan pulled away, she already missed the soft, creamy touch of her mother's skin.

When the heavyset guard at the Tiger Claw Film Company found her name on the list, he banged his way out of his cubicle and opened the gate for her.

Once through the gate, Joan found the studio bigger than she had expected. Three large whitewashed buildings stood side by side, surrounded by big lots for the filming of outdoor scenes. Joan squared her shoulders and headed toward the building nearest to her.

Inside, she stepped into a dark, high-ceilinged room, cool and cavernous. Joan watched from the door, nervous and uneasy, her eyes momentarily blind in the dim light, as costumed actors brushed past her, hurrying from one makeshift set to another. Joan strained to see if she recognized any stars, but their faces blurred before her adjusting eyes. Hammers pounded out a hollow rhythm, while voices echoing from every direction made Joan dizzy.

"Are you looking for someone?" a woman's high, tight voice asked.

A short, thin woman about her own age was carrying an armful of ornate robes and bloodied rags.

"Yes, yes, I am," Joan answered, grateful for the help and attention. "I'm looking for the office of Mr. Chin. I'm supposed to begin working here today."

The young woman smiled. "Let me get rid of these costumes,

and I'll take you to the main building." She turned away, then back again. "Oh, my name is Jade Wind."

"Joan Lew." She smiled.

"Nice to meet you. I'll be right back."

Joan watched Jade Wind move swiftly from one set to another—individual worlds divided by thin plywood walls. From where Joan stood, she saw an emperor's throne room and a modern living room just steps away from each other. Jade Wind dropped off costumes and collected others. She returned and deposited her new armload on a wooden chair.

"It's this way," Jade Wind said, already heading out the door.

Joan hurried into the bright sun, her eyes blinking against the harsh light.

"That's the main building over there." Jade Wind pointed to the plain building next door. "You'll find the offices and classrooms where the actors and actresses train on the top floor. The building we just left and the one over there are divided into different sound-stages."

"It's bigger than I thought."

"I work in costuming. We're at the back of the building you were just in. You must be an actress."

Joan hesitated, then said, "Bit parts."

"A trainee. Well, you might see Chin more than you expect then." Jade Wind laughed. She stopped at the entrance of the main building.

"What do you mean?"

"You'll see. The offices are just right up those steps." Jade Wind glanced at her watch. "I've got to go. We'll talk again soon."

Jade Wind smiled reassuringly before she turned around and disappeared between the two buildings.

It didn't take Joan long to learn what Jade Wind meant. She was given a stack of rules and procedures by Chin's secretary, Mei, a slightly older, statuesque woman with a serious demeanor.

"You're to report next Wednesday morning at wardrobe for a crowd scene in *The Blind Swordsman*, Stage Eight." Mei eyed Joan up and down. "Mr. Chin would prefer it if you didn't date other personnel at the Tiger Claw while working on a movie together. And when you aren't scheduled for any set work, you'll be attending voice and acting classes and be assigned other duties to help Mr. Chin."

"Of course," Joan said, clutching the papers in her hands, wondering just what those duties were. "Will I be meeting Mr. Chin?"

Mei smiled. "Not today."

By the end of her first week, Joan learned her duties included fetching a tray of tea and cake for C. K. Chin, and opening and closing the door as quietly as possible when she left his office. The tray of hot tea Joan was carrying felt heavier by the minute. Her quick, solid knocks on the large wooden door echoed through the hollow building. Each deep strike resonated through her body as she nervously waited. Jade Wind had warned her that wearing a cheungsam was not conducive to carrying trays of tea and running errands. So, while most of the other actresses still wore cheungsams, Joan began wearing wide, Western-style skirts with matching cardigan sweaters. She shuffled from one foot to the other, waiting for the door to open, so she could finally come face-to-face with Chin. Instead, Joan heard a muffled voice telling her to come in. Her sweaty hand gripped the doorknob as she balanced the tray she was carrying in her other hand. She stepped forward and pushed, only to realize the door opened outward. "Bloody hell," she whispered under her breath.

The tray rattled as she stepped back and pulled open the door. The room was dim and reeked of smoke. Framed posters of Chin's movie successes hung along one wood-paneled wall. Among them was Ming Li in *The Woman from Swan River*. Chin sat at his desk flicking ashes from his cigarette into a silver ashtray. Through the haze, Joan saw that he was thin and balding, looking every bit his sixty years. He waved his other hand and talked rapid fire at the two men who sat beyond his desk. His secretary, Mei, in a tight red silk-satin cheungsam, sat to one side, taking notes.

"Your tea," Joan said in a loud, clear voice.

"Put it right here," Chin said, sucking on a cigarette and waving at the side of his large desk.

Joan did as she was told.

"Good, good," he mumbled, waving her off.

As she turned to leave, Joan caught Chin giving her the once-over, his narrow bird's eyes sliding quickly from head to toe and back again.

Classes were held in small, windowless rooms upstairs in the main building. "Mr. Chin doesn't want anyone distracted," the thin, serious acting coach explained at Joan's first class. Most of the other eight trainees gathered around the large table in the middle of the airless room were slightly younger and had been recruited by Chin or someone else from the studio. While they nodded or greeted her politely, Joan noticed each person kept their distance. She sat at the far end of the table near the door and felt nervous and fragile in the hard wooden chair.

The acting coach walked down the length of the table and passed out a short script to each of them.

"Take some time to look at your scripts. They're all different excerpts from *A Streetcar Named Desire* by Tennessee Williams. Most of you must be familiar with the play or movie. Then, I'd like you to come up front and read your assigned piece," the coach said, his hands grasping the back of a chair.

Joan stared down at her excerpt and smiled. It was from one of her favorite scenes. She closed her eyes and imagined herself as Vivien Leigh playing Blanche Dubois.

Joan followed two other actors. "Miss Lew," she heard her name called out.

"Yes?" she looked up startled at the sound of her name, her heart beating fast when she saw all the staring eyes.

"Would you like to take a turn?"

Joan scraped her chair back, stood up, and took off her cardigan sweater, draping it over the back of the chair. She was glad she'd worn a loose chiffon dress, a simple string of pearls. At the front of the room, Joan raised her chin, fingered her pearls, and read loud and clear in her best Blanche Dubois:

> ". . . *Physical beauty is passing. But beauty of the mind and richness of the spirit and tenderness of the heart—increase with the years!*"

When Joan finished, she felt chilled with perspiration, her legs weak and wobbly. She looked around. The room was completely silent, the faces of the other students engrossed, upturned. All Joan heard was the richness of the words she'd spoken, still alive in her mind.

The Blind Swordsman was a period piece in which Joan was to play one of the frightened villagers. On her way to costuming, Joan walked past the sets of various movies. Costumed martial arts scenes seemed to be on the day's agenda. Joan marveled at the actors' elaborate, antique costumes—the thick, rich white makeup recreating the ghostly past, the bodies jumping from trampolines, flipping through the air, and landing gracefully as if in a dance. She knew fantasies were realized through the construction of fragile sets, held together by nails and glue, castles and monasteries built and torn down within hours, men and women changing costumes and makeup to play different characters in the same movie. While Joan had lost her belief in the movie magic she had worshiped on the screen, she was still fascinated by all that was created through illusion.

Jade Wind worked in a large, cluttered back room that was the costuming department. Clothing and ornate robes hung from racks lining the walls, spilling over on tables and chairs. In the midst of it all, Joan found Jade Wind busy sewing beads on a robe.

Joan was happy to see her friendly face again. "I guess I've found the costume department."

Jade Wind looked up and smiled. "The one and only. Are you here for a fitting?"

"I'm a villager in *The Blind Swordsman*." Joan laughed. "Not exactly the glamour-girl role I had hoped for!"

"This does seem to be Chin's month for martial arts movies." Jade Wind stood up, put down the robe, and browsed through a rack near her. "Four so far, and the three of us in costuming can barely keep up!"

Joan glanced through a rack of silk and lace cheungsams. "Have you worked with Ming Li? I loved her in *Swan River*."

Jade Wind nodded, pulled out a mud-stained black cotton tunic and pants. "She has quite a temper, especially when she doesn't get what she wants." Jade Wind rolled her eyes. "I'm just glad she's between film projects. Here, this is your costume. You can try it on over there." She pointed to a fitting room.

"Really? She's that difficult?" Joan asked, unable to hide her disappointment.

Jade Wind picked up the robe and sat down to finish beading. "It's a shame that some actresses aren't as sweet as the roles they play. Oh, and beware of the extras. Keep to the front of the crowd scenes, or you'll be swallowed up by all those trying to get in camera position."

Joan grasped the tunic and pants close to her. "Thank you," she said gratefully.

"Small tricks of the trade." Jade Wind pulled at a knot in her thread. A few beads clicked to the floor. "Just wait, I've only begun to tell all!"

Sometimes, after a long day at the studio, Joan caught a taxi after work and went to visit Auntie Go. At her knitting factory Joan lamented the lot of a bit-part actress and errand girl.

"You don't have to stay," Auntie Go said, pouring Joan a glass of sherry. "You know how your Mah-mee worries about you."

"What else can I do?" Joan asked, sipping the smooth, sweet wine and feeling its heat run down her throat.

Auntie Go smiled. "You can always come back to work for me."

Joan paused. The knitting business had grown larger each year, and she remembered Mah-mee saying the other night that Auntie Go was moving from the Wan Chai District to a larger building. "Did Mah-mee say you're moving Western Wind to Kowloon side?"

Auntie Go poured Joan more sherry, then refilled her own glass. "We've outgrown this place. I hope to make the move in the next few months."

Joan knew Auntie Go dreamed of having either her or Emma working at her knitting factory. Joan watched her tall aunt and felt a wave of admiration for her. Auntie Go had made a successful life for herself without the benefit of marriage. Joan only hoped she could do the same.

"You're turning the Western Wind into a knitting empire!" Joan smiled, then lifted her glass. "Here's to your continued success!"

Auntie Go blushed, sipped her sherry. "It's nothing, nothing."

"It's everything!"

Joan drank down the last of her sherry, but knew in her heart she wasn't ready to give up on acting. Cold and calculating as the profession was, there was still some silent voice within her that she needed to share with an audience.

Joan felt a pleasant warmth rise to her cheeks. "Can you give me more time to answer your offer?"

"You know you have my lifetime."

Early the next morning Joan walked straight to C. K. Chin's office. His secretary, Mei, wasn't at her desk yet. Joan wondered if the growing rumors of Mei's sleeping with Chin were true. Late mornings after late nights. She had been his fifth secretary in as many years. Unlike other producers, Chin paid no attention to his actresses; he preferred his secretaries to keep him company. He had a long-suffering wife and four children living in Repulse Bay, who drowned their sorrows in a ten-room mansion and a variety of cars, including the latest-model American Cadillac.

Joan had read in the Chinese movie magazines that though Chin appeared older than sixty, he was known to have the constitution of a man thirty years younger. No matter what event or private meeting kept him up late into the night, he was always at his desk by eight o'clock every morning, except Sundays. On Sundays, he worked deals from his Repulse Bay office at home. Joan imagined he had to visit his family sometime.

Joan's tongue flicked across her red lipstick. She swept back her hair, touched the darkened mole above her lip, then straightened the silk blouse and capri pants she'd purposely worn. Without further hesitation, she knocked solidly on Chin's door. No answer. Maybe Chin hadn't come in early after all. Maybe he wasn't the "creature of habit" the magazines proclaimed he was, possessive of his private morning hours. Just as she turned to leave, Joan heard his voice mumbling, "Come in." Carefully she stepped back and pulled open the door.

Chin sat behind his large, wooden desk across the room. He looked small and less intimidating in the morning light. As she stepped closer, Joan tried to keep this first simple vision of him in mind. Only then would she get through with what she wanted to say to him.

"Excuse me, Mr. Chin, I'm one of your actresses, and I was wondering if I might speak with you?"

"Yes, what is it now?" Chin answered, not looking up from the morning paper he was reading. A thin blanket of cigarette smoke lingered just below the ceiling.

"I am a very good actress," she said, her voice sharper and louder than she had intended. "I deserve to have a larger role in one of your films."

Chin's eyes finally strayed away from his paper toward her. He took the burning cigarette from his lips and dropped it in the half-filled silver ashtray. Again, she felt his eyes move from her head to her toes and back again.

"And what makes you think you can act?" he asked, leaning back in his chair.

Joan felt hot and sticky. She wished she could turn around and leave, but instead, folded her arms across her chest.

"How do you know I can't?" she asked back, keeping her voice steady. "Just come watch me in one of my classes. I'll show you how good I can act."

Chin stared at her for a long time, his eyes narrowing. Scrutinizing, Joan thought, but she didn't budge. She felt perspiration trickling under her collar. Then a slow smile spread across Chin's wrinkled face.

"You're right. I can't know unless you show me." He picked up his cigarette and sucked in a deep breath. "Tell me, is that mole on your lip real?"

Joan's fingers instinctively touched it. "Yes. And so are my acting abilities."

"What is your name?"

"Lew. Joan Lew."

"Joan Lew." He smiled. "Ah, yes. The perfect Blanche Dubois. Or so I hear." He lit another cigarette. "Well, we shall see what becomes of you, Miss Lew." He turned away and picked up his paper.

Weeks, then months, flew by without a change. Joan wondered if she'd ever be seen on film without fifty other people crowding around her. Occasionally, she saw Chin glide onto a set, speak to a director, then disappear back into his office.

The first time Joan saw herself on film was at the Queen's Theatre in *The Blind Swordsman*. Mah-mee and Auntie Go waited anxiously for her crowd scene, while Joan wondered if she was even in the shot. She'd tried to stay in the front of the crowd, but a persistent actress kept blocking her way. There were more behind-the-scenes battles going on than were written in the script.

"There she is!" Auntie Go whispered.

"Where? Where?" Kum Ling asked, grabbing Joan's arm.

Joan's mouth went dry when she saw herself for a split second, in mud-splattered clothes, pushing and pulling against the crowd, her dark eyes frantic as she ran for her life, as if the camera could save her.

Joan was just about to give up when Chin cast her in a small "woman in distress" role in another martial arts film. The first thing Joan did was write Emma, who she knew would be anxious to hear of her good fortune. *You may one day see me in Hollywood after all,* Joan wrote. *I'm finally getting to open my mouth and say something, even if it's only to scream for help!*

Mah-mee was still skeptical, but Auntie Go was encouraging, and Foon stopped brewing her teas. After so long, Joan was finally finding a direction in her life.

In one small role after another, Joan usually felt hidden beneath the costumes and makeup. She screamed and yelled on cue and once in a while actually uttered more than a word or two—her longest line being "You won't get away with this!" right before she met her untimely death saving her mistress. Even if her scenes were trimmed or removed altogether, Joan pinched herself to think she was really in the movies. And, as insignificant as her roles were, her latest death scene was enough for Chin to see that she did have talent. He signed her to another year's contract.

Almost a year and a half after setting foot into the Tiger Claw Film Company, Joan graduated to larger parts, mainly playing the lady-in-waiting to Chin's heroines. At the same time, Joan became a regular member of Chin's film family, finally acknowledged by others in the company. It wasn't long before she found many of the younger actresses jealous and spiteful, eyeing her suspiciously, whispering insults behind her back. How she had "slept with Chin" or had "bought her way in with family connections." Joan much preferred the more established actresses, who simply ignored her. By the beginning of her second year in films, Joan was fully aware of the realities of the business—the long hours, the backstabbing rumors, the positioning for each shot that might gain her more notice. Still, nothing was more thrilling than seeing herself transformed into someone else on-screen.

*   *   *

One of the first things Joan had to learn was how to handle all the unwanted attention that came her way. Not long after she'd joined the company, many of the actors and directors began to pursue her with flowers and dinner invitations. "You have to eat," they said, or, "I'll make sure your next part is bigger and better." She grew sick and tired of their empty words and sweet-smelling colognes. When polite refusals didn't work, Joan began to look them straight in the eyes as she refused, until they couldn't help but turn away. Soon, they were too intimidated to ask her out. Joan deliberately kept her distance, even at the risk of being known as "stuck-up" or a "prima donna."

Jade Wind became Joan's closest friend and confidant at the studio. Whereas she put up false fronts with the other actresses, she and Jade Wind traded gossip and laughter whenever they found time to have lunch or tea together in the small courtyard behind the large buildings.

"Look how much weight she's gained," Jade said, raising her eyebrows toward another young actress crossing their path. "She can barely fit into her costume. I had to use pins to hold it together." She laughed. "I can't imagine how she'll be able to do her fight scenes."

"Pretty soon, she won't be flying through the air with such ease," Joan added, picking up her bowl of noodles. "At least, that's what I hear."

"You mean . . . ?"

Joan nodded. "It's rumored the father is the director of her latest film."

Jade lifted noodles to her mouth. "But I heard that he couldn't . . ."

"Apparently he can." Joan laughed.

She wanted to tell Jade that on at least two occasions she had had her own problems with this director, but thought better of it. Joan had learned that the Tiger Claw Film Company was a world within itself. Sometimes, they were no better than squabbling siblings. You could never be too careful. It was one thing to pass on existing rumors, but another to start unwanted ones about yourself.

The next day Joan anxiously waited all morning for a scene to be set up in her latest movie, *The Price of Love,* starring Bai Guang, one of her favorite actresses. It was Joan's biggest part yet as a singsong girl, the escort-girl and songstress role that seemed to be growing in popularity. A Hong Kong dance hall had been replicated, only to have the scene postponed by the director at the last minute. As she wasn't scheduled for any other scenes that day, Joan was able to go home early for the first time in almost two years.

The flat felt cool and inviting. The lingering scent of Mah-mee's Shalimar still remained, though Joan knew her mother was probably out to lunch before playing mah-jongg at an auntie's apartment, or in one of the restaurant's private rooms.

Joan flipped through the mail on the dining room table and found a letter from Emma. Foon was nowhere in sight, so Joan kicked off her heels and sat down on the sofa to read Emma's letter.

> *I can't wait to come home during the holidays to see you in one of your movies. I'm so proud of you! I've told the girls in my dorm that my sister is a genuine Chinese movie star, and they want to know when you'll be as big as Joan Crawford. I told them to give you another year, then you'll be as well-known as Lucille Ball! I went home with a classmate, Maggie O'Leary, and saw the television show* I Love Lucy *for the first time. I still can't understand how you can actually see moving pictures in such a small box. But Mrs.*

*O'Leary says it's transmitted through airwaves. So maybe
one day you'll actually have your own television show in
Hong Kong!*

Joan felt herself blush, but read on.

*I wish you could come to visit me. You would love San
Francisco. The weather is so mild, I sometimes can't tell the
difference from one month to the next. I try to go to Chinatown whenever I can, though the food barely resembles what
I had at home. Even the Chinese food here is Americanized.
Sweet-and-sour sauces on everything. Still, it's better than
our dormitory diet, which consists of large portions of
tasteless, overcooked meats and potatoes with lots of
ketchup. What I miss the most, besides all of you, is rice for
dinner. The girls eat stacks and stacks of plain white bread,
until I think they're all going to explode!*

*I hope Mah-mee and Auntie Go are well. I'll write them
all separately, including Ba-ba. How I miss Foon's wonderful cooking. Isn't it strange how you have to go away to
really appreciate what you have.*

Joan put down Emma's letter and went to look for Foon. She listened closely for any signs of her old servant's whereabouts, but
there was only a strange, flat quiet, uninterrupted by the usual rush
of voices in the courtyard, or the clinking of pots cooking on a
fire. Joan's throat felt dry. She hadn't really had a conversation
with Foon in a long time. Frequently, when Joan came home for
dinner, it was already late. She usually ate, then retired to her room
to prepare for a scene she was in the next day.

"Foon!" Joan called out. She opened the kitchen door, but the
room was empty. Maybe Foon was off on an errand, or downstairs
in the courtyard, squatting over a large tub doing laundry.

Joan looked out the back door to the stone courtyard, but it too was empty.

"Foon!" Joan yelled again, though she didn't expect an answer. She returned to the kitchen, redolent of garlic and Foon's strange herbs. It was the room in which Joan had always found the most warmth and comfort. She reached out and touched the stone counter, polished smooth from years of cleaning, then picked up Foon's old cleaver and balanced its weight in her hand. She smiled to herself remembering how Foon had told her several times that the edge had been sharpened so much over the years, it had lost an inch off of its width.

"You home early." Foon's voice startled her.

Joan turned around to see Foon emerging from her closet-size room next to the kitchen. A sliver of Foon's gold tooth glimmered as she spoke. Wisps of gray hair stood away from her head. Joan wanted to go and hug Foon, but didn't make a move.

"They let us off early." Joan replaced the cleaver on the stone counter. "Trouble with one of the scenes."

"Too soon to cook." Foon looked down at the cleaver.

"Is Mah-mee playing mah-jongg?"

"At Auntie Hong's."

Joan smiled. "I was just wondering what you were doing. Maybe I could help you with something?"

"Everything done."

"Do you need anything from the market?"

Foon buttoned up her padded vest. "Already went this morning."

Foon poured water into an old kettle and placed it on the fire. "Afternoons quiet now. With you at the studio, and moi-moi in America . . . At first it's the voices you miss most. The rest follows."

Joan paused, not knowing what to say. "No matter what paths we take in life, you and this flat will always be home," she said, taking down two of Mah-mee's good teacups from a shelf.

Foon remained quiet, busying herself by breaking off a small piece of tea from a large circular cake of dried leaves. "Why two?" she asked, seeing the cups Joan had taken out.

"I thought you might like some too," Joan said, never taking her eyes off her old servant.

Foon looked at the delicate porcelain cups, then slowly nodded her head, raining just enough dark tea leaves into each one.

Rendezvous —

1954

Auntie Go

Auntie Go felt a stiffness in her left knee as she paced her hotel room waiting for Emma to arrive. This was her second overseas trip in a year, and Go detected the small signs of her travel's effects on her body. Besides the stiffness that came and went, she had trouble sleeping, which invariably led to terrible headaches. Now, every time Go left on a business trip to America or Europe, she could hear Kum Ling's voice telling her over and over, "You're not so young anymore! Let someone else go for you."

Not yet fifty years old, Go refused to let her cousin dissuade her from her travels. She loved all the new sights and sounds, had grown used to traveling alone. The droning hum of a plane, and the screeching metal wheels of a rattling train, had become just as much a part of her life as the steady swishing sounds of her knitting machines. In a strange way, the raw mechanical noise of travel set her free, took her away from her daily life and into uncharted territory.

Still tall and striking, Auntie Go dressed in Western-style clothing when she traveled—tailored calf-length dresses with matching hats and handbags. At home in Hong Kong, she disregarded the fashion trends, preferring comfort to American and European designer labels, which most Hong Kong *tai tai*s fancied. At the Western Wind, she usually wore a tunic and pants in alternating sets of black and blue.

Many of Auntie Go's meals abroad were taken with clients, some of whom she'd come to know well. She was often invited to their homes to have a pleasant dinner with their families. Out of friendship, and sometimes loneliness, Go accepted these invitations.

"But you don't really know anything about them," Kum Ling warned when she first found out.

"They have been kind to me, and they order sweaters from me. That's all I have to know," Go answered.

Kum Ling watched her carefully, then spoke in clear, precise words. "Just so the gods know I've warned you. A face worn to work is not always the same face worn at home."

Auntie Go had smiled, then dismissed her cousin's words with a silent shake of her head.

Kum Ling couldn't know how friendly most of her clients were. There were so many big and small happinesses in Go's life. She was proud of the Western Wind's success, and the many friends she'd made. Auntie Go also learned to enjoy eating a mixed variety of Western foods—thick slices of salty ham from a can, mashed potatoes, corned beef and cabbage, casseroles of noodles and cheese. Lately, she had even drunk an occasional glass of hot milk before she slept. Still, Go had to laugh at the thought of Foon's face were she to see the jumble of dull colors and tedious tastes.

What Auntie Go kept from Kum Ling was that sometimes Westerners were uncomfortable seeing her eating and traveling alone. She could tell by their darting eyes and low whispers. Go was immediately set apart, left dangling. In Hong Kong, she'd always been part of a larger group—second mother to her two nieces, owner of the Western Wind knitting factory, a member of Kum Ling's mah-jongg group.

Go deliberately kept a slight smile on her lips, a universal language she found everyone understood. It protected her from sideways glances when she ventured alone into expensive restaurants and disarmed sly assessment of her mother's deep green jade ring where a wedding ring should be.

Now Auntie Go smiled and glanced at her jade ring, the only jewelry she wore on her travels. "Jade will always protect you," she heard her mother's soft voice telling her. Go wondered if her mother also knew what great comfort the ring had given her.

She looked at her watch, then at the white walls of her hotel room. It might be a room anywhere in the world, except that a glance through the windows at the Golden Gate Bridge reminded her it was San Francisco; Emma would arrive at any moment. Auntie Go had specified a suite, in case Emma changed her mind and wanted to stay with her for a few days. After all, Go was the only family member attending Emma's graduation. The sitting room was large and comfortable, with a sofa and two oversize chairs. Now, looking at it, Go wondered if she'd been too extravagant.

Emma had returned to Hong Kong only once—the first summer after she'd left for college. Auntie Go remembered the sweltering heat of early August, and how they had sat around the dining room table in cotton housecoats, drinking iced tea and relentlessly fanning the thick, still air.

During the hot, sticky month, Foon stayed in the kitchen and cooked all Emma's favorite dishes—fried rice with salted fish and diced chicken, Chinese mustard greens with mushrooms in oyster sauce, and scallops with garlic and ginger.

On the nights when Joan was working late at the Tiger Claw, Auntie Go and Kum Ling hovered closely over Emma, making sure she ate enough, greedy for her to fill in all the blank spaces of her past year in San Francisco. Emma smiled wearily, lifted her hair away from her sweaty neck, and repeated much of what she'd already written them in letters.

"I go to classes from eight in the morning until about four in the afternoon," Emma said between bites of rice and diced chicken with pickled vegetables.

"When do you eat?" Kum Ling asked.

"Between classes."

Kum Ling eyed Emma closely. "No wonder you've lost weight. Running around and not eating!"

"You look good," Auntie Go interceded. "Much more grown-up."

Emma looked at her aunt with a grateful smile. "It's different being on your own. Everything seems clearer, more immediate."

Auntie Go continued, "You must have made some good friends in the dorm where you stay?"

"They're very nice to me. There are a couple of girls I'm close to. One of them is a Hong Kong girl. But I do miss Foon's cooking," Emma said, raising her voice so that Foon would hear.

"Then you should stay home," Kum Ling snapped. She laid her chopsticks across the rim of her bowl, then picked up her fan and opened it with a quick flick of her wrist.

Emma stopped eating and looked up at her mother. "Sometimes

I think about coming home, but I've really come to love San Francisco," Emma said, her words measured and self-assured. "Besides, I'm determined to finish my bachelor's degree in art, even if I starve to death at Lone Mountain!"

Auntie Go smiled to herself.

Kum Ling remained silent for a moment, then she too smiled, dishing more chicken into Emma's bowl. "How did both of my daughters get so stubborn?"

"Look who their mother is!" Auntie Go laughed.

Kum Ling nodded in rare agreement. She turned to Emma and said, "Well, then, you better eat while you can."

After that summer, Emma stayed in San Francisco to work, even when Auntie Go offered to send her a ticket to come home. There was always work to do, Emma said, or exams to study for, that kept her across the Pacific. At the same time, Auntie Go sensed it had to do with the increasing noise and crowds of Hong Kong. Like her, Emma needed the distance, the calm.

"Do you think moi-moi's growing further away from us?" Kum Ling had asked one day with a sigh.

"Emma's growing up, not away from us," Auntie Go had gently answered.

Auntie Go couldn't believe how quickly time slipped through her fingers—a good year since she had seen Emma. Go had had to cancel their last scheduled visit because of trouble at the Western Wind, exchanging only quick words at the airport as she passed through San Francisco on her way back to Hong Kong from New York. Auntie Go had slipped a red envelope with lucky money into Emma's hand and couldn't forget her slight figure waving good-bye from the gate.

There'd been talk of a strike and an imminent shutdown of the Western Wind if she didn't get back to Hong Kong right away. She remembered thinking, *Give them what they want. They work hard enough for it!* But the company had grown too big for her to make that decision alone. Auntie Go had to meet with her managers, lawyers, strategists. "You'll never make money giving in to them!" voices roared at her.

But Auntie Go had made money, more than she could ever imagine, and many of the knitters had been with her since the beginning, when she didn't know the difference between a Fair Isle pattern and a tuck stitch. Old Sum had taught her how to operate the machines, Mei-mei how to read patterns. They'd become her working family, faces as familiar as those of her own blood relatives. *Give them what they want,* she kept thinking, just as she would give everything she could to Kum Ling, Joan, Emma. In the end, the voices calmed. They had met her working family halfway.

Go remembered entering the Western Wind after everything had been settled. She was greeted by the smiling faces of her workers, who nodded their heads and thanked her. The hundred or so machines, lined up in uniform rows, were running again, the sharp swish of wood against metal filling the large, open room. A bright light filtered in through the skylights above, as if everything were caught in the flash of a camera. Auntie Go blinked, rubbed her nose against the motes of wool and cotton that floated through the air. She stopped to inspect a rack of cotton pullover sweaters. Were the stitches even? The design and colors perfect? The Western Wind's reputation was based on quality work. Satisfied, Go climbed the wooden stairs to her office, looking down at a blur of motion that made her eyes water.

At the end of the day, Old Sum approached Auntie Go. She knocked and entered Go's office, eyes averted, and refused to sit down. Her fingers darted in and out of the pocket in her black tunic. "You know if it had been up to me, none of this would have happened," Old Sum said, her voice timid and shy.

Auntie Go smiled at her longtime worker, well into her sixties.

"Sometimes, things must be shaken up in order to fall right again. Do you remember when you first taught me to use the machines? You told me to relax, that my mind and fingers would soon memorize how to thread the yarn and press the right buttons, without my even thinking. I believe in the past year I've been operating the Western Wind in much the same fashion. It's time to begin thinking again."

Old Sum glanced up, her eyes bright. "But the workers should have talked to you, instead of sneaking around behind your back."

"We need to let go of the past. What matters is that we now look toward the future."

"To a prosperous one!" Old Sum smiled, her crooked, discolored teeth protruding.

Auntie Go poured a glass of sherry and handed it to Old Sum, then poured another for herself. "To a long and prosperous future!" Go said, then sipped, the warm, sweet liquid soothing her throat.

But this trip to San Francisco held special importance. Nothing would keep Auntie Go from attending Emma's graduation, even if the Western Wind stopped production. Already it had been a journey riddled with difficulties. Tickets reserved, then canceled. Joan was all set to accompany Auntie Go, until C. K. Chin himself cast her in a movie, which she tried unsuccessfully to postpone.

"What can I do?" Joan had asked, pacing the floor of Auntie Go's office. "It's not the starring role, but *Gone Forever* is a good family drama, with a strong part for me as Lin Yu's best friend. And most importantly, Chin asked for me himself."

During the past year, Joan had won larger roles, and audiences were beginning to take notice. She played second to the lead actresses in her most recent movies, *The Dream Chamber* and *The Three Phoenixes*. Kum Ling and Auntie Go were holding their breath as to when Chin would give her a starring role.

"She does make you believe," Kum Ling had said as they walked out of the Queen's Theatre after seeing Joan's latest movie, *The Three Phoenixes.* "Don't you think Joan was convincing as the younger sister?"

Auntie Go laughed. "Joan's had moi-moi to draw from all her life!"

"But it's one thing to know a person, it's another thing to become them."

For the first time, Go heard the sharp edge of pride and hope in Kum Ling's voice.

Auntie Go sat and listened to Joan, nodding her head with sympathy, pouring hot tea and sipping it slowly. "Then you have no choice but to stay," Go said, and made a mental note to cancel her niece's plane ticket.

"Do you think moi-moi will ever forgive me?" Joan asked, looking dark and serious.

"Of course she will."

"I'll send her a telegram tomorrow. Will you tell her how sorry I am, and that I'll make it up to her?"

"Yes, you know I will."

When Joan turned toward her with a sad smile, Go couldn't get over how much she resembled Kum Ling.

Auntie Go had also tried tirelessly to convince Kum Ling to fly to San Francisco with her. But her cousin wavered, afraid to commit herself, citing Lew Hing's health. She backed out only days before they were to leave.

"You go and explain why," Kum Ling had pleaded, sitting at her dining room table. She tucked a pair of pearl earrings and a gold bracelet into a red, embroidered silk pouch and pushed it into Auntie Go's hand. "Please, Go, give this to moi-moi for me. Tell her that her ba ba is not feeling well, and I had to stay in Tokyo with him."

Go stroked the smooth silk pouch. What Kum Ling said was only partially the truth. Yes, Lew Hing had been under the weather lately, but Go knew Kum Ling's reason for not going to San Francisco had more to do with her fear of flying than anything else. Kum Ling could barely tolerate the flight to Tokyo. Before, when they had traveled together, Go remembered her strong-willed cousin, white-knuckled, gripping the arms of the airline seat until they landed. There was little chance she would cross an entire ocean.

"It seems a feeble excuse," Go persisted. She wasn't about to let Kum Ling off so easily. "Moi-moi is the first one of us to graduate from college. It's not a small event to miss!"

Kum Ling made a clicking sound with her tongue, fingering loose cake crumbs on the table. "It's such a long distance. She'll understand," Kum Ling said, more to herself than to Auntie Go. "I'll write her a letter explaining."

In the silence between them, they heard Foon in the kitchen—chopping, pouring water, clapping a pot onto the fire.

"Write it tonight." Go stood up. "It will be faster if I take it to her."

Quick taps on the door roused Auntie Go from her thoughts. She rubbed her left knee and rose slowly. Emma was waiting in the hallway, smiling. Auntie Go drew a breath and let it out slowly. In the year since she'd last seen her niece, Emma had grown up remarkably well, her youthful chubbiness giving way to sharper, leaner features. She'd cut her hair short—above the shoulders with bangs—and was dressed in a blue cardigan sweater, flare skirt, and saddle shoes. She looked fresh out of college. In comparison, Go hated to think how she must have aged in Emma's eyes.

"Moi-moi . . . I mean Emma." Go laughed. "You look wonderful! Very American."

Emma hugged her. "I'm so glad to see you. I can't believe you're really here," she said in an excited flow of words.

"Come in, come in," Go said, taking Emma's arm. "We have so much to catch up on."

"I'm so glad to see you," Emma repeated as she sat down on the sofa. In her voice there was a hint of the young girl Auntie Go knew so well.

"We're very proud of you. I'm sorry we all couldn't be here."

"How many people can say their sister's busy making a movie?" Emma laughed too quickly. "And how's Mah-mee?"

Auntie Go handed her Kum Ling's letter and red silk pouch. "Your mah-mee had to be in Tokyo to look after your ba ba. She'd be here if she could."

Emma nodded, held the red pouch in her lap, but didn't open it. "And Ba ba? How is he feeling?"

Auntie Go shook her head. "He has been under the weather for the longest time now."

"He wrote me to say he was fine, and for me not to worry about him," Emma said, her voice strained.

"Then you should listen to his words," Auntie Go said reassuringly. "You should also know that your mah-mee would be here, but she's afraid of flying in an airplane for so long. Kum Ling just doesn't trust the fates. She never did."

"But you do."

Auntie Go laughed. "I've never been smart enough to do otherwise."

With two days before graduation, Auntie Go was thrilled to have Emma all to herself. They were free to do whatever they pleased in one of the most beautiful cities in the world. Go was determined to make it a weekend Emma wouldn't forget. She wanted to climb all the hills she'd read about—Nob Hill, Russian Hill, Telegraph Hill. . . .

* * *

Auntie Go sat in the fifth row of the overcrowded St. Dominic's hall at Lone Mountain College and watched as her younger niece was about to graduate with honors. The room was stifling, filled with murmuring voices, thick perfumes, hairspray, and perspiration. "It's too damn hot in here," she heard a man's voice say, followed by a louder "Sshh!"

Auntie Go smiled. It *was* too hot in the crowded hall. She'd taken the longest time trying to figure out what to wear, finally deciding on a burgundy knit suit, complete with matching purse and shoes. Go never did like to wear gloves. They somehow made her feel as if her hands couldn't breathe. Still, she looked just as she felt, a proud mother watching her daughter graduate.

Go took off her knit jacket, fanned herself with the green and gold-edged program, and checked again to see if her envelope for Emma was in her handbag. Within the card was a thin piece of white parchment paper that conveyed 25 percent of her Western Wind ownership to Emma. The same would go to Joan. The rest of the company would be theirs to use as they wished upon Go's death. She swallowed the thought. The future would sort itself out.

Auntie Go sat squeezed between two sets of parents who craned their necks looking forward and backward. They fidgeted so much in their seats, Go wanted to tell them to "freeze" like in one of those children's games. When Emma's name was called, it echoed and filled the enormous hall. Auntie Go felt everything around her stop. The sting of hot tears welled behind her eyes. Emma, in black cap and flowing gown, which matched those of the nuns, moved carefully across the stage and reached for her diploma. Then, just as she approached the edge of the stage, Emma turned, her eyes seeking and finding Auntie Go. A grateful smile spread across Emma's face as she lifted her hand and waved.

A
Dream
of
Spring —
1955

EMMA

The pungent smells of fresh fish, sweet fruits, dried herbs, and cig-arette smoke mingled in the air as Emma got off the Stockton Street bus in Chinatown. She walked briskly down the block, weaving around the throngs of people in her way. Outside the numerous small markets that lined the street, men and women laden with shopping bags gathered in front of chaotically displayed wooden crates, picking and choosing oranges, tangerines, and Chinese grapefruits for the New Year. Their hurried, high-pitched voices re-minded her of Foon and the other servants gabbling at the market, or washing laundry together in the courtyard. Emma imagined that most Americans must think the Chinese language sounded like arguing, but she knew it was a way of life, a clash of voices fighting to be heard, erupting in a chorus.

Except for occasional dinners at the Kuo Wah Restaurant or the Pacific Cafe with other Chinese students, Emma hadn't been to Chinatown very often while she attended Lone Mountain. Yet, each time she did venture down to its bustling, noisy streets, all the small similarities brought her a sense of comfort, as if she weren't so far from Hong Kong and her family after all. It always amazed Emma how bits and pieces of her childhood could follow her so closely into her present life.

Emma paused in front of the Golden Harvest Market, where a large red and gold 1955 calendar hung on the plate-glass window. An oversize head of a ram with spiraling horns stared at her, surrounded by the eleven other animal signs she could never fully remember—dragon, monkey, horse, tiger, rat, boar, rooster, rabbit, snake. . . . Her eyes drifted away. Emma watched the crowd push and pull to buy the best fruit. She remembered being a small girl, holding the warm, smooth hand of her mother as they walked through the bustling marketplace before one Chinese New Year. Mah-mee appeared so out of place with her immaculate makeup, and in her silk cheungsam, but Emma had never been happier, smelling Mah-mee's sweet, flowery scent as she leaned over and whispered, "A secret, moi-moi . . . the oranges with smooth, thin skins are always the sweetest." She handed Emma one, waxy and shiny as the moon. Emma carried their secret around like a gift, only to discover later that Joan had known about the smooth-skinned oranges for years.

Emma smiled at the memory and wondered if all these people were vying for the same sweet, thin-skinned oranges as they inched forward toward the crates. Emma wrapped her overcoat tighter around her body and kept walking. February was cold, with a sharp wind that stung. She couldn't wait until spring.

She turned up Washington Street for her job interview at the Chinese Recreation Center. She had graduated from Lone Mountain College almost eight months ago and, except for a string of temporary office jobs, had had no luck in finding anything permanent.

Emma remembered the days before graduation, when she and Auntie Go spent an afternoon in Golden Gate Park—the sweet scent of the flowers and freshly cut grass intoxicating. By late afternoon, they stopped for tea at the Japanese Tea Garden. They sipped the bitter green tea and nibbled on rice crackers, gazing out to a large pond with a wooden bridge across it.

"What are your plans after you graduate?" Auntie Go asked, reaching out for a tiny square cracker.

Emma shrugged. "I'd like to stay in San Francisco and work for a while. I know Mah-mee won't be too happy about it. But now that I'm going to graduate, I'd love a little more time to explore this city. There just seems to be so much here. Maybe for a year or two. Secretarial or very light bookkeeping. Something that would allow me to keep taking drawing classes in my spare time. Do you think Mah-mee would be very upset?"

Auntie Go sipped her tea. "Your mother will make a fuss, then accept it," she answered matter-of-factly. "She misses you, moi-moi, even if she won't say it aloud. And now with Joan at the studio all day . . ."

"I miss all of you, too. You can't know how much it means to me to have you here."

Auntie Go touched Emma's hand. "I wouldn't have missed it for the world."

Emma smiled. "So, Joan's finally found some happiness on the big screen. I just hope that one day she'll find time to come visit me here. Maybe when she's a big star!"

"It never hurts to keep your fingers crossed," Auntie Go said, cradling her clay teacup in the palms of her hands.

"For me, too."

Auntie Go lifted her crossed fingers and said, "Just for added protection. You're a college graduate now. You're going to be fine, moi-moi."

The wind felt like ice on her face. The Chinese Recreation Center was Emma's third job interview in the past week. The other two had also been clerical positions, one for an insurance company, and the other for an accounting firm. Both offices were large and cold, leaving Emma, at twenty-four, to question her decision to stay in San Francisco to work. Her office skills were limited at best, but being a woman and an art major left her with few other opportunities.

The past two months had been financially tight. Emma didn't want to upset Mah-mee, so she wrote home saying, *There are always temporary jobs whenever I need them*. With Ba ba not well, she knew her mother had financial worries of her own. But the truth was, Emma struggled through the shorthand and typing and hadn't been called back in the last month. She'd been living on her meager savings, and a flow of "lucky money" that came every month from Auntie Go.

It was still hard for Emma to believe that her college days were over. She'd just begun to relax and enjoy the student life when the ordered rhythm of classes and studying came to an end. Emma recalled her first six months at Lone Mountain as being the most difficult. Sometimes, when she felt especially homesick, she reread bits of letters from Mah-mee, Joan, and Auntie Go, hoping their words would take away some of the emptiness.

Auntie Hong's niece is getting married next month, Mah-mee wrote. *She's the one with the long face that some say resembles a horse. But you know what they also say, that if you resemble some kind of animal, you're sure to bring good luck*. Or Auntie Go's calm voice: *The*

Western Wind is doing well. I hope to come visit you in San Francisco at the end of the year if everything goes as planned. And finally, Joan's words telling her, *I can't believe I'm really working for C. K. Chin. My first crowd scene was a success, even if you can barely see me! Keep your fingers crossed that somebody notices me next time.* Each time Emma read Joan's words, she couldn't help but cross her fingers.

Emma slowly began to fit into her new life with the help of two new friends—Sylvia Lu and Margaret O'Leary. They were as different as night and day, and each in some way came to represent Emma's old and new lifestyles. Sylvia was short and petite, full of energy, and from a rich Hong Kong family. She spent her free hours shopping instead of studying, "buying time," she said, laughing, until she could graduate and return to Hong Kong.

"Why did you come here?" Emma had asked one evening when they were having dinner in the dark, stately dining hall.

"Ba ba wants me to have a good education," Sylvia answered, reaching for her purse and clicking it open. Her tray of gray meat loaf, canned green beans, and lumpy potatoes was barely touched.

"It doesn't seem like a bad idea," Emma said, picking at a white mound of potatoes.

"He's hoping I gain some character out of the experience." Sylvia laughed, pulling out a silver compact and lipstick.

Emma wasn't sure if she should laugh or not, until Sylvia nudged her softly with her elbow.

"It's okay," Sylvia said, "I'll have all the brains that my father's money can buy. Anyway, San Francisco isn't such a bad place to be." She flipped open her compact, powdered both sides of her nose. "I do miss my family, sometimes."

Emma swallowed; a dull ache moved through her body and stopped at her heart. "Me too," she whispered, then asked, "What surprised you the most when you first arrived here?"

Without missing a beat, Sylvia answered, "Everything was

smaller than I expected. Even the city itself. Not to mention that the dorm rooms are no bigger than my closet back home! How about you?"

"The tasteless food," Emma said, pointing at her tray. "And sometimes they're so casual here. The students walk around barefoot. And saleswomen call me 'honey' or 'dear' when I don't even know them."

Sylvia nodded and laughed. "And what do *you* like most about San Francisco?" Then, twisting up her ruby red lipstick, she applied it to her full lips.

"Its openness," Emma said, the words slipping out without thought. "I feel like I could be anything I want here."

"Everything I want is back in Hong Kong," Sylvia said, snapping her compact closed.

Still, with their similar roots, she and Emma spoke and laughed about people and places that brought back childhood comforts. Sylvia knew of C. K. Chin and the Tiger Claw Film Company when Joan's letter arrived with the news of her job there. And Sylvia also introduced an extra element into Emma's life—dating. But after several double dates of dinner and dancing, Emma realized Sylvia's friends were like all the spoiled Hong Kong rich boys Joan had dated. As "The Tennessee Waltz" and "Apple Wine and Cherry Blossom Time" played over and over in her head, Emma vowed never to go on another double date with Sylvia again.

Maggie O'Leary was opposite from Sylvia, not only in personality, but in her sheer physical height. From good Irish Catholic stock, she had flaming red hair and stood almost a full head taller than Emma. She was serious, scholarly, and driven to succeed.

Emma celebrated her first Thanksgiving dinner at Maggie's Richmond District house in San Francisco. Then she watched the miracle of *The Milton Berle Show* on their Philco television.

At dinner, Emma sat between Maggie and Mrs. O'Leary. The five younger O'Leary children, who seemed intensely interested in Emma when she first arrived with candy and flowers, had since turned their attention to the table of food.

"And what are you planning to study, Emma?" Mrs. O'Leary asked. She was a big-boned woman with red hair and a kind face.

Emma chewed her piece of dry turkey, which she cautiously kept away from what they'd told her was a sweet, red cranberry sauce, and swallowed. "Right now it looks like art," she answered, then sipped some water.

"Emma's sister is an actress back in Hong Kong," Maggie offered.

"Really? An actress! Is she famous?" Mrs. O'Leary asked.

"She's going to be." Emma grinned.

"Our Maggie's going to be a doctor," Mrs. O'Leary said proudly. "All she ever wanted to be. And to think I never even finished high school! It is a wonderful country we live in."

Emma simply nodded and smiled. She sometimes wished she could have her own life as well planned as Maggie's. She had no idea what she would do with an art degree, but art gave her a great deal of gratification. Emma glanced quickly around the cluttered, comfortable room, her eyes resting on the rows of porcelain figurines that lined the shelves against the wall behind Mrs. O'Leary. Most of them were of animals—turtles, horses, swans, and birds.

"Another?" Mrs. O'Leary smiled, lifting a slice of turkey in the air. Emma politely declined the slice, which was quickly snapped up by one of Maggie's younger brothers.

There were so many younger O'Learys that it took the entire evening for Emma to get all the children's names straight. In descending order, there were Patrick, Daniel, Barbara, Sean, and the youngest, Mary. For the first time in her life, Emma realized what it was like to be in a big, unruly family, with each child fighting for attention. Even Maggie came alive when she was with her family, as if some secret door had been unlocked and a flood of boisterous voices streamed into the room.

Every time Emma had dinner with the O'Learys, she couldn't help but think of Joan and wish they'd had more brothers and sisters to keep Mah-mee busy.

Sylvia had returned to Hong Kong, and Maggie had been accepted to medical school. Life had gone according to plan for them, while Emma felt as if she were floating. As a young girl, there were so many places she'd wanted to see, things she wanted to do. Now, her days were fixed on finding a job so she could pay her rent at the Bellevue Apartments for Women, where she'd been staying since she graduated.

Emma always knew that when her reserves were gone, she could wire Auntie Go for help. For the time being, she had no intention of giving up. Still, if Emma didn't find a steady job soon, Mah-mee would ask her to return to Hong Kong. Already the words echoed through Mah-mee's letters in less than subtle ways: *Now that you have seen some of the world, it's about time you came home and settled down;* or, *Joan doesn't listen to a word I say! Maybe when you come home, you can talk some sense into her. She insists on staying in this acting business.*

Every time Emma returned to her apartment, she felt hot and nervous at just the possibility of a letter from Mah-mee waiting for her.

Emma had returned to Hong Kong just once in the five years since she'd been in San Francisco. She could almost smell the thick heat of that summer, walking with Mah-mee into the suffocating flat with all its wonderful and familiar scents—her mother's perfume, salted fish, herbs, and the welcome aroma of Foon's cooking. But, in that instant, the longing that had gripped Emma all year disappeared in a few short steps.

Foon had come out of the kitchen, taken one look at her, and said, "You too skinny."

"I've missed your cooking," Emma practically blurted out. "They need you in the kitchen at my school!" She wanted to hug her old servant, but knew Foon was more likely to accept words with greater ease.

Foon smiled, the glint of her gold tooth a welcome sight. "I cooked one of your favorite dishes tonight. Stuffed bitter melon."

Aside from Foon's cooking, Emma's biggest thrill was finally getting to see Joan on the big screen. And though Joan's role had been small—a woman in a crowd scene who screams and faints when her child is taken away from her—Emma knew Joan had *star* written all over her the moment the camera lingered on her beautiful, haunting face. Emma sucked in her breath, not daring to let it out until the short scene was over.

"You were so beautiful! So tragic!" Emma exclaimed when the lights came on. The audience around them stood up and moved toward the door, the faint smell of dried plums and Chinese beef jerky filling the air. Emma sat next to Joan, still clutching her arm, while Mah-mee sat on the other side of her. Auntie Go wasn't able to get away from the knitting factory for the afternoon showing, but would meet them later at the Peninsula Hotel for tea.

"It was a much bigger role this time," Mah-mee said, adding her approval.

Joan smiled. "Less of me ended up on the cutting-room floor."

"Does that really happen?" Emma asked.

"More than you know, moi-moi!" Joan laughed.

That evening Emma and Joan were able to spend a rare evening alone together. Mah-mee and Auntie Go had gone to a birthday banquet, and Emma and Joan came directly home from the Peninsula. Emma's head was still spinning from having seen Joan on the big screen. Foon had prepared them a dinner of Chinese mushrooms with bok choy, and sliced beef in oyster sauce, which they ate leisurely before moving to the living room to drink Ba ba's expensive sherry.

"I feel like I've been away for years." Emma sipped her sherry, and the sweet, warm liquid slid down her throat. "I can't believe how much Hong Kong has changed in just a year! There are new buildings everywhere, not to mention all the people."

Joan nodded. "We've been more of a magnet since the war, and then with the Communist takeover . . . I guess nothing ever stays the same for long."

"Just look at you!" Emma laughed. "You're a real movie star!"

"You mean a movie extra."

Emma raised her glass. "I mean an up-and-coming movie star!"

"What a year! I never thought my life could change so drastically."

"I knew you could be whatever you wanted."

Then Joan raised her glass. "And to my lovely sister, who will be the first one in the Lew family to graduate from college. If Professor Ying could see you now!"

Emma leaned back against the sofa and laughed. It sounded good, if she could ever make it. She sipped her sherry and relaxed. "Did you ever think we would actually get this far?"

Joan smiled and poured herself more sherry. "Do you remember the time you went to collect money with me?"

"Of course."

"I was afraid you'd think I was a failure if I wasn't able to collect anything."

Emma looked at her sister, flushed. "How could you think that? There's never been anyone braver than you in the world. Then or now!"

Joan blushed. "I hope you're right. I just don't want to fail now. I wish Mah-mee had as much faith in me as you."

Emma placed her empty glass on the table. "Just give her a little time. She'll come around when she sees what a big star you're going to be."

"I hope we'll both be shining soon," Joan said, squeezing Emma's hand tightly.

The Chinese Recreation Center was an old redbrick building between Powell and Mason Streets, according to what the man on the phone had told her. Emma was early for her two o'clock appointment, so she lingered at a few Chinese antique shops up the street until time for her interview.

Emma found the administrative office down a small, dark entry hall past a bulletin board. The dirty-looking green door banged open and a young Chinese boy of about twelve or thirteen stepped out carrying a basketball, which he bounced once or twice between them. He smiled shyly.

"Wilson will be back in a minute. He told me to wait here for you."

"Thank you." Emma smiled back. The boy was thin, but almost her height. His flattop glistened with sweat, the sides of his head shaved so closely, she could see the pale white of his scalp. A thin line of sweat ran from his hairline down his jaw. He stepped back and awkwardly held out the ball with both hands in the direction of two wooden chairs.

The office was small and crowded, the desk cluttered with papers. Three tall, gray file cabinets lined one wall. The opposite wall was lined with black-framed photos of past Chinatown championship basketball teams. All the boys in the photos resembled the one before her—skinny, long-limbed, more comfortable with a basketball than with a girl. A 1954 calendar still hung to one side.

"You can sit and wait here. Wilson will be right back," the boy repeated.

"Thank you." Emma smiled again and sat down.

The boy seemed relieved as he turned to leave. "He won't be long," he said reassuringly, and closed the door behind him.

A moment later, the door banged open and a short, wiry man wearing a white T-shirt, brown slacks, and a brown cardigan sweater entered. Around his neck hung a silver whistle.

"Miss Lew, I'm Wilson Chang. I'm sorry I'm late. We had a little problem in the gymnasium. I hope you haven't been waiting long?"

"No, not at all."

He shook Emma's hand. His hand was surprisingly warm and smooth. He pulled a manila folder from a pile on his desk and sat down.

"Sorry I'm so disorganized, but you can see that's why I'm looking for someone to take care of the office." He glanced up and smiled.

Emma nodded. She held her purse tighter on her lap and shifted in her chair while he studied her file.

"You don't have much experience doing clerical work," he said without mincing words. "College grad. In art. We could use some color around here," he said, his eyes remaining on her file.

Emma wanted to just get up and leave. First, he had made her wait, then he hadn't the decency to have at least glanced at her file before she arrived. Sometimes, Emma thought that Americans were *too* casual. She tried to smile and sat tight.

"You were born and raised in Hong Kong. I assume that means you speak fluent Cantonese?"

Emma gripped the handle of her purse tighter. "Of course I do," she snapped, no longer caring if she was polite or not.

He glanced up at Emma over her file. "I see. All right, you've got the job if you want it. It's important that you speak fluent Cantonese here, since most of our calls come from the parents of kids from the old country wanting to know about our programs. It pays sixty dollars a week until further notice."

Emma was stunned. She stood up so quickly, she almost knocked over her chair. "Are you sure?"

"Never more. You look like someone who can straighten out this mess and answer the phone." He waved his arm across his desk.

"When do I begin?"

"Is tomorrow morning at nine o'clock too soon?"

"Tomorrow would be fine." Emma smiled awkwardly and turned to leave. Hesitating, she turned back toward Wilson Chang. "I think it's only fair to tell you I'm not a very fast typist."

"Neither am I," he said, rising from his chair. "But can I trust you to be here on time and help clean up this mess?"

Emma looked around the small, crowded office and smiled. "Yes. Yes, you can."

"Then I'll see you tomorrow morning," he said hurriedly. "I'm sorry to rush you, but we've got a game in ten minutes."

When Wilson extended his hand to Emma, she again marveled at its warmth, which clung like a glove when he let go.

On her way home, Emma stopped at the Golden Harvest Market, hungry for some home cooking. Over the years, she felt less and less homesick, comfortable in her new life, but an occasional memory of some dish Foon had made would make her mouth water and send a deep craving through her. Emma shuffled through the dusty, crowded aisles of the store, which smelled faintly medicinal, and bought all the ingredients to make Foon's stuffed bitter melon specialty. In a brown bag she carried home on the bus were the necessary ingredients: black mushrooms, lean ground pork, the fist-size, torpedo-shaped bitter melon, and a bottle of oyster sauce. Emma had seen Foon and Joan make it so many times at home, she was certain she wouldn't have any problems.

Hours later, Emma gave up and sat down to a dinner of white rice, debating whether to drop a sunny-side-up egg on top. Through the thin walls she heard *The Jackie Gleason Show* blaring on the television next door. She couldn't quite make out what was being said, only the occasional rise of voices, followed by organ music, and mechanical-sounding laughter. In front of her was the overcooked melon and gray meat blended together. It didn't even faintly resemble what Foon and Joan had made at home. Emma reviewed what she'd done—peeling and hollowing out the middle of the melon of its seeds, mincing the garlic and mushrooms before mixing them with the pork, then filling the cavity with the pork mixture and slicing it into inch-thick circles. Emma looked at the watery, overcooked mess in front of her. She must have scraped the melon too thin, then left it cooking on the stove too long. Unlike Joan, her cooking skills were minimal at best.

Emma glanced at Joan's last letter on the other side of the table, next to a copy of *Anna Karenina* and yesterday's newspaper. The headline read, *President Eisenhower Authorized to Defend Formosa.* Emma didn't expect Joan to have much time for cooking now, especially when she was on the verge of movie stardom. She'd written to Emma of her new contract with the Tiger Claw Film Company: *Can you believe it? Chin has promised me that I'll have a starring role in one of his films within a year's time.* Emma smiled at the excitement in her sister's words. She picked at the melon and pork, flat and tasteless, already planning to fly back to Hong Kong for the premiere.

Emma began working at the Chinese Recreation Center the following morning, arriving half an hour early and staying until almost six o'clock. For the most part, Wilson Chang told her what and what not to do, then stayed out of her way, preferring to be with the kids in the gymnasium, rather than sitting behind his cluttered desk. He had an old desk and chair brought up from the basement for her. They squeezed it into a small alcove next to his office. Emma returned phone calls and organized his papers into alphabetized files in the cabinets. It was easy enough, and Wilson was grateful, though he shyly tiptoed around her without saying much.

By the end of Emma's first week, she could see some semblance of a working office. As she put on her coat and started for the front door, Wilson appeared from the gym, looking as young as some of his basketball players in a T-shirt and tennis shoes.

"Don't forget," he said, "to add on all the extra hours you've worked this week."

"But I . . ."

"You've done a good job so far," Wilson said, his voice kind and calm. "Have a good weekend then."

"You too." Emma smiled.

They teetered in a moment of awkward silence before Wilson turned around and disappeared into his office.

c h a p t e r 12

What
Price
Beauty?—
1956—57

JOAN

Joan knocked against the makeup table in her dressing room, rattling the many jars and bottles. Almost thirty, Joan was on the verge of stardom. She was preparing for the final scene in *The Longest Day,* hopefully her last film in a supporting role. Sometimes, in her deepest imaginings she could hear the roar of applause, feel the slow crush of the crowds, the hot lights and cameras flashing a snow-white blindness. It frightened her to think that her movie career was actually materializing after years of persistence and hard work. Joan bit her thumbnail and didn't dare to think what would happen if her upcoming movie, *A Woman's Story*, in which she was to star, failed.

A sudden slapping sound made Joan jump. She turned around to see the pages of her *Movie Mirror* magazines fluttering on the table by an opened window. The smooth, glossy pages were a gentle reminder as to who the real movie stars were—Elizabeth Taylor, Marlon Brando, Kim Novak, William Holden.

Lately, everything made Joan anxious. In the past few weeks, she'd felt a strange sensation moving through her body. It was as if a fever grew and surged through her blood, leaving her warm and flushed most of the time. Last year, Joan had seen similar symptoms in Mah-mee, who was constantly perspiring and complaining of the heat. "Like an oven that suddenly turns on inside of you," Mah-mee had said, fanning herself vigorously. Joan knew the heat marked a time in life after which her mother would no longer be able to have children.

Before, children were not something Joan thought much about. She could barely keep up with her own life. All around her, old classmates she knew were having their second . . . third child, hiring amahs to take care of them while they resumed their life of luncheons, shopping, and afternoon teas. Joan never understood the need to have children you barely saw. But now, every time the heat surged through her blood, she couldn't imagine not having them.

Joan stared into the mirror, searching for any distinct changes. She felt a sudden wave of warmth move through her body, rising to color her face pink. She leaned closer to the mirror. The warm glow enhanced her pale, smooth complexion, dark eyes, the mole above her lip, which had become her acting trademark in the last few years.

Still, the feverish flush frightened her. Joan wondered if anyone noticed that this was happening to her too soon. She was too young. Yet, no one seemed to observe any difference in her. Mah-mee and

Auntie Go hadn't said anything . . . no "Are you feeling all right?" or "Do you have a fever?" . . . no strong black teas coming from Foon.

In the heart of winter, as the wind and rain raged outside, Joan drank down iced tea and coffee, soy bean milk, both sweet and salty, and took special care to eat "cold" foods—fresh tofu, fruits, and vegetables—to control her body temperature. At dinner, she waited until her soup and rice turned room temperature before eating them, giving detailed accounts of her day—the actor who broke his leg swinging through the air in a fight scene, or the actress who froze and forgot all her lines—to entertain Mah-mee and Auntie Go, so they wouldn't notice her food getting cold. Only Foon shook her head, but she didn't say a word. After a week, she simply waited until the end of dinner before bringing Joan a bowl of lukewarm soup to drink.

There was a hollow knock on Joan's dressing room door, followed by a high, anxious voice. "Miss Lew, you're needed on the set in five minutes."

"Yes. Yes, I'm coming."

Joan pulled her hair back into a chignon, then buttoned the top frog of her cheungsam, looking very much like the *tai tai,* the married woman she played in the film. In reality, Mah-mee had all but given up in the past few years, her matchmaking dwindled to a standstill. She was content that Joan would at least have a career to fall back on. She'd heard her mother telling some aunties at one of her mah-jongg games, "My older daughter is an *act-tress*"—always stressing the syllables—"and my younger daughter has graduated from college in America. With honors."

Just when everyone had finally grown comfortable with this modern arrangement, Joan felt the smallest whisper of dissatisfaction. Despite her growing success, her emptiness increased. The more Mah-mee accepted the fact Joan wouldn't marry, the more unsettled Joan became. She tried hard not to show it, but found herself imagining that what her mother really thought was that she had somehow failed to do what was expected of her. She saw again her mother's tight smile and searching eyes. And sometimes, even when she knew it was foolishness, Joan finished the sentence she really thought Mah-mee meant to say: "My older daughter is an *actress* . . . because she couldn't find a husband."

Joan traced the beginning of her sudden fever back to last month at the studio, just after she'd heard the news of the actress Lily Wong's death from Jade Wind. For almost a decade, Lily Wong had been one of the most beautiful lead actresses to grace the Hong Kong movie screens. Originally from Shanghai, she'd migrated to Hong Kong after the war, along with a second wave of actors and directors in 1948. She immediately established herself as a major presence in the Hong Kong film industry, making both Mandarin- and Cantonese-speaking movies. She had been under contract to another large Chinese studio, though rumor had it that C. K. Chin spoke endlessly of signing her with Tiger Claw as soon as her current contract was up. Only in her midthirties, Lily was at the height of her career and was even rumored to be courted by the likes of David O. Selznik for a big-budget Hollywood film.

"How did she die?" Joan had asked. Jade Wind was busily hemming a long, white robe Joan would have to wear in her next scene.

"Committed suicide," Jade Wind mumbled, pins pressed between her lips, talking out of the side of her mouth. "Cut her wrists. Her servant found her. She was lying in a pool of her own blood. Already dead."

Joan sighed and looked away, her eyes beginning to burn. She'd read about Wong's unhappy love affairs with actors and directors, most of them never lasting more than a few months at a time. Joan could easily imagine what it was like, the euphoria that comes with hope, then the letdown. Hadn't she been through it before? Still, it was hard to believe anyone so beautiful, in the prime of her career, could simply end her life so senselessly.

"Does anyone know why?" Joan asked.

"Rumors." Jade Wind removed the last few pins from between her lips. "Some say she was pregnant, others say she was having another unhappy love affair. I say it was probably the love affair, because a friend of mine had fitted her for a film just before, and she was as thin as a piece of straw."

"Love," Joan mumbled to herself.

"What did you say?"

Joan pulled the robe closer around her body. "It's a shame."

Another knock on her small dressing room door and Joan closed the window. She glanced one more time into the mirror, finding just the right expression for her role as a happily married woman—lips rising up into the smooth curve of a waxing moon, eyes as bright and content as stars.

In March, Joan had her first scheduled meeting with Edward Chung, the director Chin had chosen for *A Woman's Story*. Somewhere in his late thirties, he was reputed to be a demanding, difficult director to work with. Joan had no great illusions of liking him.

"Be careful of that one," Jade Wind had told her. "He has been known to send more than a dozen actresses crying from the set before a movie is finished."

Joan brushed off her fear with laughter. "Well, he'll have met his match with me!" she said defiantly.

She had prepared herself for all-out war, but Edward Chung surprised her by being tall, thin, and mild-mannered in his gold-rimmed glasses. He remained completely silent during their first meeting in Chin's smoke-filled office. When she glanced in his direction, Joan caught him watching her and couldn't help but think, *You might as well not be here at all.*

It wasn't until halfway through the meeting that Joan realized her fever had disappeared. It was as if her body had found balance again. The heat that had left her perspiring throughout the winter had departed as suddenly as it came. Unconsciously, Joan smiled, then found herself laughing out loud with relief.

"What's so funny?" Chin asked, his cigarette burning between his lips.

Edward Chung remained silent, watching.

Joan looked over at Chin's drooping eyelids, his tired face. "Oh, nothing. I'm sorry," she quickly apologized, imagining the heat rising out of her body like steam.

Only when they were finally about to leave did Chung pause in front of her, take off his glasses, gaze directly into her eyes, and ask, "Are you ready?"

Joan assumed he meant starring in the film, and her reply was just as short and curt. "Of course."

But at home that evening, Joan ate her dinner and drank her soup steaming hot, still troubled by Chung's question. She began to doubt herself, knowing her career would depend on the outcome of this film. It made her angry to know that he already had this power over her. Joan knew it was in his eyes, the way he looked at her— with an unrelenting steadiness. Unlike so many other men, who sometimes squirmed, then looked away when she walked by or entered a room, Chung didn't seem at all intimidated by her. Joan drank down another hot bowl of soup Foon had brought her, certain that she was as ready as she'd ever be.

A few days later, Joan was surprised to find a message from Chung waiting for her when she arrived at the studio:

> *Would you be free for tea this afternoon at four o'clock to discuss the movie? I'll be waiting at the Peninsula Hotel, unless I hear otherwise.*
>
> *Edward Chung*

Joan thought of a hundred different ways to tell him she couldn't make it, but instead, watched the clock all day, then rushed out of the studio in order to make it to the Peninsula Hotel on time.

Chung was already sitting at a table when Joan arrived. He was dressed casually in khaki slacks, white shirt, and ascot. The large, open room was filled with people standing in line, waiting and watching for an empty table. Joan made her way through the thick crowd of *tai tai*s in designer suits, seeking refuge from shopping, and the intense businessmen who met regularly at the Pen for afternoon tea. Joan knew that certain preferred customers had designated tables held for them every day, so she couldn't imagine how Chung had managed to get a table snugly in the corner, away from the center of the storm.

As soon as Chung saw Joan walking toward him, he lifted his hand up in a slight wave, fingers spread evenly apart as if he were raising his hand in a classroom. Immediately, Joan felt another kind of warmth flush through her.

Chung stood up and smiled. "I'm glad you could make it," he said, offering her a chair.

"You wanted to discuss the movie?" Joan sat in the chair across from his and kept calm, distant.

"Yes, I do." He raised his hand again to call a waiter over. "Tea or coffee?"

"Tea, please."

After a waiter arrived and scribbled down their order, Chung wasted no time in getting down to business. He leaned forward against the loud hum of voices surrounding them and asked, "What do you expect from this movie?" He removed his glasses and watched her with a steady gaze.

All morning Joan had wondered what he might ask her. She had practiced her answers throughout the day, as if it were some kind of exam, and now answered without hesitation. "That it be a movie better than what they have at the theatres now. Something different from the usual family soap operas you see being made."

"A movie can only be as good as its story," he said, his gaze still focused on her. "And by the way it's interpreted. How do you think this story should be interpreted, Miss Lew?"

Joan smiled. *Try to remain calm. Try to remain calm*, she thought to herself, but said, "Please, call me Joan. I can only show you what my character feels in the world around her. The rest will have to be up to you."

"I see." Chung sat back in his chair. "But, what if this is a story that's determined by your character?"

The waiter returned carrying a silver tray with their tea and a three-tier stand of finger sandwiches and cakes. Across from them came the low hum of voices.

Joan cradled her teacup and leaned forward. "Is that what you think?"

He smiled. "I'm beginning to."

"My character is a survivor," Joan said, selecting a cucumber sandwich from the tray. "She has learned how to pretend all her life to get what she wants, yet hates herself because she isn't strong enough to leave a man she doesn't love, for one that she does." Joan bit into her sandwich.

Chung laughed. "How can you make an audience like your character?"

Joan swallowed, leaned back in her chair. "Because I'll show them that, beyond everything, she's ultimately honest about who she is."

Chung smiled. "And what do you expect this movie to do for

your career?" He snatched a finger sandwich from the tray and placed it entirely into his mouth.

Joan paused, not certain what she should say. She wished the twenty questions would end. "Perhaps if I'm good enough in this movie, it'll lead to other opportunities."

Chung glanced away from her out into the flurry of the room, then back at Joan again. "I'm sure you will be." He smiled at her.

Now Joan was the one to look away. She drank down her tea too quickly, the hot water singeing her tongue.

After their first tea together, there had been a lunch or two, then several dinners, which led to a string of articles written about them in the Chinese movie magazines. Auntie Go was the first to notice their picture plastered on the cover of the most widely read, *Chinese Movie Digest*.

"Is there something you want to tell us? I picked these up on my way home from Western Wind." Auntie Go smiled, placing two copies of the magazine on the dining room table.

Mah-mee immediately reached over and picked a magazine up, studying the photo. "He looks like an intellectual type."

Joan laughed. "He's the director of my next movie. We were just discussing film strategy."

"Look, Go," Mah-mee said, pointing at the photo. "They call it 'film strategy' now."

Joan tried to laugh it off, but later stared at the photo, somehow taken during their first meeting at the Peninsula Hotel. She had to admit, it did show them in a compromising position. It looked as if they were nestled close, whispering intimately to each other. At the time, nothing could have been further from the truth. Chung had remained a perfect gentleman, soft-spoken and polite. She had always conducted herself in the same manner. But even then, the photo told a different story.

Of course, things had progressed since the photo was taken. What had been a perfectly innocent meeting was growing into something much more complicated. Edward had since loosened up with her, telling her of his childhood growing up in Shanghai. "The most exciting city in the world," he called it. And how he was going to return there to make movies again once the industry got back on its feet. "Real Shanghai movies," he said, "that aren't filmed on phony back lots dressed up to be Shanghai."

Joan knew it was only in the past few years that many of the Shanghai directors had finally begun setting their films in Hong Kong, with stories tackling the daily problems of the society they'd migrated to. What about Hong Kong? she wanted to ask him, before his dark eyes caught hers, and the thought drifted away.

By their third dinner together, Joan knew she was in trouble. Not since Joseph had she felt this need to be with someone. She began to daydream and wonder what Edward was doing when she wasn't with him, hoping he thought of her in the same way. Joan found herself going to the studio early, even when she wasn't needed, hoping for a glimpse of him. A quick wave from across a set would last her the entire day. She knew he had to meet with Chin to discuss the final movie schedule before they began filming in two weeks. Joan paced back and forth in her dressing room, then went to look for Jade Wind.

"What's wrong with you? It's like you're a thousand miles away," Jade Wind teased as they sat eating lunch.

Joan blushed. "I was just thinking about the movie," she quickly said, her chopsticks resting between her fingers.

"What's to think about? You're going to be a big star. Chung's films have all done well. He has a big following in Shanghai, and now, in Hong Kong."

Joan smiled, putting her bowl of noodles down. "There's always a first time."

"It won't happen." Jade Wind laughed. "After all, Chung won't allow someone he's interested in to star in a flop. Just remember, there are a handful of actresses here who would kill to be in your position. You should hear the rumors flying around here. That you *seduced* the role out of him, that you're carrying his *love child*, that you're to be *married* once the film is completed!"

Joan laughed. "You know that affairs are notorious on these sets. I told you, there's nothing to those magazine photos. You'll be the first to know if anything does happen between us. It's just a way for them to sell copies."

Jade Wind slurped up the rest of her noodles. "Then they've succeeded," she said between bites.

When Joan returned home, she was surprised to find Edward Chung waiting for her. He had sat patiently in his car watching for her, calling out her name when Joan stepped out of a taxi. The wind carried it like a whisper to her, grazing the back of her neck just below her ear.

"What are you doing here?" Joan asked, her heart beating faster with every word.

"I needed to see you," he answered, his characteristic reserve weakened.

"About the movie?"

"About us."

When Joan got into Chung's car, she knew she was stepping into something that she no longer had any control over. She felt a great emptiness inside of her finally being accounted for, and the feeling was so warm and astounding, Joan was afraid she might start crying. Familiar streets sped by in a dream, as she rolled down the window and let the warm wind fill the car. Joan turned when she faintly heard him saying something, saw his lips were moving, but couldn't hear beyond the quick rush of wind as she leaned her head closer to the open window. All the way down the winding roads, Joan prayed that he would finally open that part of her that she had held closed for so long.

Chung drove her to a small apartment he kept on Kowloon side, near the studio. He still had a place in Shanghai that he considered his real home. Ever since he'd migrated to Hong Kong in 1948, he was simply waiting like so many others for the day when he could return to Shanghai. His Kowloon apartment was small and almost bare, except for a table, two chairs, and a sofa. From the living room, she could see his small bedroom, dominated by a large bed. Joan flinched at the sight of the disheveled bed, but Chung quickly apologized, closed his bedroom door, and went into the kitchen to make some tea. When he returned, carrying a teapot and two cups, Joan tried to relax as they sat at the table.

"What did you need to talk about?" Joan gathered her strength to ask.

"I think about you all the time," he simply answered, looking straight into her eyes.

Joan's heart was racing faster as each moment of silence passed. "Me too," she finally said.

When Edward Chung touched her hand for the first time, Joan felt a spark move through her body. Then, he leaned forward and kissed her once . . . twice . . . more.

The rest came so smoothly and easily, Joan thought she might be dreaming. He took her hand and led her to his bedroom, opening the door he had just closed, and placing her gently on his bed. He removed his glasses and suddenly appeared to her much younger, softer.

For a moment, it was as if Joan had risen out of her body and were watching everything from above. He was gentle as he removed her clothes, unsnapped each frog of her cheungsam from her neck down, touched her in hidden places and made her shiver, though the warmth of his body covered her like a blanket. She touched his back, letting her hands feel the softness of his skin, the curves of his shoulders, listening for the soft sighs, the deep intake of breath. She tried to concentrate, relax, felt him enter her with a sharp sting, the slow rocking movements of a dance, followed by a blinding warm release that spread through her.

Joan felt each day after pass in a haze. She spent all the time she could with Edward. Even when she wasn't physically with him, her thoughts twisted and turned around him. They had to work hard not to draw undue attention to their relationship. From the studio, she would either take a taxi to his apartment or meet him at a designated location from which they'd return to his place together. Until the movie was completed, Edward told her it was better for them to keep a low profile. "Chin won't like it," he said.

Joan knew he was right. She remembered the speech Mei had given to her when she first came to work at the Tiger Claw Film Company. How Chin disliked any kind of personal interaction to occur when one of his films was being shot. "Leads to nothing but trouble," he had once warned all of his actors. "Not to mention time and money if the love sours."

Yet, Joan grew tired of pretending, shying away from Edward at the studio, and keeping her feelings hidden from Jade Wind, Mah-mee, and Auntie Go. What did it matter if they were seeing each other? For all C. K. Chin knew, they might actually be married by the time the movie was completed. Joan had waited so long for the right person to come into her life that now the secret burned through her.

Sometimes, when Joan grew restless, she thought about writing Emma. The distance would provide protection. She began a letter,

Dear moi-moi, the words floating from her pen, *I've met someone. I'm in love,* then stopped. Seeing the word *love* startled her. At first it felt foreign, like a new taste, but she gradually grew used to it. Joan began another letter and then another, finally letting one slip from her fingers into the mailbox.

They were to begin filming in late April. Joan arrived at the studio early in the morning, hoping to talk to Edward before the others arrived. At that moment, she didn't know what she felt more excited about, seeing Edward or acting in her first major movie role. A warm rush of happiness moved through her in anticipation of both. But these thoughts vanished when she saw a note in her dressing room summoning her to Chin's office. She glanced at the note again, held it in the sweaty palm of her hand, and felt a tinge of fear.

When Joan knocked lightly on Chin's door, his response was sharp and immediate. She quickly entered the dark, smoky room, ready to deny any wrongdoing. She wouldn't be lying. In the photos, they were simply discussing the film project. Neither of them had mentioned anything of a personal nature. Edward had been a perfect gentleman; besides, at the time she wasn't interested in a relationship. Her career had been foremost in her mind, Joan thought to herself. Chin had nothing on her, except a glossy eight-by-ten photo showing them whispering so close together, you couldn't fit a piece of paper between them.

Chin was sitting at his desk, looking stern and serious. The first thing Joan noticed was that his hands were resting palms down on top of his desk. A ribbon of smoke rose from the cigarette burning in the ashtray next to him, instead of dangling from his lips.

"You asked to see me?" Joan's throat felt dry, parched.

"Come in, come in," Chin urged, smiling too widely.

He pointed to a chair that Joan had seen directors, actors, and producers sitting in, but never her. That morning, she had prepared herself for spring, dressing in a pale green dress, pink scarf wrapped loosely around her neck, dark sunglasses. She sat down in the chair, felt awkward, out of place.

"Is there anything wrong?" she asked, not bothering to hide.

Chin smiled. "It's been brought to my attention"—he paused and cleared his throat, a raspy, hollow sound. A smoker's voice—"that you've become quite good friends with Mr. Chung."

Joan let out a quick breath. "All just movie-magazine rubbish," she heard herself saying, though all her life she'd sworn by them. "We were just discussing the movie. You know how noisy it can be at the Pen. We sat close together in order to hear each other."

Chin nodded his head, watching her. "It makes me feel much better to hear you tell me this. You know I never listen to rumors without going straight to the persons involved. This company is built on trust and respect. We are like a family, and family members can be honest with each other. . . ."

Joan's thoughts drifted. She wondered if Chin had talked to Edward yet, then remembered she had been the first one in that morning. If he also denied any wrongdoing, Chin might be satisfied. He was just giving them a warning, not wanting to jeopardize the movie.

". . . Marriage being a sacred bond, it doesn't look good if one of my married directors is, let's say, keeping time with one of my unmarried actresses. . . ."

Joan's head jerked up. "Married?" she asked under her breath.

"What did you say?"

The room reeked of smoke, made her feel sick to her stomach. "Nothing," she said, swallowing. "Just that you're right. The last thing needed during the filming is a scandal. There're enough things to worry about." Joan felt the bitterness on the tip of her tongue.

"I knew you would understand." Chin picked up another cigarette and lit it. "This movie is going to make you a big star. I would hate to see anything happen after you've come so far."

Joan nodded and stood up. Her legs felt rubbery. "There's nothing to worry about. There's nothing between us." She forced a quick smile.

Chin picked up his cigarette and inhaled. He blew out a cloud of smoke that rose up toward the ceiling. "Good, good. It's what I thought. These rumors are just a nuisance."

Joan took a step toward the door, willed herself to walk out of Chin's office. She'd given him the best performance of her life. Once the door was closed behind her, Joan leaned against a wall for support. She closed her eyes and tried to clear her head of Chin's words, which swept over her again like a tidal wave. *Married!* How could she be so stupid? Why hadn't anyone ever mentioned he was married? Even Jade Wind didn't know. It was as if Joan's lungs were slowly filling up with water. *Breathe, breathe,* she thought to herself, forcing air in and out. In the near distance, she heard a door open . . . close, then felt a cool breeze rise up and brush the back of her neck, chilling her to the bone.

From that morning on, Joan threw her heart and soul into making *A Woman's Story* and herself a success. The fate of Lily Wong loomed heavily in her mind as she sat nervously waiting for Edward at his apartment.

Her once soft, loving words turned quick and hard. "Now that we've begun filming, I don't think we should see each other," she said, furious, yet unable to accuse him of being married. The word still felt thick and heavy on her tongue.

Edward's eyes grew wide with surprise as he reached out for her, held her at arm's length by the shoulders. "What are you talking about? What's going on?"

Joan lowered her eyes, away from his stare. "I have to go!" she said, knocking his hand from her shoulder, her voice breaking, shattering like glass.

Joan tried to remain as detached and professional as she could, refusing to speak to him unless it was about the movie, anesthetizing herself from every aspect of Edward Chung that had once given her such happiness. It hurt to hear his soft voice even as her director telling her to "move a little to the left" or to "brush your hair away from your face." It was still too intimate, as if it were just the two of them together again. And like a last dance, Joan gave a perfect performance, allowing her emotions to emerge through her acting. She laughed, cried, and screamed on cue.

"Love you? I've never loved you! It's just been a stupid game I've been playing," she rehearsed her lines over and over.

According to Jade Wind, there were already rumors circulating that Joan was giving the best performance of her career, and that this movie would certainly secure her rise to stardom.

On the set during a break from filming, Chung pleaded with her, "Talk to me! If this is about Chin, don't let him scare you. He knows all the rumors will just generate more publicity for the film."

Joan glared straight ahead. She noticed Edward had waited until the set had completely cleared. Anger welled up inside her to think that he was still protecting himself.

"There's nothing to talk about! Let's just make the best movie we can and forget everything else," she said coldly. She glanced sideways at him, saw that he was upset, his usually calm face flushed.

"What's going on?" He grabbed hold of her arm. "Will you talk to me!"

Joan pulled out of his grasp. "Let's just say I've wised up. I trust you can keep our relationship on a professional basis from now on." She turned away from him. "I have to go. I'm late for my costume change."

Chung didn't give up. He followed her from one set to another. "Leave me alone," she snapped.

"What's wrong with you?"

Joan swung around unexpectedly. "Save the concern for your wife!" she hissed.

Chung stopped and fell back a step as if he'd been hit. Still, he didn't miss a beat. "How do you know? We haven't been together in years."

"Are you still married?" Joan asked, her eyes straining against tears.

Chung looked away from her. "Yes. But she lives her own life in Shanghai."

Joan summoned all her courage. She could feel the warmth of his body standing there, hear the soft sigh as he released a breath. Joan didn't dare look at him as she said in a businesslike voice, "Then it's settled. From this moment on, completing this movie is our only reason for having to speak to each other. When we've finished it, I don't want to ever see you again!" She spit out the words as hard and final as stone.

Joan turned around and kept walking. This time Chung didn't follow her. For a brief moment, Joan thought she heard some soft whisper telling her to stop, though it was lost in the wind whistling through the hollow set.

Joan had returned home late almost every evening since *A Woman's Story* began filming. Mah-mee and Auntie Go were just finishing dinner when she entered the dining room.

"You look tired," Auntie Go said, putting down her bowl.

"What is that director doing making you work so late?" Mah-mee asked, scooping rice into Joan's bowl. "I have just the thing for those dark circles under your eyes."

Joan's eyes burned. Her mouth felt dry and sour. For the past few days she had felt nauseated. "I'm not very hungry," she managed to say.

"Nonsense! You have to eat. How are you going to complete this film if you don't keep up your strength?" Mah-mee spooned more chicken into her bowl.

Joan fell into her chair. How was she going to finish making this film? She forced herself to eat what was in her bowl so she wouldn't have to talk. They couldn't know that acting was the only thing keeping her going now or else she would simply wilt away.

Foon brought her a bowl of soup made out of astragalus roots and wild berries. "Give you strength," she whispered, her voice unusually gentle.

Again sleep eluded Joan. At moments it teased her, allowing her to forget, to rest her eyes for a short while. Then, the smallest sound would awaken her—the distant barking of a dog, a door creaking open, a sudden sigh. The less she slept, the more acute her hearing became. After days of not enough sleep, there was a constant dull throbbing at the back of her head. She lay in bed watching the light turn slowly from a soft black to gray, the outlines of her room growing into focus. Her head throbbed with the need to be part of his life, the thought of his touch, his body lying next to her. *If I could just sleep,* she thought to herself. *If I could just close my eyes and forget.*

"Drink this," Foon said as soon as Joan came home the next evening. Her devoted servant took her script, her purse, her sweater, peeling away the layers of her day. "Drink!" she commanded again. Joan drank, tasting the bitterness, then the relief of being guided in a direction, taken care of. She was led to her room by Foon, helped to undress, and laid gently down on her bed. As Joan closed her eyes, her head began to throb and her stomach felt queasy, yet she could feel the unexpected and comforting presence of Foon sitting beside her. She smelled garlic and herbs, heard Foon saying, "Sleep, sleep," in a light, careful command. Joan tried to say something back, but her voice felt thick and fuzzy. "What would I do without you. . . ." echoed through her head. She wanted to thank Foon, but instead slipped into sleep with such ease, she barely had time to think about wanting it.

Forever

Waiting —

1957—58

EMMA

Emma sat on the scuffed hardwood floor of her studio apartment on the first weekend in October and tightly bound another orange crate filled with her books. For the past few weeks, she'd been dragging back empty apple, orange, and banana crates and boxes from the Golden Harvest Market around the corner from the Rec Center. After nearly three years at the Bellevue Apartments for Women, Emma was ecstatic to be moving into a larger apartment of her own near Lone Mountain, off of Geary Boulevard.

Wearing an old shirt tied at the waist and a pair of baggy jeans rolled up at the cuffs, Emma forced herself to pack the next shelf of books, which ranged alphabetically from Austen to Wharton, without stopping to examine or flip through each one. She was rarely without a book tucked under her arm or stuffed into her handbag when she rode the bus to and from work in Chinatown. The old childhood habit stayed with her right through college and into her working years. Each story still cast a spell on her, sent Emma soaring through history and countries, fighting wars and falling in love.

Lately, she'd realized more than ever how much she needed these precious books. The pages helped to fill an increasing void in her life. At twenty-six, Emma was still working as a secretary at the Chinese Recreation Center. Not that it wasn't a good job, mostly due to Wilson Chang, who was not only a wonderful boss but had also become a close friend. But something had changed in the past year, a feeling of stagnation had crept into her bones like a dull ache. Her temporary job had become fixed in cement. Half of the time Emma wondered what difference it made to have a college degree.

Then as summer moved into the bittersweet days of autumn, Emma decided it was time to move. She hoped that if the walls around her changed, her life would too. She wrote Mah-mee . . . *I've outgrown the small studio* . . . then could almost hear her mother's sharp voice asking Auntie Go, "When will she forget all this nonsense and just come home?"

"Is there anything wrong?" Wilson asked, his presence a sudden surprise.

He stood at her open doorway as Emma quickly jumped up amidst her jungle of boxes and crates. She'd forgotten he had volunteered to help her move. As always, Wilson was wonderful, giving her Friday off from the Center to pack, and now arriving bright and early on Saturday morning to help her move. Emma knew that somewhere along the line, he was the brother she had never had.

"No," Emma said, brushing her hair back with her fingers, hooking it behind her ear. "I was just thinking about the move."

"I have this theory about thinking too much." He smiled. "It only gives you a headache."

Emma smiled back and nodded. Wilson always had kind, comforting words.

"I brought a friend along to help," Wilson continued. "He's downstairs waiting with the van."

"How can I thank you," Emma said, turning serious. "I don't know how I would have managed—"

"What's in these boxes?" Wilson broke in, picking up a crate and straining against its weight.

"The orange crates are my books." Emma laughed. "I like to read. You haven't even gotten to my art books yet, just wait till you get to the banana boxes!" She pointed to another stack.

"Ever heard of the library?" He smiled.

"I like to own the books I read. Come on, a big, strong jock like you shouldn't have any trouble with a few books."

Wilson laughed, and a boyish grin spread across his face. If not for his thinning hair, it would be hard to guess that he was already thirty-five.

"You owe me," he said, stacking two boxes next to the door.

"Dinner at Mel's," Emma offered.

"I was thinking Ernie's or Alfred's." Wilson stood straight, rubbing his back.

Emma laughed. "Only if my boss gives me a raise."

"Mel's it is," he said, boosting an orange crate to his shoulder and heading downstairs.

Emma returned to packing. The last of her large art books filled a thick, sturdy Chiquita-banana box. Lately, she'd saved money to buy mostly art books—Degas, Klimt, Manet, Matisse. Their glossy pages full of line and color excited and inspired. In her spare time, Emma had begun to draw again, a remnant of her art classes that grew increasingly urgent. It afforded her a sense of freedom her everyday life couldn't provide. Mostly, she worked in charcoal on cheap paper, shaping and shading the faces of her models—the boys who passed through the Rec Center program.

From memory, Emma also drew her family—Ba ba in a dark business suit, Mah-mee at a mah-jongg table, Auntie Go in front of the Western Wind, Joan reflected in a mirror. Even Foon watched her from the walls of her small room. But when their faces became too oppressive, too much a reminder of how her life had ground to a full stop, Emma carefully took down each drawing, wrapped them in tissue paper, and put them all in the closet. She now laid them on top of her art books and quickly sealed the box.

In the closet Emma found a box of letters from her family and Lia. She fingered the neatly tied stacks, slipped out a few envelopes, and opened them in her lap. Time stopped again as the voices of her family whispered over her, embracing Emma. Ba ba's words floated back from last winter, brief but haunting. . . . *It seems the days pass by so quickly. My bones grow brittle with the cold. I've decided to return to Hong Kong in two years or less. Your mah-mee insists that I slow down. It may be time to listen. Perhaps then we will visit you in San Francisco.* Emma stopped reading. It was dated May of this year. With luck, she would still have time to establish a new career before her parents arrived.

Emma smiled at the other letter in her lap. It was Lia's pink envelope and her large, bold writing, postmarked just a month ago. They'd last seen each other more than ten years ago, but the soothing lilt that sang through Lia's words never failed to make Emma happy. Lia was married now, with two small children and another on the way. She worked part-time as a nurse's aide and still hoped to become a full-fledged nurse one day. Emma peeled back the sticky flap of the envelope and glanced at the first page. *Joan's movie* A Woman's Story *just opened here. All Macao is excited. I left the boys with Mamae and took the bus downtown to see it. You would have been proud to see the line in front of the Rialto. She is so* bonita *and is certain to be a big star!* Emma stopped reading. Whenever she thought of Joan's success, a small knot wound tighter in her stomach. She didn't want to jinx Joan's good fortune with her unhappy thoughts, but lately her sister's achievements only emphasized her own deficiencies.

Emma skipped through the rest of Lia's letter to the last page. *After two boys, if this baby is a girl, we've settled on naming her Carmelita Emma Alvarez. I've decided to face these family superstitions head-on. Mamae says it will bring back bad memories that will haunt her grandchild, but I say, how could anyone hurt her own namesake? Besides, she will be named after two strong women. What better way to enter this world? And maybe it will bring you to Macao again.* Emma put down the letter. After so many years, a stabbing ache of homesickness overwhelmed her.

Emma wiped her eyes with the back of her hand when she heard footsteps on the stairs. She didn't want Wilson to see her upset. Quickly she tucked the letters into an opened box and turned around in surprise. Not Wilson, but a taller, thinner man in jeans and a sweatshirt stood in the doorway. He watched her intently, dark eyed and dark complexioned with diluted features that made him appear both Chinese and Caucasian at the same time.

"Hi. You must be Emma. I'm Jack Leung, a friend of Wilson's." His voice, low and soothing, startled her with its warmth and made her flush.

"Yes," she said, standing up and extending her hand. "Thank you for coming to help. I'm really grateful."

"You aren't from San Francisco, are you?"

"Hong Kong." Even with jeans and a shirt on, she was given away by the trace of her accent.

"I was there for a few days several years ago." Jack smiled. "Always wanted to go back."

"You liked Hong Kong then?"

"Yes, very much." He smiled again, a gleam of straight teeth. "Better get to work before Wilson wonders what happened to me.

Are these ready to go?" He pointed at the boxes Wilson had just stacked.

"Yes," she nodded.

He smiled at her, picked up a box, and moved swiftly out the door and back down the stairs.

By late afternoon, her fruit crates and boxes were correctly stacked in the rooms of her new apartment. The place felt huge and hollow—with one bedroom, a living room, a small kitchen, and a breakfast nook.

In the kitchen, Emma unpacked the boxes she'd filled just that morning. All her kitchen utensils, so cramped in her studio at the Bellevue Apartments, scarcely filled the yellow drawers and cabinets. Emma liked the smell of Mr. Clean, and the walls papered in a pattern of yellow and green squash. The apartment felt lived in and comfortable, but scrubbed clean. She smiled to think that Foon would approve.

Emma could hear Wilson and Jack talking in her living room, waiting for her to find cups for their Coca-Cola. She dug through an apple box and found the two blue plastic tumblers she'd bought at Woolworth. Emma fumbled with the bottle opener, flipping the cap off and across the green linoleum. She dropped ice cubes into the tumblers, poured the fizzy cola, filled a plate with peanuts, and hurried into the living room.

"At last!" Wilson said, sitting on one of her yellow vinyl kitchen chairs in the middle of the room. Jack sat next to him, legs crossed, as if they were waiting at a doctor's office.

"You're a slave driver!" Emma laughed, thrilled to be using one of the many slang terms she'd learned since coming to America.

Emma would never forget her early confusion with the English language. It still plagued her, though she understood and spoke as well as most American-born Chinese. She still had some problems with reading the slang-filled, abbreviated newspaper headlines . . . *Elvis Shakes His Pelvis, Freed's Radio Show Rocks 'n' Rolls 'em, Troops Flood Little Rock. . . .* During her first year in San Francisco, Emma felt as if she were learning another language.

"Do you have a radio?" Jack asked, his tennis shoes tapping lightly against the muted brown carpet. His dark eyes followed Emma from the moment she entered the room.

"In one of those boxes," she answered, blushing, careful not to make eye contact with him. She felt hot and slightly uncomfortable.

Emma searched in an apple box in the corner, but Jack lifted her square, brown RCA radio out of a banana box and plugged it in. Static filled the room and grated against their ears.

"Turn it off!" Wilson yelled, laughing.

"Hold on." Jack sprawled on the rug and played with the knob until Pat Boone's syrupy voice leaked into the room crooning "Love Letters in the Sand."

"Please, anything but Pat Boone!" Wilson said, his swirling ice click-clacking against the sides of the tumbler.

Jack spun the dial again through a blur of voices until he found Buddy Holly singing "Peggy Sue." He turned it lower so they could hear each other talk, only to have them all suddenly grow quiet.

"Peggy Sue, Peggy Sue, I love you." Jack's fingers tapped against the top of the radio. Emma couldn't take her eyes off his ring, gold with some kind of insignia etched on it.

"What do you say I take us all out for dinner?" Wilson suggested. "Chinatown? North Beach? Your choice."

"It's my treat, remember?" Emma said, glancing first at Wilson, then at Jack. "You've both been so nice to help with the move."

Jack drank the remainder of his Coke, then raised himself off the rug. "I'd love to, but I'm afraid I'll have to take a rain check. I'm on duty tonight."

"Duty?" Emma asked.

Wilson answered, "Jack's in the army. He's stationed at the Presidio. A real Korean War hero!"

"Get out of here," Jack teased back. He arched his back, then stood up straight, tall and square-shouldered.

Emma now wondered how she could have missed all the clues. He even stood like a soldier at ease, feet spread apart and hands clasped behind his back. Standing next to him, Emma felt short, though she reached his shoulder. Wilson, at five feet six, was scarcely an inch taller than she.

"Give me a call," Jack said to Wilson, who remained seated.

"In a day or two. Thanks, buddy."

Emma walked Jack to the door, stood in the cool breeze, and pulled her cotton cardigan tightly around her. She extended her hand for him to shake. "Thank you again for all your help."

He shook her hand, then, still holding it, leaned closer and whispered, "I really mean it about that rain check for dinner. I'll talk to you soon."

Jack stepped back and winked, then walked quickly down the concrete steps, the warmth from his hand still tingling in hers.

The weariness pulled at Emma as soon as Wilson brought her home from dinner and left her alone in her new apartment. She walked through each room, trying to dispel the strangeness, the boxes stacked and waiting to be unpacked. She boiled some hot water to make tea and drank it sitting in the living room on the same vinyl kitchen chair Jack had sat on. She wondered what he looked like in his uniform and smiled to herself. A soldier. Emma sipped her tea and thought about the way Jack's dark eyes followed her around the room, how quickly he moved, working as hard as any of them, though he didn't even know her. Why hadn't Wilson ever mentioned this friend before?

Just a few hours earlier, she and Wilson had sat in his DeSoto and ate hamburgers and french fries at Mel's Drive-in. She thought of their easy conversation, the greasy smell of onions and fries, the coolness of the strawberry milk shake sliding down her throat. Emma didn't want to ask too many questions about Jack, but did manage to nonchalantly inquire, "How long has Jack been in the army?"

Wilson chewed thoughtfully before answering, "Enlisted right out of high school. He was the younger brother of a friend of mine. Half-Chinese, half-Portuguese. Always a good kid. He's a second lieutenant, career officer. Some kind of sonar specialist now, I think. Good-looking, huh?"

Emma grew warm, began nibbling on a french fry. "It was nice of him to come help move."

"Jack's a good guy. We made sure to keep in touch, especially after his brother was killed."

"In Korea?"

"No. In a Chinatown shooting. Got mixed up with the gangs in high school. One of the reasons I got involved with the Rec Center." Wilson stuffed the last of his hamburger into his mouth.

Emma remained quiet. She couldn't begin to count how many different worlds revolved around her. How awful it must have been for Jack to have his brother killed. Even worse than the pain Lia must have felt when her brother died. After all, she didn't even have the chance to know him. And how important it was to have someone like Wilson to provide programs that kept kids off the streets. He was probably one of the nicest guys she'd ever meet, so different from the Hong King boys who had been weaned on their family's money.

"I have a friend whose brother choked to death. But he was a baby, and it was an accident. I can't imagine what I'd do if something happened to my sister, Joan." A shiver moved up Emma's spine.

Wilson shook his head. "It's scary to think how easy it is to lose someone you love."

Emma heard the slurpy sound of Wilson's straw sucking up the last of his chocolate shake. He picked up the bill when it came, taking a rain check for a home-cooked dinner when Emma was ready to test out her new kitchen. *Rain check* seemed like such a silly word to define her new social life.

When Emma finally lay in her familiar bed in the strange new bedroom, she closed her eyes and roamed from room to room, through the blur of the last few days. Sleep finally came as a dream in which Emma was falling, falling. Below her she saw only darkness, felt the continuous flight downward. Only when Emma surrendered to the void did she feel her descent slowed down, feel a pair of strong hands break her fall. But close as they held her, Emma couldn't see in the dark whose face it was.

Jack came to her in a whirlwind at the end of the following week. She was sitting at her metal-gray desk next to Wilson's office and jumped when the front door banged open with a gust of cold wind. *Those kids again,* was her first thought. Emma sprawled forward on her desk, trying to hold down stray papers. Her bag lunch hit the floor and a jar of pencils scattered after it. When she looked up, Jack was standing in the doorway. He looked handsome and official in his army uniform, even with the large rubber plant he carried in one arm. He set it on the floor beside her desk.

"I'm sorry. The wind's a wild thing today." He turned to close the door and she stood up, hastily adjusting her cardigan. "How are you? Getting settled into your new apartment?" He set her lunch sack on the desk.

Emma gathered a bunch of pencils, cleared her throat. "I'm fine," she managed to say, staring at his pressed dark green jacket, beige shirt, and slacks.

"I thought I'd bring you a small housewarming gift."

"Thank you." Emma touched the rubber plant, stroked a thick, green leaf. "It's beautiful."

He glanced at all the team photos lining the wall behind her. "Looks like Wilson's doing a great job."

"He is. Do you want to see him?"

Jack pinched the creases in his hat and frowned at it. "Well, actually I dropped by to talk to you."

Emma grew warm, certain her face had turned scarlet. "You did?"

He licked his lips. "I was wondering, if you weren't busy Saturday night . . . if you might like to go to dinner?" He crossed his arms below a single row of red and yellow ribbon.

Emma snapped a rubber band around the bunch of pencils, turned them around and around in her hands. "This Saturday?"

"I could pick you up at seven," Jack added with a smile.

"I . . . Yes." Emma pulled a pencil out and wrote down her phone number. "Here." She handed him the paper. "Just in case you need to get hold of me."

"Thanks." Jack slipped the piece of paper into his jacket pocket. "Saturday at seven." He smiled wide and backed up, then raised his hand in a cockeyed salute.

When he opened the door, the wind played around Emma again, rustling the papers that lifted from her desk like happiness and floated gently to the floor.

When Emma left work on Friday afternoon, she didn't mention her dinner plans with Jack to Wilson.

"See you Monday," he said as she was leaving. "Got any hot plans, or are you just going to stay around the apartment?"

Emma grabbed her coat. "I'll probably do some unpacking,"

she answered, her voice catching. She opened the drawer to re-
trieve her purse.

"Yeah, sounds good." His fingers played with the whistle around
his neck. "Have a good one then."

"You too."

Wilson nodded.

All the way home on the bus, Emma couldn't read a word of
her book, *Peyton Place*, without wondering why she just didn't
come out and tell Wilson about her dinner date with Jack.

On Saturday, Jack arrived promptly at seven, wearing a dark
jacket and tie instead of his uniform. "Only when necessary," he
said, registering her quick stare. "I prefer to look like everyone
else."

"Would you like something to drink? Coke? Coffee or tea?"
Emma asked, surprised he knew what she was thinking.

He glanced at his watch. "We have seven-thirty reservations.
Better get going." He held the door open for her. "By the way, you
look great."

Emma blushed, muttered a quick "Thank you."

She'd spent all afternoon deciding what to wear, finally settling
on a blue silk cheungsam. She hadn't worn one since she'd double-
dated with Sylvia Lu in college. When Emma first stepped into the
cool silk and snapped each frog, she felt strange and foreign in it.
Glancing into the mirror, she no longer looked like the Hong Kong
girl who first came to San Francisco. Still, she certainly wasn't the
American one who danced to Elvis Presley and swooned every
time he shook his hips. Emma hovered just beyond the both of
them.

*   *   *

Dinner was at the New Pisa restaurant on upper Grant Avenue in North Beach. Emma sat across from Jack, the candle between them flickering a soft yellow light as she sipped the too tart glass of wine, which went straight to her head. She found herself telling him all about her family. Ba ba in Tokyo, Mah-mee in Hong Kong, Auntie Go and the Western Wind, her sister, Joan, the actress, and of course Foon and her wonderful cooking.

"They sound wonderful," he said, cutting into his cannelloni. "I'm afraid my life hasn't been nearly as exciting. I grew up with my mother and brother. My father took off by the time I was five. My brother, Frank, was almost ten. We lived in an apartment just outside of Chinatown."

"Your mother is Portuguese?" Emma asked, spearing a ravioli, the sauce potent and garlicky.

Jack nodded. "Her family's from Macao originally. She met my father over here."

"We lived in Macao during the occupation. It really was a safe haven."

"My mother left there when she was just a little girl." He took a sip of his wine. "Tell me what you liked best about being there."

Emma swallowed some water. So many things came to mind— Lia, music, St. Paul's, the lazy tropical days, the language. . . . "The people. And their kindness."

At the door Jack held her hand in his for the longest time. They hardly spoke, but she felt cold when he released her hand and broke the connection.

Later that night, Emma rummaged breathlessly through her box of letters, looking for the one she'd received from Joan several months ago. When she found the thin white envelope, the faint smell of My Sin still remained. Emma skimmed the short letter to the last lines. *I've met someone. He isn't at all the type you'd expect me* to have fallen for. *Much more serious and intellectual. Mah-mee and Auntie Go don't know a thing. I can only tell you that he's in the business and that I'm in love.*

Emma slipped the letter back into the box, her rapid thoughts already making plans—tell Wilson on Monday about Jack, unpack the rest of the boxes, wait for Jack's call, write another letter to Joan saying, *I know exactly how you feel.*

chapter 14

A

Woman's

Story —

1959—61

JOAN

Joan waited in C. K. Chin's office. The morning sunlight bleached the room in a harsh light. She sat in one of the new black leather chairs in front of his desk. Not even the rich smell of leather could overcome the years of stale cigarette smoke embedded in the rug and walls. Joan glanced down at her watch. Chin was late.

After Joan's success in *A Woman's Story* came two more films, *Day After Day* and *The Final Hour.* Posters of all three movies hung on the dark wall in Chin's office, a space he reserved for his most successful films. She could scarcely believe it was her own face staring back at her. From where she sat, Joan saw traces of Mah-mee watching over her. She looked at her watch again and was just about to get up and leave when the door banged open and Chin hurried into his office.

"Joan, Joan . . . I'm sorry to be so late." Chin leaned over and kissed her on the cheek. "Problems on the *Typhoon* set." He sighed, his breath stale with smoke.

"You needed to see me?"

Chin hesitated, sat down in the chair next to hers and crossed his legs. Away from his desk, he looked awkward and out of place. "I need to ask you a little favor." Chin smiled, his eyes narrowing. "I have the perfect movie for you, only . . . only it can't wait until you return from your trip."

Joan stood up. "No. My sister's expecting me in San Francisco in two weeks, and that's final."

Chin reached out, touched her arm, his hand moist and sweaty. "Postpone it. It will be worth your while. Joan, do this for me, and it'll make you a bigger star than you already are."

"Another singsong girl?"

"Not exactly." Chin laughed. "Though the character is a woman who struggles to be understood by society. But believe me, it's an entirely fresh approach to the theme. Just take a look at the script."

"No," she repeated, grabbing her purse. "Now, if you'll excuse me, I'm late for an appointment."

"I'm not asking you to make up your mind now. Take a day or two. I'll have a script sent to you. Just remember, an actress's fame can be fleeting. It's always wise to strike the iron when it's hot." Chin rose, flipped open his gold cigarette case, and reached for the gold lighter on his desk. He flicked it twice before the flame flared up and lit the cigarette dangling from his lips.

Joan hadn't expected her meeting with Chin to take so long. She dashed through Kai Tak Airport, late and out of breath by the time she reached Gate 2A, where a small crowd waited. Ba ba's plane had just landed. Joan leaned against the wall beside the window, her sundress sticking to her back, her dark glasses sliding down her nose.

Outside, waves of heat rose from the black surface where the Pan Am plane had rolled to a stop. Just then, she saw the door slide open, and one by one the passengers walked carefully down the silver steps and across the tarmac to the terminal. Joan dabbed at her forehead with a tissue, afraid to blink and miss Ba ba. She hadn't seen her father since he'd returned from Japan for the premiere of her first starring movie, *A Woman's Story*.

"Make sure you get there on time," Mah-mee had told her the night before. "Are you certain I shouldn't take a taxi and meet you there?"

"I have a meeting with Chin at the Tiger Claw. I'll pick Ba ba up afterward and bring him right home," Joan said, her voice calm and gentle. She was looking forward to spending some time alone with him.

"Just be there on time," Mah-mee insisted, pacing back and forth between the sofa and the terrace doors. "You know Ba ba hasn't been well."

Joan looked twice before she recognized his gaunt, pale figure walking down the stairs from the plane. Her heart ached to see how much he had aged in the last two years. She took off her sunglasses, brushed her hair back. "Ba ba!" she called as soon as he stepped into the building. When he looked up, she saw a hint of the handsome man he had been.

"How is my movie-star daughter?" he asked, dropping his briefcase and hugging her tight.

"She's awfully glad to see you." Joan felt only skin and bones through his jacket. "Let me take that." She grabbed his briefcase, then took his arm and led him to the baggage claim.

As their taxi wound through Kowloon and back to Hong Kong, Ba ba stared out the window for the longest time. After a while, he sat back and murmured, "So many people." Then, as if remembering Joan was next to him, he turned and asked, "Isn't your studio somewhere around here?"

Joan nodded. "A couple of blocks that way." She pointed past him out the window. "Now that you're home again, I'll take you on a tour."

Ba ba smiled, wiping his forehead with his handkerchief. "You know, at first I wasn't terribly happy when you wanted to become an actress. I was afraid that you might be disappointed by such a difficult business."

"But . . ."

Ba ba put his thin, veined hand on hers. "But, I've always remembered how well you did collecting my receipts before the war. I knew you could do whatever you set your mind to. Both of you girls. It is a hard enough world without having your family against you."

"What if I had failed?" Joan said softly, more to herself than aloud.

Ba ba heard. "But you didn't."

Joan swallowed, a lump in her throat. The hot, humid air was suffocating. She closed her eyes behind her dark glasses. As they glided through the narrow, crowded streets of Kowloon, Joan took her father's hand in hers and held it tight.

Six months after Ba ba returned to Hong Kong, Joan moved into her own apartment on Magazine Gap Road. It had a large living room, two bedrooms, and a narrow kitchen she rarely had time to cook in. Usually, she ate out or, at least three times a week, had dinner with her parents and Auntie Go. Every time she ran up the stone steps at her parents', she could smell Foon's cooking and almost guess which dishes she had made for dinner. Tonight, they were having beef with garlic and ginger. When she opened the front door, Joan heard low voices coming from the living room.

Mah-mee stood by the piano. It hadn't been played since Emma left for America. Mah-mee's eyes were swollen, as if she'd been crying. Auntie Go sat quietly on the sofa.

"What's the matter?" Joan asked, her mouth dry. "Where's Ba ba?"

Auntie Go answered, "He's in the room resting. We received a telegram from Emma today."

"Is she all right?"

Mah-mee's voice, tight as wire, rang through the room. "Your sister was married three days ago." A small vein on the side of her forehead throbbed.

"To Jack?" Joan asked, caught off guard.

Mah-mee's eyes darted back to her. "You know?" she asked accusingly.

"Then she's known him for a while?" Auntie Go asked, a sliver of relief in her voice.

Joan put down her jacket and purse. "Emma's been seeing him for the past year."

"And you've kept this Jack person a secret?" Mah-mee continued, her eyebrows rising.

"I promised—"

"You might have prevented this marriage!" Mah-mee accused.

"Kum Ling, listen to yourself," Auntie Go interrupted. "Joan was just doing what moi-moi asked her."

Mah-mee pressed her lips tightly together, crumpled the telegram in her hand. "After she graduated, I should have insisted she return with you, Go. All this art nonsense. And then wasting time working in San Francisco. I could have found her a good match here! Now she's married to a person we know nothing about. Who's his family? What does he do?"

Joan watched the tiny wrinkles that spread from the corners of her mother's mouth. "Emma loves him. Isn't that enough?" Joan's words slipped out before she had time to think.

Mah-mee glared at her. "No, sometimes love is not enough. She should have never gone to America in the first place!"

"The best thing that could have happened to Emma was going to America! Why can't you just be happy for her? For anyone?" Joan said, her anger rising.

"Just because you're a big movie star doesn't mean you know everything about life!" Mah-mee drew in a breath, then spit out, "Or love!"

"I know more than you'll ever realize!"

Mah-mee's eyes narrowed. She turned away from Joan and said in a dead tone, "If that's what you think. Both my daughters seem to think they know everything!"

Auntie Go stood up and walked over to Mah-mee, taking the telegram from her, then folding it neatly along its creases. "You can't dictate fate, Kum Ling. Whether you agree with them or not, everyone has their own life to live."

"You can agree all you want, Go," Mah-mee snapped. "Owning your own business doesn't give you authority over my daughters!"

Then Mah-mee turned and walked out of the living room, her heels clapping against the wood floor. Her bedroom door whined open, then slammed behind her.

That night Joan soaked in a hot bath until her pale skin turned pink from the heat. The water covered her breasts and leveled just under her chin. She allowed her body to float upward—her toes, a patch of dark hair, her nipples rising to the surface.

"Moi-moi's a married woman now. A wife . . ." Joan said the word aloud, getting used to the taste of it in her mouth. Other words followed, ones that lay heavy on her tongue . . . "single, spinster, old maid." They felt muffled, softer in the thick fog of the steam-filled bathroom.

"Single, spinster, old maid!" Joan said louder, laughing to herself. At thirty-three, she refused to accept titles that sounded like children's games.

Joan floated in the warm water. She still thought about Edward Chung, who had returned to Shanghai two years ago. Rumors circulated that he was trying to revive the Shanghai film industry to its former glory, but was having difficulties with the Communist government. Joan placed her hand on her flat stomach, wondering how her life might have been if she'd had the child. It wasn't until several weeks after they'd finished shooting *A Woman's Story* that she even realized she was pregnant. Joan had panicked, then felt nauseated every morning, and tried to hide it from Mah-mee and Foon. She wanted to tell Auntie Go, but decided to put her trust in Jade Wind.

"What do I do?" Joan asked, closing the door to her dressing room.

"How far along are you?" Jade Wind asked.

Joan shook her head. "I'm not sure. The month of filming and then three weeks afterward. Close to two months."

Jade Wind paced back and forth, then stopped abruptly. "I can find out where to go to get rid of it. Several of the actresses here have had it done. And they're fine. . . ." Her voice trailed off.

Joan leaned against the door, beginning to feel sick again. "I can't," she whispered.

"Are you going to tell him?"

"I can't."

Two days later Joan woke up with a terrible cramping. By the time she made it to the bathroom, the problem had solved itself. But time and again since then, she had felt the soft pull of life that had been inside her.

Joan held her breath and slid down under the water. She cleared her mind and tried to remember an early letter from Emma all about Jack. *He's a good friend of Wilson's . . . half-Chinese and half-Portuguese . . . good-looking . . . His being of mixed blood won't go over well with Mah-mee. . . . He doesn't have a college degree . . . wants a career in the army. . . . He's good and kind. . . . I've never been happier. . . .*

Joan stepped out of the tub and wrapped herself in a towel. The cool air raised goose bumps on her stomach and legs. She glanced toward the mirror, but couldn't see a thing in all the heat and steam and didn't bother to wipe it off.

She slipped into a white silk robe, then went straight to her desk to write a telegram to Emma.

> *Congratulations on your marriage. A new movie project means postponing my trip a couple of months . . . give you time for a honeymoon. You deserve to be happy.*
> *Don't worry about Mah-mee, she'll get used to the idea.*
> *Much love, Joan*

Sunrise —

1963–64

Auntie Go

Death came quickly to Lew Hing, and not without pain. The year he returned to Hong Kong from Japan, he was already thin and weak. In the hospital, when the cancer was diagnosed, Kum Ling accepted the doctor's words as if she were tasting something too cold. The words froze in midair: "In the pancreas . . . Too far gone . . . nothing we can do . . . Make him comfortable. . . . I am sorry. . . ." When Auntie Go reached out to comfort Kum Ling, Go felt a chill spread from her cousin's hand to hers and up and down her body.

In the taxi home from the hospital, Kum Ling had thawed and couldn't stop talking.

"We will take him home," she said, twisting the diamond wedding ring on her finger. "I'll move into Joan's room. He'll be more comfortable that way. I have to remember . . . remember to tell Foon to buy some . . . some cat's-paw grass to make a soup. The girls. I have to tell the girls. . . ."

Auntie Go put her hand on Kum Ling's to pull her back, slow her down. It now felt warm and clammy. "Joan is coming over later this evening. We'll tell her then. I'll send a telegram to moi-moi. There's nothing they can do now, Kum Ling. It's better not to disrupt their lives any more than we have to."

"Yes. Yes, you're right, Go."

"We'll have Foon make some *po lai* tea when we get back, and then you can lie down for a while. There's plenty of time for everything else."

Kum Ling nodded. She turned and stared out the window, her eyes fixed on the passing streets. Go watched Kum Ling's reflection in the glass, the vacant eyes, the creamy, smooth skin, the full lips pressed tightly together. At fifty-nine, she was still very beautiful, not a gray hair on her head, while Go seemed to have turned gray overnight.

"Do you remember?" Kum Ling asked all of a sudden, still facing the window.

"Remember what?"

"Our wedding." Kum Ling said, turning back toward Auntie Go.

Go smiled. "How could I forget? It was a beautiful wedding."

"I was so young, sixteen. I refused to go by sedan chair, you know. Mah-mee wanted me to, but I refused. Money was tight. 'He has seen me already,' I told her. 'What do I need to hide for?' When the marriage broker told Hing's family, they were appalled, but

Hing wasn't. He simply said, 'She's right.' How could I have not loved him for all these years, through all the good and bad?"

"He's a good man," Go whispered.

"I haven't always been easy. Not for any of you."

Auntie Go didn't know what to say. For so many years they'd been arguing on different sides of the wall, it felt strange to be sitting close to each other now in total agreement. "Neither of us has been easy," Go said, "but, can you imagine our lives any other way?" Auntie Go gave her cousin's hand a squeeze.

Kum Ling smiled. Her lips parted to say something, but froze again. Instead, Auntie Go felt Kum Ling move closer, closing the small space that still divided them.

"Eat, eat!" Foon commanded. "No use to Lew *seen-san* sick." She dished rice into Kum Ling's bowl and stood beside her until she raised her chopsticks.

Joan leaned over and whispered to Auntie Go, "Do they know how long?" It was the first full sentence she'd said since hearing the news about her father. The words came out sharp and sad.

"Six months, more or less," Auntie Go whispered back.

"But that's so little time," Joan mumbled, more to herself than to Auntie Go.

"What was that?" Kum Ling asked, cradling the untouched bowl of rice in the palm of her hand.

"I think it might be better if I move back home for a little while," Joan quickly answered.

"Nonsense!" Kum Ling snapped, her old spirit returning. "You have your own apartment now. An actress needs a quiet place to study her lines."

Auntie Go smiled hearing the same advice she had once given Kum Ling now repeated in her cousin's voice.

"But, you'll need . . . " Joan protested.

"If I need anything, I'll ask," Kum Ling said, ending the small struggle.

Joan picked at her food. "What about Emma?"

"I was going to telegram her tomorrow," Auntie Go said. "She must have her hands full with the baby and their move to the new house."

"Please," Joan asked, "please let me do it?"

Auntie Go watched Joan's face, flawless as her mother's. After all her years of pretending before a mirror, she'd become a big star in her first starring movie, *A Woman's Story*. Since then, Go detected a profound change in her. Joan's nervous energy had calmed. It seemed she had discovered something much more important than fame—an understanding of who she was, and what she could do.

"Of course." Auntie Go smiled. "Tell her not to worry, he's being well taken care of."

Joan nodded. With her chopsticks she raised a piece of Chinese mustard green to her mouth, then let it fall back to her bowl.

Kum Ling refused to let Auntie Go spend the night with her. "I'm all right, Go. Foon's here. You have a business to run and have to be up early. Tomorrow I'll make arrangements with the hospital to bring Hing home. Please, go home."

Auntie Go hesitated, then saw in Kum Ling's eyes that she meant what she said. "I'll talk to you tomorrow morning."

"Fine, fine," Kum Ling said, holding the front door open. "Thank you, Go," she whispered as a cool November wind whistled up the stone steps. "For all these years." Then Kum Ling quickly closed the door between them.

Auntie Go started to walk down the block to her flat, then changed her mind and caught a taxi to Kowloon. Her keys jingled on the ring as she unlocked the door of the Western Wind. When she stepped in and turned on the overhead lights, the bright, white glare startled her. The slightly sour smell of wool and metal reached her first. The idle machines were silent. Just the sight of them brought back the phantom swishing sounds that filled her days. Go had no idea why she had returned to the factory at this time of the night, but she locked the front door behind her and with slow, deliberate steps climbed the stairs to her office.

"Why here?" Auntie Go whispered to herself, though she didn't have an answer. She entered her office, flipped on a softer lamplight, poured herself a sherry, and sat down at her cluttered desk. Auntie Go sipped the sweet wine, then leaned back in her chair, closing her eyes as the alcohol flowed through her blood, warming her body.

Go thought of how some memories hung on like small burdens. Even held back, they pushed forward, reentering her life as if they belonged in the present. And now was no exception. She knew why she had returned to the Western Wind. It was here in her office that Lew Hing had come to see her so many years ago. Auntie Go counted back the years. It was over fifteen now, though she could still feel his presence as if it were yesterday.

He had knocked and entered her office so quietly, she might not have looked up if it wasn't for the sudden loud waves of swishing and the strong, sweet scent of his cologne, which preceded him.

"Hing!" Go had said, surprised.

He smiled, put down his suitcase, and stood there pressing the rim of his hat between his fingers. "I've just flown in from Tokyo. I came here straight from the airport."

"Is there anything wrong? Kum Ling? The girls?" Auntie Go asked, half rising from her chair.

Hing shook his head, lifted his hands in explanation, but they remained suspended in the air. "I . . . I came to talk to you."

Auntie Go sat back down, relieved. Her next thought was that he'd come about the job offer they'd discussed months before. She gestured for him to sit down, but Lew Hing fingered a button on his overcoat and remained standing.

"We could certainly use your help here," Go said, hoping to ease into the conversation and make him more comfortable, "A man of your business sense—"

"You don't understand," Hing interrupted. "What I'm about to say comes after a great deal of thought. You know that I love Kum Ling with all my heart. . . ."

Auntie Go stood up slowly, matching his height. "What are you trying to tell me?" she asked, hoping to the gods that what she feared was just some kind of misunderstanding.

He ran his fingers through his hair, looked Go in the eyes, and said, "There's been someone else for a long time now."

Go stood there, stunned. In their younger days, Kum Ling had traveled with him as much as she could, even when her fear of flying increased, and she left the girls with Go and Foon for weeks at a time. But as the girls grew older, Kum Ling elected to remain in Hong Kong, while Lew Hing conducted his business in Tokyo. Go could well imagine that they might have grown apart over the years.

"Is she in Tokyo?"

"No," he answered, looking away. "She's here."

Go felt the heat of anger rising. She leaned forward, her arms braced against her desk. "Here! How?" She tried to steady her voice.

Lew Hing clutched his hat tighter. "Here. Right here in this room." A smile transformed his face.

For a moment, Auntie Go didn't understand. Then she stepped back. "What?" she whispered.

"I've loved you for a very long time." Hing's words came quickly now. "You needn't say anything, Go. Lives are fated to take different paths. I know this. Kum Ling will always be my wife whom I dearly love. But, I couldn't let my life pass by without saying what I feel. Have always felt."

Auntie Go sat down, speechless, her mouth dry and bitter. She had known Hing most of her life, was only fourteen when he and Kum Ling had married. Go loved him as a brother. He had no right to change that. She didn't dare look up at him, even when she knew he was putting on his hat, picking up his suitcase, turning to leave.

"I'll leave now. I won't ever speak these words again, Go. You needn't worry."

Then he let himself out of her office as quietly as he had entered, leaving behind the flowery scent of his cologne.

In the five months after Lew Hing came home from the hospital, Kum Ling became another person, shedding her makeup and silk cheungsams in favor of tunics and pants. Go stood by as her cousin nursed Lew Hing, doing everything in her power to ease his suffering—endless cool cloths, soothing teas, soft words.

His pain took its toll on all of them, but Auntie Go and Joan grew increasingly worried about Kum Ling's health. She refused to slow down and slept only a few hours every night, preferring to sit by her husband's bed in case he needed anything.

"You need to sleep," Auntie Go pleaded. "Joan or I will stay with him."

"What if he needs something?"

"I'll wake you."

"I don't know," Kum Ling said, shaking her head slowly, a frantic look in her eyes.

"Emma called yesterday. She's concerned about you. Baby or no baby, she says she'll fly back if you're not taking care of yourself," Auntie Go threatened.

After almost two years of Kum Ling's barely speaking to Emma, the birth of Kum Ling's first granddaughter broke the silence between them. In place of anger at Emma's marriage came joy in a new generation.

Now Kum Ling relented. "My grandchild needs her mother. Tell her I'm fine." She sipped the tea Foon had brewed with mulberry branches and dragon's-eye meat to help her sleep. "You promise to wake me?"

Auntie Go smiled. "Of course I will. And Joan will come to help you, first thing in the morning."

Kum Ling's smile flickered and faded. Fine lines had deepened of late across her forehead, spread like angry creases from the corners of her eyes.

Two nights later, Auntie Go sat by the window of Lew Hing and Kum Ling's bedroom, listening to his raspy, labored breathing. She and Lew Hing had rarely been alone since his confession years ago. Always the girls or Kum Ling stood between them to erase the words he had spoken, to cover her shame and confusion. Auntie Go made sure of it. And true to his word, Hing treated her as before and never mentioned that day again. Go was grateful for his restraint. Yet, she could never step into this bedroom without feeling slightly uncomfortable. Now, in the darkness, the room felt cold and sterile, the strong smell of rubbing alcohol, medicines, and herbs making her eyes water.

Right here in this room, Go thought, *he'll take his last breath.* The doctor had said it was just a matter of time. He was already comatose. *What does that mean?* she had wanted to ask the doctor. *Weeks? Days? Hours?* Hing already lay withered and stripped as branches under a blue sheet and blanket.

"This is what I've always known, Lew Hing, that you are a kind man." She spoke aloud, wanting him to hear her. "Your daughters are doing well, and I'll always take care of Kum Ling. You needn't worry." From the courtyard below she heard the high, whining snarls of the neighbors' cats, which masked for a blessed moment his thick, struggling breaths.

*   *   *

Auntie Go was awakened sometime before dawn, stiff from sleeping in a chair. She could have sworn someone had touched her shoulder, had gently shaken her awake, but she found herself alone in the darkness. Go stood up, straightened her aching back, rubbed her eyes, then listened to the silence of the room. Heart beating in her throat, she moved closer to the bed. Go bent down to touch Hing's hollow cheek, thin wrist, only to feel a coldness. A small cry escaped her. She sat down again to wait. In a few hours it would be sunrise and she would wake Kum Ling.

Song

on

a

Rainy

Night —

1964—65

EMMA

Emma sat in the living room of their new house sipping a cup of *lok on* tea. The warm afternoon sun streamed a hazy light into the room, making her drowsy. She looked at the empty white wall across from her; just that morning, Jack had said, "We could put a bookcase right over there." Emma smiled. She knew Jack was happy with the house by the way he carried on about building her bookshelves for the boxes of books still stacked in the garage. "I don't plan to be hauling them around again for a while," he said, laughing.

Before, Jack would have been content to stay in apartments. "I'm comfortable in small spaces," he had told her. All of his life, Jack had lived in cramped, solitary rooms, first with his mother and brother in an apartment on the outskirts of Chinatown, then in assigned army quarters that were no more than a room and bed, and finally in her apartment on Geary Boulevard after they were married in May of 1960.

When Emma discovered she was pregnant with Emily a year later, she insisted they move to a house by the time the baby needed more room to play and grow. Just past Emily's second birthday, Emma had gotten her driver's license and gained a new sense of freedom. In Jack's green and white Ford convertible, she drove around San Francisco neighborhoods—Sunset, Noe Valley, Richmond, Twin Peaks—past rows of houses, some alike, while others were as unique as the charms on her bracelet. Emma finally found a white Mediterranean-style house in the Richmond district for sale. It reminded her of her family's Macao house and was also near a quiet park and grocery store, which she presented to Jack. Emma hadn't given him a choice. Even if the house was more expensive than planned, she wanted to give her baby as stable a home as she could, since Jack was determined to stay in the army. "This is the house I want Emily to remember growing up in," she had told him—grass in the front and back yards, Emily's own cream-colored room, a bright yellow kitchen where Emma would teach Emily a few Chinese characters when she grew older, and a large, light-filled living room.

Adding to the appeal, they only lived a few blocks from the O'Learys' house. Emma heard Maggie was now living and practicing medicine in Portland, Oregon, but Emma had never forgotten her first Thanksgiving there.

"What a wonderful surprise!" Mrs. O'Leary had said when Emma brought Emily over to say hello. "You are a wee cute little lady." Mrs. O'Leary tickled Emily.

"She takes after her daddy." Emma smiled. Emily had Jack's dark coloring, his high, straight nose.

"But she has her mother's pretty eyes," Mrs. O'Leary added.

"How is Maggie?"

"Likes it up there with the trees and nature! Maggie's life is medicine. No time for babies she says. But if she could see your little precious one, I'm sure she'd change her mind."

Mrs. O'Leary had aged since Emma had last seen her. She still had the same easy smile, but her red hair had dulled with gray. She had also put on a bit of weight, now that all the kids were grown and out of the house.

Emma smiled. "Maggie's fulfilled her dream. Not many of us can say that."

"Looks to me like you have a little dream right there in your arms. I can see you with a couple more like her in a few years."

Emma laughed out loud. Emily had been such a difficult birth, she often wondered if she dared to have another baby. The long, horrendous labor, followed by the tearing, cutting, and stitching, had left her unable to walk for days. Emma had decided to leave any more children up to fate.

Two weeks after they moved into the new house in November, a telegram came from Joan saying that Ba Ba had cancer. Emma felt a chill spread throughout her body. *Oh, Ba ba, I've been waiting all these years for you to come,* she thought. She managed to put through a long distance call to Mah-mee, whose voice sounded small and distant.

"Do you need me to fly home?" she asked, wanting Mah-mee to tell her what to do. Her mind raced. Should she take Emily? Could they afford the trip?

"No, no, there's no reason. Ba ba is comfortable. You have your own family to care for, and we can't know how long . . ." Mahmee's voice drifted across the ocean.

Emma gripped the receiver, studied the beads of winter rain

running down the kitchen window. "Will you tell Ba ba we send our love," she said, sounding more like an American greeting card than she wanted.

"Of course . . ." Mah-mee's voice answered, then faded into the static void.

For the next few days, Emma could hardly eat and felt a heaviness pressing against her heart. All the old superstitions from her childhood returned. Mah-mee had always said that bad news came in threes. Every time the phone rang or the mail arrived, Emma was sure it was from someone who had bad news to deliver.

As the months crept by, Emma forgot all about her fears and superstitions. Life in their new house took on a comfortable permanence. Jack was working hard, and she and Emily settled into a routine in their new neighborhood. A walk to the park every day, followed by Emily's nap, while Emma cooked, cleaned, wrote letters to Hong Kong, and took out her sketch pad more and more to fill her spare moments. She had finished a series of charcoal drawings of Emily and was just beginning a sketch of Jack when the phone rang. She wiped her hands quickly before answering it.

"Hello?"

There was a loud click on the other end, and the unmistakable, low, sultry voice of Joan saying, "Thank you, operator." Then she said, "Moi-moi?"

"Joan, is that you?" Emma asked, feeling a warm stab of joy in hearing her sister's voice.

"Yes, it's me," Joan answered, the hollow static of distance flowing between them. "Emma, I have bad news," she quickly said.

"Ba ba?" Emma said, knowing, always knowing, the call would

come. The words slipped from her tongue before she had time to hold on to them, to taste the words fully one last time before letting them go. Emma covered the mouthpiece, held her breath, then let it out slowly as she listened.

"He died in his sleep. By the time Auntie Go checked on him, he was already gone." A sudden, crackling white noise cut into Joan's words. ". . . bury him . . . here in Hong Kong . . . day after tomorrow . . . Emma? . . . Are you there?"

Emma held the receiver tighter. "Yes, yes, I'm still here. How's Mah-mee?"

"As well as can be. She's strong. They both are."

Emma knew Joan meant Auntie Go when she said "they." Emma suddenly wanted to see them all so badly she began to cry, the warm, salty tears stinging her eyes. Instead, she cleared her throat and said, "Will you give them my love? I miss you all. I wish I could be there."

"I wish you could be too. How're Jack and Emily?"

"They both can't wait to see my famous sister. *I* can't wait to see my famous sister."

Joan laughed. "One way or another, I don't expect another year to go by without our doing so."

The static grew stronger, reminding them of the distance, the years that had grown between them.

"Are you happy?" Emma blurted out. The words seemed so simple.

Joan's slow response traveled through the crackling static. "I'm not only happy, I'm hopeful."

That night Jack wrapped his arms around Emma in the chilly San Francisco night. He pressed her close to his body, kissed her on the forehead, his minty breath grazing her ear. "It's all right to cry," he whispered. Emma gave him a quick squeeze back, then waited until she heard the measured breathing of his sleep before her tears came.

Since her marriage, Emma had been receiving invitations to a weekly coffee circle, which Jack persuaded her to attend. "You might even have fun," he had said. "I'm sure Mrs. O'Leary will watch the baby."

Emma went once in a while because Jack wanted her to, though she never felt comfortable having coffee and cake with the wives of other career officers from the Presidio army base. Their smiles were too tight and they spoke too fast. The gossip and small talk reminded her of Mah-mee's mah-jongg groups.

"It's a hot spot," one of the officers' wives had said just yesterday afternoon.

"We need to go over to Vietnam and show them who's boss," another wife said, swinging her arm and almost hitting the woman sitting next to her.

Emma listened as another voice changed the subject. "Say, did you hear Bill Harvey's wife left him?"

Emma tried to look interested, drank the bitter coffee, and smiled as the voices revolved around her. Though the women were nice to her, Emma felt uncomfortable among them. She remained quiet the rest of the afternoon. She wanted to hear more of what they thought about Vietnam, but knew no one would speak the truth and risk jeopardizing her husband's career. Still, Emma's head buzzed with what she'd heard just the other day on the radio. Dozens of GIs had been killed over in Vietnam, and as tensions mounted, so did her fear for Jack's safety.

* * *

At first Emma thought she had heard wrong when Jack telephoned home from the Presidio to tell her he was being sent south. "The army wants me trained in the latest radar-detection equipment. Then I'll be returning to the Presidio to teach all the newest techniques. For now, it means not being shipped overseas." His voice sounded light and happy.

"Los Angeles?" she asked, cradling the heavy, black receiver in her hand. It still smelled faintly of Jack's cologne, which she imagined floating in waves over the thin wires and through the multitude of tiny holes of the receiver to her.

Jack laughed, sweet and low. "No, honey. I'm being sent to the Deep South—Augusta, Georgia. It shouldn't be for more than three months."

"When?"

Jack drew in a quick breath; let it out again. "The beginning of February."

"Au-gus-ta," Emma repeated. In less than three weeks. Her thoughts raced. Jack would be on the other side of the United States, far away from San Francisco, from her and Emily. "Can we go with you?"

He paused. "It wouldn't make sense for such a short time. I can stay on the base, and you and Emily won't have to be uprooted. Anyway, I'll be in class all day. There won't be anything for you to do there. . . ." He rambled on. Emma knew it was something he had prepared to tell her.

"The beginning of next month?"

"I'll know for sure in a few days. We'll talk more about it when I get home tonight. How's Emily?"

Emma lightened. "She's fine. She's taking a nap."

Jack covered the phone and mumbled something to someone else. "Gotta go, honey. Give the baby a kiss for me. I'll see you at dinner." With a quick click the receiver went dead.

Emma leaned against the wall and closed her eyes. "Augusta, Georgia!" she said aloud, wanting to scream at the thought of Jack's being so far away. Still, Emma was grateful he wasn't going to Vietnam.

That night, Emma had difficulty falling asleep. She hated the fact that the army could disrupt her life. As she lay in bed, the warmth of Jack's body beside her, Emma tried to swallow her fears, then remembered the time Emily had had a fever that rose to 105.

Emma still shivered every time she thought of what could have happened if Jack hadn't acted so quickly. Emily had cried throughout the night with a fever. Emma sat up with her next to the crib, dozing off and on. Sometime in the middle of the night, Emma woke up in the dark, frightened by the eerie quiet. She listened, her heart racing when she couldn't hear Emily's breathing. She reached down to touch Emily's forehead, knowing when her fingers stroked her skin that she was too hot.

"Jack, wake up." Emma shook him, not caring if he had to be at the base early the next day. She knew so little about babies, and until then, she had thanked God that Emily was healthy. "Jack, the baby's burning up!"

Jack stirred. "She'll be all right. All babies have fevers. Helps them grow. You better get some rest," he said, turning back to sleep.

Emma shook him harder, frantic. "Oh, God, Jack, Jack, she's too hot!" She ran back to the crib, picked up Emily, feeling the heat of her small body spread through her.

Before Emma knew what was happening, Jack was beside her, lifting the baby from her arms and screaming for Emma to fill the tub with cold water. "Now!" he yelled.

An hour later, Emily's plunge into cold water had brought down her temperature enough that when the doctor arrived, he'd said,

"You did the right thing. Fever's broken. She'll be fine in a few days."

As the room filled with a soft gray light, Emma watched her sleeping baby. She watched her husband change out of his wet pajamas into his uniform. Emma couldn't imagine what she'd do if Jack wasn't there.

Emma was always afraid Jack might be sent overseas; when they were first married, she once asked him to leave the military.

"You don't have to stay in the army," she pleaded. "You're thirty-two and you have a family now. You've also been to Korea. You've served your country."

Jack smiled, his fingers touching her cheek lightly. "I have a career to think about."

Emma knew there was no use begging. The army had been Jack's life since he graduated from high school. He would no more disobey the army than abandon his family. But in a strange way, that was exactly what he was doing.

Jack left for Augusta, Georgia, early in the morning, on the third day of February 1965. The sky was still a dark, dusty gray, as if the day hadn't developed yet. Amidst the crowds of families and departing soldiers at Travis Air Force Base, Jack dropped his green duffel bag on the black asphalt. In his other arm he carried Emily.

"You take care of them while I'm gone," he said, giving Wilson a hug.

"Don't even think otherwise," Wilson said.

"And you, my sweetheart," Jack said, hugging Emily, "you take care of Mommy." He kissed Emily on the cheek, then blew in the palm of her hand, which always made her laugh, and handed her to Wilson.

"Say 'Bye-bye, Daddy,' " Emma heard Wilson telling Emily.

"Bye-bye, Daddy," Emily repeated. Her plump hand rose up

into a fist, her fingers opening and closing, opening and closing.

Emma had promised herself she wouldn't cry, but the tears came anyway. Jack folded his arms around her and said, "You are my life. I'll be back before you know it." Then he kissed her, wiped the tears from her eyes.

"It won't be forever," Jack said softly.

Emma shook her head. "No, it won't," she said, taking Emily into her arms and hugging her close in the desperate cold. The top of Emily's head brushed against Emma's chin, smelling sweetly of baby shampoo.

Even as Emma watched Jack climb the stairs to the plane, she wanted to cry out, "Don't go, you can still turn back," but instead bit her lip until she tasted blood.

After Jack left for the South, Emma began to tell Emily stories about Hong Kong. It made her feel less lonely, as if her family weren't so far away after all.

"Pao pao, Auntie Go, Auntie Joan, and Foon live on an island called Hong Kong. That's where Mommy comes from," Emma said, the pungent smell of incense and salted fish coming back to her. "Way across the Pacific Ocean. One day, Mommy and Daddy are going to take you there to meet them."

"Pao pao . . . Auntie Go . . . Pao pao . . . " Emily said, repeating the sounds as if she were singing a song.

When Jack's first letter arrived, Emma read parts of it to Emily, even when she knew her daughter couldn't possibly understand. Just reading Jack's words aloud was like filling the room with his voice.

> *Honey—*
> *I guess I'm fortunate. The weather here is much cooler than I expected. A couple of guys have told me I'm lucky*

to be in Augusta during the winter instead of summer. You can't breathe it's so hot and humid. Small favors. It's different here. I still can't get used to the WHITES ONLY or COLORED ONLY signs in the windows of diners, Laundromats, even above drinking fountains. "Where does that leave me?" I keep asking myself. For the first time in my life, I realize how the lighter color of my skin still places me in a category above others. Luckily, I spend most of my time on base, which is like a world in itself. You're right, I don't know how I ever survived in such cramped quarters!

The classes are interesting. There are some good old boys here, and some not so good, like everywhere. I went out with a couple of the guys for a quick dinner in town the other night. I half expected someone to block my path into the diner, like Governor Wallace blocking integration at the University of Alabama. A few heads turned, but that was it. Best meat loaf I've ever eaten!

I miss you more than words can say. Kisses for Emily. Love and more to you.

Jack

The beginning of March brought unusually cold winds that whistled through the house and whipped their faces raw. In the month since Jack left, Wilson and Mrs. O'Leary had come by several times a week, often for dinner or tea.

"My youngest boy, Sean, wants to enlist," Mrs. O'Leary had said the day before, sitting in Emma's warm kitchen. "He doesn't use the brain the good Lord gave him!"

Emma had never seen her so upset. "Maybe it's more talk than action. You know how college kids are. One day they're burning their draft cards, the next day they're signing up."

At thirty-four, Emma felt old. Every day the nation became more polarized on the Vietnam War issue. From her experience, war didn't solve anything. It only destroyed lives and separated loved ones. She poured Mrs. O'Leary another cup of tea, refilled the plate with butter cookies.

Mrs. O'Leary shook her head. "He always was the difficult one. Always chasing dreams. Never finding them." She sighed, reached out for another cookie.

"I'm sure it will all work out," Emma said, taking Mrs. O'Leary's hand, a trace of cookie crumbs remaining. She wondered what Jack would say to someone who grieved at the fact her son wanted to join the army that he loved. Until now, it wasn't something they had had to face.

"It's not like your Jack. A career officer."

Emma nodded.

"That there should be such a thing as war," Mrs. O'Leary said, reaching for another cookie.

The next day, while Emily napped, Emma flipped on the radio to hear the endless commentaries on the escalating troop deployments to Vietnam, then clicked it off again. She sat down and began a letter to Jack. His last letter had hinted that his training might end earlier, which meant his returning in mid-April. Emma kept her fingers crossed that it might be true.

After a lunch of hot soup and crackers, Emma put a heavy jacket on top of Emily's two sweaters. A weak sunlight had emerged after days of cold gray. Behind their backyard was a large, open piece of land with rows and rows of pine trees. After months of staring out her kitchen window at the tall, majestic trees, Emma thought it might be nice to collect some of the pinecones to paint for ornaments. They could spend some time outside and also begin an art project in the afternoon.

The knit mittens and hats Emma had bought at the base PX protected them from the icy wind. She held on to Emily's hand and they ran across the yard. Emily giggled, her pink-mittened hand swinging up and down, her round, dark eyes peeking out from under the hat. Three-year-old Emily was growing taller every day.

Hundreds of pinecones lay scattered on a soft bed of pine needles. Emma took a deep breath. The sharp scent reminded her of some tea Foon might have brewed.

"Pinecones like this one, Emily," Emma told her, holding out a spiny, oval-shaped cone for her daughter to drop into the brown bag Emma had brought along.

"There!" Emily ran after one. "And there!" she yelled, almost tripping as she picked one up in each hand.

"Get one for Daddy," Emma called out, watching her daughter run in small circles and pick up one pinecone after another.

"One for Daddy," Emily said, placing another one into the bag. Then, much to Emma's surprise, Emily continued to rattle off names for each pinecone: "For Pao pao, Auntie Go, Auntie Joan, and Foon." She laughed at the funny sounds that rolled off her tongue.

With their shopping bag filled with pinecones, Emma took Emily's hand and walked back to the house just as the wind began to swirl around them. All afternoon they painted the edges of the pinecones red, orange, yellow, and green, then tied them together with colorful ribbons and hung them all across the living room like lighted lanterns.

By April the weather warmed, though the nights were chilly. When the phone rang, Emma jumped. She had just put Emily down to sleep and ran to grab the phone before it woke her.

"Hi, honey, how's everything?" Jack's voice was an instant relief. He sounded as if he were in the next room.

"I didn't expect you to call tonight. Is everything all right?" Emma asked, an edge of fear in her voice.

"Everything's fine. Better than that. If I hitch a ride back to San Francisco with one of the guys driving back, I can be back a few days earlier."

Emma's heart raced. "But it's such a long drive."

"Give or take five days. It beats waiting around here until they fly me out. Besides, it'll give me a chance to stay in some of the motels this buddy of mine has been telling me about. How's the Tuck Yourself Inn sound? Or the U Drive Inn? Or my favorite of all, the Moby Dick Boatel, with portholes instead of windows?"

Emma laughed. "Well, I'd hate for you to miss seeing the real America!"

"I knew you would agree." Static played a Morse code across the line. "One . . . of the . . . reasons . . . I . . . love . . . you. Can't wait . . . see you . . . again. Ten days . . . and . . . counting."

"I love you too," she said as the line went dead.

When two grim-faced officers from the Presidio knocked on the front door, Emma had no idea why they were there. She heard, "I'm sorry to inform you . . . " before her life froze on that April morning in 1965.

Two days later, Emma was no less paralyzed. Jack had died in a freak car accident just outside Livingston, Alabama. A truck had lost control and careened into the passenger side of the car where Jack was sitting. The worry and anxiety Emma had lived with from the day Jack left melted to nothingness. He died in an accident, not in the terrible war brewing a half a world away. There was no sense to it. A cold, hollow blackness spread through her body, extinguishing any of the colors that filled her life. Emma wanted to cry, to scream, but it was as if her voice had frozen too.

Wilson and Mrs. O'Leary helped to take care of Emily. They wired her family in Hong Kong, spoke soft words that she could barely hear . . . *need to eat . . . get some sleep . . . feel better.*

Something did flicker in Emma's heart when Emily crawled up into her lap and said, "Mommy, don't be sad." She held Emily tight, felt her warmth that burned at the touch, kissed the back of her neck, unable to look at the face that reminded her so much of Jack.

The perfume reached her first. The sweet scent of My Sin brought back a rush of childhood memories. Emma suddenly longed for the rich simplicity of Foon's cooking. The ceaseless clacking of mah-jongg tiles, bowls, and abacus beads filled her head. She remembered walks in Happy Valley along the crowded street stalls that sold everything from potted plants, to bubbling pots of noodles, to rows of hanging ducks with shiny, crispy brown skin.

Emma stood up, listened harder to the soft murmuring of Wilson talking to someone. Moments later, there was a knock on her bedroom door, a rush of sweet-scented air, followed by Joan.

"I caught the first plane out when I heard," Joan said, closing the door softly behind her. "I'm so sorry, moi-moi. I . . ." She stopped.

"You're really here?" Emma asked, surprised at the sound of her own voice, dry and parched as sand.

Joan put down her handbag, moved closer to Emma. "Yes, I'm here."

Emma touched her unwashed hair, the wrinkled shirt and slacks she'd slept in the past two nights, her swollen eyes. "I'm a mess," was all she could say, her voice breaking.

Joan opened her arms and wrapped them around Emma and whispered, "It will get easier, I promise."

Emma breathed in her sister's perfume, makeup, the slight oily smell of sweat, the light touch of cashmere. The money-collecting days floated back to her like another life, but here Joan was again, protecting her. Emma saw that Joan was even more beautiful with age, closed her eyes, and blinked them open again. She looked past Joan to the slats of sunlight coming through the half-opened blinds, to the cheap three-way lamp she'd been wanting to give away, to the unmade bed she had shared with Jack. She swallowed, felt something hard inside her suddenly melting, then her entire body trembled as a rush of tears swelled to the surface.

chapter 17

Home Sweet Home — 1965

AUNTIE GO

Rows of cars already crowded the Kai Tak Airport by the time their taxi pulled up in front. "We should have left earlier," Kum Ling mumbled as she clicked her compact closed and dropped it back into her handbag.

"There's still plenty of time," Auntie Go said, paying the taxi driver. "Besides, it's not as if they don't know their way around Hong Kong." Auntie Go laughed, patted Kum Ling's hand.

Kum Ling nodded, swung open the taxi door, and stepped out. "Come on, we're going to be late." She smoothed down her skirt, trying to hide the irritation in her voice.

Auntie Go smiled and followed her cousin. She knew that Kum Ling had been anxiously waiting for this morning for the past week. When Joan's telegram had arrived saying she was returning with Emma and Emily, it was the first time Go had seen Kum Ling at a loss for words. She sat down, held out the telegram to Go like an offering.

Auntie Go's heart raced. Lately, she'd come to fear the thin yellow sheets with careful, uniform type that brought them more bad news than good. Her eyes glanced over the spare lines.

"It's wonderful news," she said, relieved.

Kum Ling remained seated. "Was I wrong?" she suddenly asked Go.

Go knew her cousin meant her disapproval of Jack, the thin years of silence. "Yes," Go said without hesitation.

Kum Ling sighed. "I've only wanted the best for both my daughters."

Auntie Go sat down next to her, faced her cousin with a tired smile. "In the end, Kum Ling, Joan and Emma have found what's best for themselves. You gave them direction, but they've had to find their own way. We all do."

"And now?"

"Don't look back." Go smiled. "Just be thankful that we're all going to be together again."

A large crowd already waited outside immigration. Go watched Kum Ling glance nervously from left to right, hoping they hadn't missed Joan and Emma. Each time the door slid open and people emerged, Kum Ling stood up on her toes, craned her head forward to see. By the time Joan and Emma did appear, it was Auntie Go who spotted them first.

"There they are," she whispered to Kum Ling.

"Where? Where?" She stood straight, craning, pushing her way forward.

Joan had tied a scarf around her head, wore dark glasses against any reporters watching for her. Emma walked next to her, thinner than Go remembered, looking tired, fragile. She held on to the hand of Emily, who, except for her darker coloring, resembled Kum Ling.

Auntie Go stood back, let Kum Ling reach them first, throw her arms around Emma, say over and over, "I'm sorry, I'm sorry."

When Emma finally pulled away, she stepped over to Auntie Go for a quick hug, then smiled. "And this is Emily."

"Pao pao?" Emily asked, looking at both Kum Ling and Auntie Go.

"She knows me already!" Kum Ling said happily.

"Let's get out of here," Joan said, pushing the cart ahead of them as someone's camera flashed in her face.

Foon was waiting at the door when they arrived at the flat, her gold tooth still glinting as she smiled and patted Emily on the head. Then she took Emma's hand and held it for just a moment before letting go.

"Made all your favorites," Foon said. Not looking at Kum Ling or Auntie Go, she hurried back to her kitchen.

"It's nice to see some things don't change," Emma said as Foon disappeared into the kitchen.

At dinner that night, Auntie Go watched the smiling faces of Kum Ling and her nieces as they sat around the dining room table. The room was alive with voices. The almost fifteen years they were apart dissolved into the rich aromas of Foon's cooking. One by one all of Emma's favorite dishes covered the table—the diced chicken and salt-fish fried rice quickly becoming Emily's favorite also. She ate two bowls and held out her bowl for more.

"Aii-ya, she is a good eater," Foon said happily.

"Another one to follow in your footsteps," Joan said.

"Don't encourage her," Mah-mee snapped, then caught herself and also held out her bowl for more rice.

After dinner Joan stood up from the table. "I'd better be going. Chin expects me at the studio tomorrow. He has another script he wants me to look at." Joan leaned over and gave Emily a big hug, squeezed Emma's arm.

"How can I ever thank you," Emma said, standing. "I don't know what I would have done if you hadn't come to San Francisco. Your wonderful cooking, all the gifts—"

"You're my sister," Joan interrupted, giving Emma a quick hug.

Emma held tight. "The gods have been good to me," she whispered.

"To both of us." Joan pulled away and said, "I'll call you tomorrow."

Mah-mee cleared her throat, her eyes soft and liquid. "Let's walk Auntie Joan out and then get you settled into bed," she said, taking Emily's hand. Emily turned around, watched Emma, who nodded for her to go along.

"Well, that leaves us," Auntie Go said.

Emma smiled. "At last."

Emma followed Auntie Go into the living room. Go watched as Emma moved around the room like a ghost, touching a vase, stroking a silk cushion, playing a chord on the piano. She looked blankly out to the terrace.

"It seems like yesterday," Emma said, "when I looked out to see Japanese warships filling the harbor. I can still hear the static strains of 'Home Sweet Home' they blared across the island. Now I hardly recognize Hong Kong. So many new buildings."

"More every day," Auntie Go said. "Nothing stands still here. Not for long anyway."

"How are you?" Emma asked, sitting down beside Auntie Go.

Auntie Go smiled. "Cutting back at the Western Wind, getting older by the day."

"I've always told Emily all about you. You were my Auntie Go, the Iron Maiden, so full of courage! I think Emily always liked your story best."

Auntie Go laughed. "What kind of lies are you putting in that child's head!"

Emma took Auntie Go's hand. "I just want her to appreciate what a strong and wonderful person you are. I'm glad we're here, so she can learn to treasure her family, and see Hong Kong."

"So you'll be staying?"

Emma nodded with a smile. "For now, so Emily can get to know Mah-mee and you. You should see how much she loves her auntie Joan already! Maybe we can even visit Lia in Macao. And I'd like to spend some time at the Western Wind with you."

Auntie Go's heart raced. She'd long ago given up on the idea of one of her nieces taking over the Western Wind. Now the words startled and surprised her. She squeezed Emma's hand, glimpsed the gold ring with some sort of insignia on her index finger. "I can't think of anything I'd like more."

Emma laughed. "Let's see if you still feel that way in a few months."

"Months or years wouldn't change a thing!" Auntie Go rose from the sofa. "I suppose it's time for this old lady to be getting home to bed."

"Let me walk with you." Emma stood. "I'll just be a minute."

She hurried to her bedroom and returned carrying a rolled-up piece of paper, smiling. "Let's go. Mah-mee seems to have Emily under control."

The night air was warm. In a month, the humidity would be up and Hong Kong would be stifling. Auntie Go grasped Emma's arm, moved slower, her bad knee making it much more difficult for her to fly long distances. Even now, it felt stiff and inflexible. Emma didn't seem to notice and matched pace with her.

"I'm so sorry about Jack." Auntie Go's voice filled the night air. Go would say it just once and no more. She felt Emma's arm stiffen.

"I still can't believe he's gone. . . ." Emma's voice was strained. She held up her hand with the gold ring. It glimmered in the darkness. "It was his," she finally said. "You would have liked him."

"I've never doubted it." Auntie Go stopped in front of her flat and fell silent.

"I realized as we were driving back here that part of me will always remain in San Francisco. I've grown up there, and it's a place I want Emily to know. It will always be where her father is," Emma said, her voice softening.

"Of course." In the near distance, a child's laughter filled the air.

"But I need to be home now, with all of you."

A distant memory flickered through Auntie Go's thoughts. She wanted to say something about the past, about how people never really leave no matter where you are. Their spirits stay with you, comforting, guiding you through the long years of life. But there would be plenty of time for that in the days ahead.

"Are you all right?" Emma asked.

"I'm fine." Auntie Go smiled. "And so will you be. Now, you better get back to that beautiful little girl of yours. I'll see you tomorrow." She gave Emma a hug.

"Oh, this is for you." Emma handed Go the rolled-up piece of paper.

"What is it?"

"You'll see when you get inside." Emma smiled.

Auntie Go watched Emma turn around and walk quickly back up the street. Go slowly made her way up the stone steps to her flat and clicked on the light. The soft glow cast comforting shadows around the room. She unfurled the piece of paper to see a splendid charcoal drawing of Emily. It felt light, uncomplicated, in her hands.